SHOWBIZ

A Novel

By
Ruby Preston

www.dresscirclepublishing.com

Dress Circle Publishing
New York, NY
(c) 2012

"There's no business like show business."
Irving Berlin

"It is not enough that I should succeed — others should fail."
Legendary Broadway producer, David Merrick

Scene 1

The usual cacophony of Broadway gossip and gleeful skewering of the latest shows at the popular hot spot, Joe Allen, went suddenly quiet. Scarlett, who had just moments before snagged the last free bar stool, craned her head to see the one small TV screen that had caught everyone's attention. The TV was only there to show the obligatory sporting events for the few who cared, in the otherwise strictly showbiz hangout. But that night it took center stage, as Scarlett and her fellow bar denizens took in the breaking news headline.

"Long-time *New York Banner* chief theater critic Ken Kanter was found dead in his townhouse this evening. The often-maligned journalist appears to have taken his own life."

Scarlett could hear gasps and, uncharitably but not surprisingly, some giggles. She exchanged surprised glances with a couple of other regulars perched further down the bar. As theater critics went, Kanter was famous for how quickly he could close a Broadway show with a few choice words, a dubious honor that previously had been held by his predecessors. It seemed that with each generation of critics, the nastiness-bar was elevated, and Kanter had certainly taken it to new heights.

Scarlett spun on her barstool to watch the reactions as the news of Kanter's death rippled through the dining room. The industry players were easily identified by their frantic texting, phone calling, and looks of wide eyed disbelief; while tourists continued their pre-show meals, blithely unaware that Broadway, as well as the world's leading newspaper, had just experienced a seismic shift.

It occurred to her that it was only appropriate that she would be here, at Joe Allen, tonight. The longtime theater watering hole's walls were graced with show posters from every Broadway flop that ever was. Her eyes landed on several new additions from recent seasons— shows that had opened and closed in one night, the latest victims of Ken Kanter and evidence of his real power to kill a show.

Scarlett's cell phone buzzed on the bar.

Where are you? A text from her boss, Mr. Margolies: an old-school legend in the industry that hadn't adapted to modern-day sexual-harassment laws but *had* figured out how to use text messaging to keep Scarlett at his beck and call. She regretted that she hadn't had time to order her usual drink. She had a feeling she was going to need it. Too late. She hopped off the stool with one last glance at the TV for any updates, but the news cycle had moved on.

Scarlett buttoned up her zebra-print coat and walked up the steps to the street and into the freezing February evening. Pushing her way through the pre-theater crowds, it took only minutes for Scarlett to walk the few blocks to her office in the prestigious, if non-descript, building, above her other favorite post-work haunt, Sardi's, on 44th and Broadway. Even after four years on the job, she never failed to get a thrill when she walked through the doors of her Broadway office building, where many a theater legend had walked before. *If you can make it here...* she often thought to herself.

Scene 2

Scarlett squeezed into the small elevator and steeled herself for what might be waiting at the office. She didn't know if she'd find her boss mourning or celebrating. She hadn't had time to get her own feelings in order and consider the ramifications of what had happened tonight. Kanter was known to be heartless, but suicide suggested he might have had feelings after all. Perhaps Kanter killed himself out of guilt for all the heartbreak he'd caused and the fortunes he'd lost people, she mused. It seemed the most likely, and yet the most unlikely, scenario. Kanter was known to be exceedingly proud of his status of having the "most powerful pen on Broadway."

Kanter's most recent scathing review, just last week, had resulted in a $10 million loss for Mr. Margolies, leaving more than a few bruises on his otherwise-infallible ego.

On her way into the cramped, two-room space that characterized even the most successful Broadway producing offices, she bumped into *the Actress* coming out of Margolies' private office, off the main room. It is going to be one of *those* nights, she thought.

After the abrupt close of the show, her boss had succumbed to his usual habit of easing the pain of his bruised ego and wallet with one of the ensemble dancers. It didn't hurt that his latest actress was also newly out of work and thus in search of her next Broadway gig— which Margolies might provide, if he were so inclined.

Scarlett had taken to calling her boss's revolving door of Broadway hopefuls simply the *Actress*, since it was impossible to keep up with all of them. Not that she minded, or judged. The Actresses themselves didn't seem to mind—that was for sure. It was a win-win situation, all part of the Broadway "ego" system.

Though Scarlett knew Mr. Margolies to be ruthless and calculatingly chilly in business matters, she supposed she could comprehend the Actresses' attraction, though he held no allure to her. Margolies was nice looking in that way of men who know they have power, he was rich when theater fortune blessed him—he did have the best track record of Broadway hit shows in the industry—and he had cast each of these young actresses on Broadway.

And the best part about the Actresses was that they kept Mr. Margolies' hands off Scarlett. Despite having proven to him that she held her coveted position as associate Broadway producer based on her brains, wit, and talent, she still had to waste precious energy dealing gracefully with his advances. It was a small price to pay to be where she was. And if she had anything to do with it, his office would be hers someday—without him in it. But not tonight.

Tonight as he came out of the office, smoothing his silver hair and adjusting his tailored shirt, he actually looked unnerved. Unusual for a producer of the highest order—a job which required nerves of steel. He even skipped his usual lascivious leer. He was rattled.

"You heard."

"Of course," Scarlett responded, taking off her zebra coat—which did garner the expected glance at her breasts. *I guess he isn't that rattled*, she thought.

"You need to send our condolences, flowers or whatever. Just take care of it. Right now."

Scarlett was about to make a quip about how unlikely it was that such a nasty critic had any loved ones to send flowers to, but she bit her tongue. She supposed she could send the flowers to the *New York Banner* office. If anyone missed him, it would be them. He'd certainly sold his fair share of papers with his incendiary reviews.

She glanced briefly at the *Thelma & Louise, the Musical* poster on the office wall. The most recent Broadway endeavor was, as of last week, their most spectacular flop. That was rare for Mr. Margolies, who was legendary for his unprecedented number of Broadway hits—a credit to his taste in musicals, as opposed to his taste in just about everything else. His track record was, after all, the reason Scarlett held on tight to her job, despite its drawbacks. To the latest show, however, Ken Kanter's lethal pen had dealt an instant death blow.

Who could forget Kanter's quip in the *Banner's* review: *Thelma and Louise had the right idea at the end of this ill-fated new musical. After two-and-a-half long hours at the Jackman Theater, audiences may just want to jump off the cliff, right alongside the evening's soon-to-be-unemployed leading ladies.*

"The man's dead," Mr. Margolies snapped, seeing where her eyes were. "He killed our show, and now he's dead. Artistic justice, maybe, but no excuse not to be professional."

Sure, she thought. None of the prominent producers would dare to appear as if they were enjoying the fact of his demise, though she could practically hear glasses of scotch clinking in *schadenfreude* behind closed doors all over Broadway tonight. You could probably count on one hand the people who *hadn't* wished Kanter dead at one time or another.

Here at the highest levels of show business, the best acting occurs off stage.

Scarlett pulled up the *New York Banner's* website on her computer to track down the correct contact info. The homepage was running the headline "Tragedy Strikes Broadway." Scarlett skimmed the article:

In a statement, the Banner's *senior Arts and Culture editor, Candace Gold, said: "The* New York Banner *is saddened by this tragedy which has rocked our newspaper family and the entire Broadway community. Ken Kanter was an invaluable member of our team. He will be deeply missed."*

"This ought to sell some papers," Margolies said, reading over Scarlett's shoulder, ever the cynic and hard-boiled opportunist. That's what a career on Broadway could do to a person.

Margolies' cell phone rang. He fished it out of his pocket and squinted at the display, too vain to don his reading glasses. He didn't seem surprised by whoever was calling.

"Take care of the flowers and go home," he said to Scarlett as he walked into his own office, slamming the door behind him.

Margolies hadn't ever had to learn to behave. His string of Broadway hits and resulting financial returns for both himself and his investors meant that he didn't have to play nice with anyone if he didn't want to.

To be fair, getting hired by Mr. Margolies had been the best thing to ever happen to Scarlett's career. It got her out of her suburban West Coast life in Oakland, California, and onto the Great White Way —Broadway!

She had always had the personality to be a producer. Even as a kid, she put on shows in her living room with her brother and the neighborhood kids. And she always preferred to be in charge, pulling the strings and counting the money, even if it was just nickels from the lemonade stand that served as the concessions booth. After business school, she had moved from the West Coast to the big city, against her parents' better judgment, to pursue her life-long dream of becoming a Broadway producer. Upon her arrival, however, she was passed over by several serious producing offices because, though she was in her late twenties and had a master's degree, she still looked like a chorus girl straight out of college. It was a professional liability until she met Margolies, who happened to like chorus girls straight out of college.

She hadn't been willing to give up on her dreams, despite the earlier rejections and several top producers' discouraging her, telling her the business was no place for a young woman. Then she had landed here.

As associate producer, she was basically an apprentice to Margolies. It was a job that allowed her to be in the room with the best in the business, helping Margolies make deals, cultivate investors, and get shows off the ground. It was a thrill to work with artists and stars whose names she'd known and revered all her life.

Scarlett knew that Margolies might have initially hired her with less-than-legitimate motives, based on her appearance and the novelty of an attractive young woman who aspired to be a producer. But now, four years in, she had managed to fend off his advances while holding onto her job twice as long as any of her predecessors. Out of sheer force of will, hard work, and working long hours, she had become an invaluable, if undervalued, fixture, as Margolies' right hand. The other half of the unparalleled Margolies Producing Office.

Her task for that evening—finding a florist open in the evening as well as finding a place to send the flowers—wasn't so simple, but in the scheme of things, it was one of her easier assignments. Margolies' door stayed firmly shut as Scarlett took care of the details. As she shut down her laptop and collected her things, she heard Margolies' fist hit his desk, a telltale sign of his infamous temper. Never one to miss a cue, she slipped out the door and headed to the subway stop, barely registering the glittering lights of Times Square, whose siren song had lured her to that concrete jungle in the first place.

Scene 3

Scarlett got home around 8:00 p.m. She had considered going back to Joe Allen or to Sardi's to hear the industry buzz on the evening's drama, but tomorrow was sure to be a big day and she needed to be ready for it.

She'd picked up take-out from the new Thai restaurant near her Upper West Side apartment. The studio apartment she rented was unimaginably small, despite being at the upper end of her price range, but it was perfect for her needs. She had never understood why anyone would spend time at home, with Manhattan just outside the door. She made a habit of spending as little time at home as possible, and not just because she generally hated being alone.

Tonight, though, she didn't mind. She had a lot on her mind. She flipped on the news, in case there were any late-breaking updates on the Kanter situation, though she supposed there wasn't much more to be said on the matter. She kept an eye on the coverage as she changed into cutoff sweat pants (her radiator had only two settings: *off* and *sweltering*) and brushed out her long hair, which had been tightly pinned up all day in her ongoing effort to look like a "serious" theater producer.

Scarlett clicked off the TV and picked up her phone to try her parents on the West Coast. They probably hadn't heard the news. With the time difference, they'd just be getting home from work. Scarlett had been the first to introduce them to theater beyond the community playhouse, and they had embraced it and loved hearing of her Broadway adventures—at least the ones she was willing to tell. And theater wasn't that much of a stretch for them, since her mom was a busy high-school teacher, and her dad a lawyer, both professions where theatrics could go a long way.

Her younger brother, Colin, had taken it a whole lot further. The theater bug bit him early, as it had Scarlett. By age ten he was donning costumes and appearing in weekly living-room productions put on by then-twelve-year-old Scarlett. Early productions included Colin starring as Maria in the *Sound of Music*, Dorothy in the *Wizard of Oz*, and Velma in *Chicago*, much to the admiration of their unconditionally loving parents and sometimes-horrified relatives. Now twenty-six, Colin was known on stage as "Queen Colleen" and was the toast of San Francisco's Castro district.

No answer at home. She thought about calling Colin. He'd love that news. The suicide of *the* top theater critic was good gossip of the highest order. No matter to Colin that a man had died…it was showbiz! Colin always made Scarlett laugh. The carefully cultivated drama in his drag-queen circles always put her daily drama at work into perspective.

Scarlett's phone lit up in her hand. The name *Lawrence* appeared on the screen, bringing an involuntary smile to her face. Lawrence was always a welcome diversion, though tonight he was probably looking for the inside scoop on the Kanter news, which she didn't have.

Lawrence, at fifty years old, had over twenty years on Scarlett and fit the textbook description of a rich playboy. Nevertheless, he and Scarlett had hit it off almost immediately, and she often graced his arm at an opera gala or a cabaret evening at Feinstein's or the Carlyle—events that would otherwise have been many thousands of dollars outside her budget. They always had a blast together, and, refreshingly for Scarlett, their relationship came with no strings attached.

"Hello, Lawrence."

"You were on my mind, Gorgeous," he crooned. Scarlett couldn't help but be flattered by his attention, even though she was sure that he called each of the many women in his life *Gorgeous*, probably to cut down on the risk that he would use the wrong name.

"Well, if you called for gossip about the Kanter suicide, you know as much as I do if you've seen tonight's news."

"I just wanted to hear your voice," he said. She smiled at the phone. He continued, "Though now that you mention it…"

"Aha! See? I knew that was why you called. I know you so well."

"You certainly do. If you come over, you could get to know me even better," cooed Lawrence. He was never one for subtlety yet always in the most charming fashion.

"Not tonight," she said, eyeing her sweat-pants-clad self in the mirror and her inviting bed. Such was their standard conversation, though her answer wasn't always the same.

"You've got to give a guy credit for trying," he said, unfazed. Then his tone changed. "But seriously, losing the top critic, that's some big news. What does your boss have to say? He seemed to have Kanter wrapped around his little finger. The last show notwithstanding, Margolies has racked up quite the resume of good reviews."

"I haven't heard you complaining," retorted Scarlett, avoiding the question, unwilling to gossip about her boss even to Lawrence. She may not like Margolies, but she was nothing if not professional.

"You know I love that nasty old man and every penny he's earned me," Lawrence conceded.

Scarlett had met Lawrence two shows ago, when he had invested in the Broadway revival of *Sweet Charity*, which Margolies had produced. To get a show onto Broadway required many millions of dollars which came from investors who were rich enough or crazy enough to gamble that a Broadway show would be a hit. For an art form like musical theater, where the end result was often a light evening of singing and dancing, the business side of it was anything but carefree. The stakes, risks, and dollar amounts were high.

Lawrence answered the call of *Sweet Charity's* "Hey, Big Spender" and invested a small fortune in the show. Fortunately for him, the *Sweet Charity* gamble paid off, as did several subsequent Broadway investments—which was not always the case for a Broadway show—and Lawrence became a regular in the Margolies office investing pool. He also became the unofficial "big spender" in Scarlett's life.

Lawrence was a venture capitalist by day, having made his fortune during the tech industry boom. Venture capital investing was nearly identical to Broadway investing, although Broadway was a lot more fun. Lawrence was brilliant with money but immature when it came to women, like a kid in the candy shop of Manhattan. He was far from serious boyfriend material, but that suited Scarlett just fine.

Ironically, although Scarlett worked in a business that relied on massive gambles, in the heart department she played it very safe.

However, having a man or two in her life kept her from being lonely. Plus, she always enjoyed spending time with Lawrence, and he was more than happy to introduce her to influential people whom she would need to know if she was to eventually take over Margolies' office. It was a good fit for both of them.

"Are we still on for Friday night?" asked Scarlett, trying to wind down the conversation before he talked her into coming over after all. His penthouse across from Lincoln Center was only a few blocks away—an all-too-easy walk.

"Wouldn't miss it, Gorgeous. We have 8:00 p.m. reservations at Orso, but let's grab a drink at Bar Centrale first."

She wasn't a bit surprised at Lawrence's plans for their evening. Both Bar Centrale and Orso were great places to see and be seen in Broadway circles, and Lawrence liked rubbing shoulders with the glitterati of New York theater. Not a night went by that you wouldn't see Broadway denizens wheeling and dealing—at least the ones who could afford it. Drinkers and diners paid a steep bill when they were lucky enough to snag a reservation at any of the prime real estate tables inside those restaurants.

"I'll meet you there after work," she said.

"Sweet dreams, Gorgeous."

Scarlett hung up. She could picture Lawrence on his couch looking out over the city, probably contemplating who he should call next from his little black book. She may not have even been his first call of the night, which was fine by her; though she treasured her spot as the only theater person in his glamorous circle of jet-setting girlfriends.

She finished her take-out and got ready for bed. It was a rare evening when she found herself home alone at a reasonable hour, since most nights were filled with theater obligations late into the evening. It was necessary that she keep up with not only the latest Broadway shows but also other performances and theater events around town. One never knew where the next big show or rising star would come from. She pulled her computer onto her lap to check the last of the day's emails. Theater people were famously nocturnal, she had learned, in the city that never sleeps!

There was nothing particularly urgent in her emails. She had learned long ago that working in a business that traded on theatrics meant that *urgent* and *crisis* were relative terms. In tonight's inbox, there was no *real* drama. Scarlett had a sneaking suspicion that the real drama was yet to come.

Scene 4

Candace Gold's driver dropped her off in front of the *New York Banner* an hour early the next morning. It was an impressive building, recently renovated for the bastion of journalistic excellence. Candace's entire thirty-year career had been at the *Banner*, though only half of it had been in the illustrious position of Arts and Culture editor. The *Banner* had recently moved into shiny new offices on 6th Avenue, and that's where Candace could be found nearly every day of the year, ever since her marriage and the rest of her personal life had circled and then gone down the drain, nineteen years earlier.

No great loss, she thought daily.

Her low heels echoed through the empty lobby and aggravated the pounding in her head—the result of another nasty hangover. She blamed her drinking habit on her high-stress job. Bourbon was her one comfort and only vice. After all, it was a tough time to be in journalism, and she hadn't clawed her way to a top spot at the top paper only to be a victim of the changing times.

Newspaper sales were down, online media was on the rise, and amateur reviewers and social media sites were putting critics out of business. Well, most critics. She had kept her theater critic, Ken Kanter, at the top of his game. Hiring him twenty years ago had been no accident, and Ken had eloquently stepped into the shoes of past *Banner* critics—the so called "butchers of Broadway"—ever since. Now he was gone.

Dead.

The articles and obituaries were already in the works. Her staff had probably worked through the night—not for the first time. She had kept an eye on their efforts via email, although she had been in no state to show up in person last night. But they didn't need to know that.

At least Kanter's suicide will sell some papers, she thought as she sat down at her desk. She dry-swallowed two aspirin from a bottle that got so much use it never actually made it back into a drawer.

She put her head in her hands. She needed to think, but her brain was fuzzy. She was sorely tempted to have a little hair of the dog. It wouldn't be the first time she had spiked her morning coffee, but she couldn't risk it that day. Her editor would be by any minute to find out her plans for ongoing coverage of the news, the theater industry fall out, and, most important, the critic's successor.

While she had been wishing for months that she and her managing editor could talk about something other than the fact that her department and her job were on the line, these weren't exactly the circumstances she had in mind.

And yet... as the aspirin kicked in and the throbbing in her head eased, an idea began to formulate. Maybe Kanter's death was exactly what she needed.

Scene 5

By 10:00 a.m., it was already feeling like a long day at the office for Scarlett. Margolies was in one of his black moods. He was never a nice person under the best of circumstances, but his volatile moods, which were his greatest professional asset as well as his greatest liability, had only two settings: bad and worse.

After the *Thelma & Louise* flop, Margolies intended to come back with a vengeance. His new Broadway musical, which had been in the works for nearly two years, would be by far the most ambitious project ever attempted by a Broadway producer. No one, least of all Scarlett, could question whether Margolies, of all the producers on Broadway, was up to the task. But Scarlett also knew better than anyone that that would test his professional credibility, and his finances, to the limit. It needed to be a hit of epic proportions.

"Have the final contracts for the writers and director *still* not arrived from the lawyers?" shouted Margolies to Scarlett through the doorway that separated his tiny back office from the main office room that housed Scarlett's desk, the intern's desk, and the conference table. "Rehearsals start this week!"

"They just came in. I'm going over them now, but they look pretty good," replied Scarlett. She felt like she had practically earned a law degree from the amount of time her job required her to spend with the entertainment lawyers, negotiating royalty points, billing, rights of refusal, and the many pages of details that went into the contracts of each and every person involved in a Broadway show.

"Glad to know those bloodsuckers did something right," Margolies sneered.

Scarlett couldn't resist rolling her eyes. It was a move that did not go unnoticed by the current office intern, who was making final preparations for a meeting of the creative team that was starting in their offices in half an hour.

18

"Glad to see he's in a good mood today," said the intern to Scarlett under his breath. Much like the Actresses in Margolies' life, Scarlett was hard pressed to think of their intern as anything other than *the intern*. Usually well-intentioned at the outset, these college kids were a staple in any Broadway producing office. Young aspiring producers, they would spend a semester in a producing office, doing the menial, mind-numbing tasks that are required in any understaffed and overworked office; more often than not, they got thoroughly disillusioned with the unglamorous, cut-throat, manic reality that was Broadway producing. Most were devastated to learn that every ounce of glitz and glamour that people associated with show business began and ended on the stage.

The current intern was a doughy, baby-faced college junior who claimed he was tough enough to work in the notoriously demanding and difficult Margolies office, but he had been reduced to tears by that same demanding businessman on his first day of work. To the intern's credit, he showed up the next day, and by all appearances he seemed like he was going to make it through the semester. That was not always the case.

"You'll understand when you meet the creatives. And don't forget what I told you. If I see so much as a hint of *any* of this on Facebook or Twitter, you'll be out of here before you even know what hit you." Strict confidentiality was a key quality in their office interns. It was critical because their shows often revealed the less-attractive quirks and qualities of their celebrity collaborators. The up-close and personal nature of Broadway had a way of exposing vulnerabilities that celebrities could hide more easily in the somewhat-shielded film and TV world.

"Don't think I haven't heard the stories," said the intern with a grim look on his face.

The intern was dressed up for the latest celebrity creative team. As he prepared a fresh pot of coffee, Scarlett could hear him humming a popular song by the pop-star writers of their next musical.

The name of the epic new musical project? *Olympus*. Just as the Greek gods came down to earth from their lofty thrones on Mount Olympus to titillate, confound, and awe mere mortals, Margolies was bringing the majesty of that classic myth of Zeus, Hera, Athena, and Aphrodite to the audiences of Broadway.

Margolies stormed out of his office and took up his seat at the head of the conference table.

"Let's get this damn show on the road. Where is everyone?"

Many producers favored round tables, which frankly would have fit better in their cramped office, but Margolies insisted on a rectangular table so that he could hold court at the head. It was a constant reminder that he was in charge. Just another of Margolies' personal theatrics.

Scarlett often thought that while Margolies' production of projects on Broadway came and went, his magnum opus was the production of his own personality and career. To the outside world, he seemed like a brilliant but impulsive gambler with a notoriously fiery temper. It had become clear to Scarlett, however, that his image was actually a meticulously calculated persona.

For all the pain and suffering Scarlett had been through, working with such an insufferable man, she still found him to be a fascinating character study. How much work it must be for him to maintain the façade! What must it be like, to be both revered and also deeply hated and feared? To have no family and no personal life to speak of? Scarlett could almost feel sorry for Margolies.

"Scarlett, before they get here, I want you to reprint the final contracts…but shave a percentage point off the payment royalty amounts for the entire creative team. If they don't notice and sign them, they are the idiots I think they are and don't deserve the money. If they do notice, I'll just tell them you're the idiot who screwed up the contracts."

"Yes, sir." It was par for the course. She'd take one for the team. Again.

Maybe she'd feel sorry for him tomorrow. Today, like all too many days at the office, she just felt sorry for herself. *It will be worth it, when I take over.* Her mantra: *It will all be worth it.*

Scene 6

Reilly took up his usual bar stool at the second-floor bar of Sardi's. Though several of his journalist and theater colleagues ribbed him for his loyalty to the old-school industry hang out, he still felt most at home in that restaurant, where decades of theatrical deals had been made. To some, it was corny; to Reilly, it would always be classic. It didn't hurt that plenty of theater veterans still frequented the bar.

His favorite bar stool allowed him to take in the view of the 44th Street Broadway theaters, where he always saw familiar faces coming and going, noting who was talking with whom. Familiar faces looked down on his perch as well—filling every spare inch of wall space were the famous Sardi's caricatures of famous folks from the theater world, spanning nearly the last hundred years.

It was his job as a theater journalist to stay abreast of the latest happenings. From that perch, he could keep an eye on who was climbing the stairs to his afternoon domain and decide if, through direct or overheard conversation, he could get some dirt for his daily sensationalistic column in the *Manhattan Journal*.

The first new arrival to catch his eye was an attractive young woman in a zebra-print coat. She almost looked too young to be in the bar. She barely glanced at the other afternoon bar patrons and took up a seat at a bistro table by the window. There was no table service at the bistro tables near the bar. But on a quiet afternoon, the regular bartender, a long-time fixture in the venerable institution, wearing the signature magenta Sardi's jacket and bow tie, called to her across the bar rather than making her come to him.

"You're here early today. Glass of white?"

"That'd be fabulous, thanks."

Reilly caught her eye as she turned back to her table. For his trouble, he saw a spark of recognition in her blue eyes. His column in the *Manhattan Journal* had made him a celebrity in New York theater circles.

Much to Reilly's chagrin, though, his fame was a far cry from the celebrity attained by the late great Ken Kanter. Reilly's column was a hit in New York, but Kanter had been read around the world. Cheers to Kanter, Reilly thought as he raised his glass of wine with a nod to the girl at the table.

The bartender set her glass of wine on the bar. Reilly, never one to let an opportunity pass him by, snatched it off the bar before the girl could get off her stool and grab it herself. With his most charming smile, he delivered it to her table.

"Things must be really bad in the newspaper business if Reilly Mitchell is moonlighting as a waiter at Sardi's," she said to him.

While he'd never admit it, Reilly lived for these moments when he was recognized. Proof that he was *somebody* in the theatrical rat race where he had spent ten years of his career. The fact that the recognition came via a witty remark from the lips of a beautiful young woman made it all the better.

"I expect a big tip," Reilly responded with a wink to the bartender, as he helped himself to the empty tall chair at Scarlett's bistro table and set down his own glass of wine. If his brazenness at inviting himself to her party of one bothered her, she didn't show it. A good sign. The absence of a wedding ring is also promising, he thought.

"So what's a beautiful woman like you doing here alone at 4:00 in the afternoon?"

She rolled her eyes, clearly the kind of girl who got her fair share of compliments. "Just one of those days."

"Reilly Mitchell," he said, holding out his hand, "but you already knew that."

"Scarlett," she said, giving him a firm handshake and taking her hand back quickly, despite his attempt to let their contact linger.

My second flirtatious parlay, rebuffed, thought Reilly. Yet she hasn't kicked me out.

"I'll admit I read your Broadway gossip column, just like everyone else."

"I prefer to think of it as investigative journalism, not gossip."

"Pretty words from a columnist who clearly revels in the misfortunes and tribulations of others," she retorted.

"The public has a right to know what happens in the back rooms of Broadway," he joked with a twinkle in his eye.

"I'm sure your article yesterday on the 'affairs'"—she made air quotes—"of Broadway's leading men was vital to public awareness."

"I know a few members of the public, or rather, their wives and partners, to be exact, who were very interested."

"You're terrible," she said, but she had a smile on her face. "Seriously, though, do you really get off on writing this stuff? Leaving ruined marriages and ruined careers in your wake?"

"You give me too much credit."

"You must really hate this industry."

"Actually, quite the opposite," Reilly defended himself. It was turning into an oddly candid, though not unpleasant, conversation. "I've devoted my whole career to this industry, but sometimes I don't like what I see. Someone needs to talk about it."

"Well, thank you, Reilly Mitchell, the Walter Cronkite of Broadway," Scarlett quipped sarcastically.

This girl has some attitude and isn't falling for my charms, thought Reilly. It's rare that someone has the nerve to talk to me like this. But he had to admit he was intrigued. He guessed she was an actress, from the looks of her, but that didn't explain her confidence.

Never one to shrink from a challenge and eager to spend more time with those beautiful lips and eyes, Reilly decided to up his game. He signaled to the bartender for another round for both of them. His glass was empty and hers barely touched. He'd better slow down. Then again, he was having fun, and his articles for the week were already turned in. He figured he deserved a break.

"As it happens, I'm working on a big story right now. It's going to be huge when it breaks."

"Jealous that Kanter stole your spotlight, huh? I hope you don't try to top that," she said. Reilly sensed a hint of flirtation in her voice. "May I ask what this 'huge story' is about?"

"I would tell you, but then I'd have to kill you," he said as he aimed his most charming smile in her direction.

He was saved from revealing anything further by the bartender, who, probably having heard the potential for good gossip about the previous night's suicide, broke with tradition and came out from behind the bar to refill their glasses.

Reilly raised his newly filled glass to Scarlett. "Here's to drinking in the afternoon."

They clinked glasses and their eyes met.

"So," Reilly changed the subject, "Are you celebrating or drowning your sorrows this afternoon?"

"A little of both, I guess. But I like the sound of celebrating better. I'm working on a new musical."

"Congratulations. You're an actress?"

"Producer, actually."

"Aren't you a little young to be a producer?"

"Aren't you a little old to be New York's premier investigative journalist?" She said those last two words with more than a little sarcasm.

"Touché," he said and raised his glass for another toast, to which she acquiesced. "But if you're a producer, why haven't we met before? I make it my business to know the movers and shakers around town."

"Then it's a good thing we've finally met," she said, meeting his eyes. "Are you going to investigate me now and uncover dark deeds and scandal around my new musical endeavors?"

"But of course," he responded with a playful glint in his eye. "I'm writing the article in my head right now. 'Beautiful young producer has passionate affair with New York's premiere investigative journalist.'"

That got the laugh he was going for and an encouraging comment from her: "No such thing as bad publicity."

The wine was clearly beginning to loosen her up, and they were both having a good time. People were starting to filter into the bar. A few of the new arrivals recognized Reilly but also who knew enough not to interrupt his conversation with a beautiful woman. There'll be time to catch up with them later, thought Reilly, unless I can talk Scarlett into dinner. He might have been moving fast, even for him, but it had been a while since he had found a woman who really caught his eye. So many women he met rolled over at the first hint of his charm and celebrity, or they occasionally tried to work him for a positive mention in his column. At thirty-five, he was beginning to give up on the idea of finding his match, although looking had proven to have its own rewards, if the beautiful if sometimes vapid women on his speed dial were any indication.

Having finished his second glass of wine, he decided to be bold.

"What do you say we go grab dinner somewhere we can talk a little more freely?" he asked, glancing over to the bartender, who had clearly been keeping one ear on whatever he could catch of their conversation over the rising din as the bar continued to fill up.

"Wish I could." She sounded sincere. "But I actually have to check in at the office. I've stayed too long as it is." She dug in her purse for her wallet.

"This one's on me," Reilly said. "Where do you work?"

She left $20 on the table as she got up.

"Upstairs," she said, glancing up at the ceiling. "Pleasure to meet you, Reilly Mitchell."

With a smile, she turned on the heel of her black boots. The last he saw was her black and white zebra coat as she headed downstairs to the street and into the corporate office entrance, leaving Reilly to wonder if she was being elusive on purpose or just in a hurry to get back. Upstairs? That narrowed it down to several dozen possible offices. Did she work in one of the major producing offices? That seemed like the kind of thing she would have bragged about. Well, he was an investigative journalist, after all—he'd just have to find her.

Until then, he turned his attention to the bar. Inevitably someone would be there to supply him with a healthy dose of gossip for a future column. It would only be a matter of minutes before one colleague or other would fill the now-vacant stool across from him.

Minutes later, as Scarlett made her way back up to her office, she caught herself smiling. She had to admit that she felt flattered by Reilly Mitchell's attention. Despite his much-maligned column, he was a key part of the fabric of Broadway. She was glad she hadn't let it slip that, in fact, she had been reading his column since before she had even moved to New York, eagerly devouring his insider views on everything from which shows would make it to which producers and stars were misbehaving in the boardrooms or the bedrooms.

Though she didn't really trust a man who made a living divulging the deepest and darkest secrets of her colleagues and, on more than one occasion, her boss, she found him to be surprisingly nice and refreshingly fun to talk to.

Scarlett knew that a friendship with Reilly would be a bad idea, yet she found herself wondering if she'd see him again. Both Margolies' personal antics and his productions were a frequent topic of Reilly's column—and often presented in a less-than-flattering light. Even if she could keep her mouth shut around Reilly, it wouldn't look good. She'd be smart to keep her distance, if she valued her job.

Maybe it was the two glasses of wine or the fact that he was a celebrity, but she couldn't ignore the unmistakable spark she'd felt with him. As the elevator doors opened and she headed back to her desk, she replayed their conversation in her head. She felt herself blushing, remembering how forward she'd been with him. What gave me so much nerve, she thought. She didn't even know the guy, and yet something about his snarky column made her feel comfortable being a tad snarky herself.

As she sat back down at her computer to finish typing up the notes from the morning meeting, she had trouble keeping her mind on the job. Note to self, she thought: Two glasses of wine in the afternoon, mixed with the company of a cute columnist, is a bad idea. And yet, overall, she thought, it was not an unwelcome turn of events.

Scene 7

Scarlett slid into the cracked vinyl booth at the little diner on 9th that served as the favored breakfast place for theater folks when they were meeting and didn't need to impress each other. The waiter barely slowed down as he plunked three cups of coffee on the table in front of Scarlett and her breakfast companions, Jeremy and Jeremy.

"Cheers." Jeremy raised his coffee cup for a toast. "To a bright future for our collective baby, *Swan Song, The Musical.*"

They clinked coffee cups, and Scarlett smiled warmly at the up-and-coming composer and lyricist of her first solo producing project.

"I want to hear everything about your experience at Pinter. I love the new draft of the *Swan Song* script and score, obviously. I know you're sick of hearing it, but you two are brilliant," Scarlett said.

"Oh, stop," Jeremy replied, preening himself in mock modesty.

"What would you like to know, Miss Producer?" teased the other Jeremy.

Knowing that she'd need to develop some musicals of her own if she ever wanted to be a true producer, Scarlett had Margolies' blessing to maintain her very own pet producing project, as long as it didn't keep her from doing her job. She was thrilled to have come across the Jeremys and their concept for an original musical based on *Swan Lake*. It hit the sweet spot for original musical theater, since it had the *Swan Lake* branding, which was vital in a day and age where audiences needed name recognition before they'd buy a ticket. But it was also a completely new and original retelling, similar to what *West Side Story* did so successfully with *Romeo and Juliet* or *My Fair Lady* did for *Pygmalion*.

"What kind of feedback did you get from the dramaturges on the final draft?" asked Scarlett. "I'm feeling like we have something solid."

Jeremy and Jeremy were writing partners and life partners with the unfortunate coincidence of sharing the same name. Pity the soul who tried to convince either of them to change their name to cut down on the constant confusion.

They had just spent two weeks developing their new musical at the prestigious Pinter Theater Center in Connecticut, away from the distractions of real life. Jeremy and Jeremy had been thrilled to have Swan Song chosen by the discerning selection committee for this opportunity. Getting selected was not only key for the writing of the show but also gave them cache in the industry.

Jeremy considered her question. "I think we finally solved the second act."

"We sure did. Jeremy wrote a kick-ass duet for the white and black 'swans.' You're going to die when you hear it!" bragged Jeremy.

Scarlett had mentally renamed Jeremy and Jeremy for her own convenience.
"Jersey Jeremy" was the composer of the couple. Though claiming to be a native Manhattanite, he was actually from New Jersey. He had been a gawky carrot-topped band geek in high school. Fortunately, he moved into the city to go to grad school at NYU Tisch for musical theater writing, and there reinvented himself as a musical genius whose smile and proclivity for writing beautiful love songs on the piano had transformed him from geek to god among his classmates. By graduation, however, he was writing love songs for only one person...

"Buff Jeremy," was a lyricist extraordinaire. His words had been a perfect fit for Jersey Jeremy's music, for the past five years. Buff Jeremy did his best brainstorming at the gym. Upon first glance, he looked like he might be more at home on a fashion runway than huddled over sheet music in a black box theater.

Scarlett had discovered Swan Song and its creators several months earlier at a reading at a tiny theater near Union Square, where actors had read and sung through the show standing on stage with their scripts and scores in hand. Scarlett had been there since part of her job was scoping out future Margolies projects by attending readings like those.

Of the several new musical readings she went to in a week, the vast majority failed to impress her. Writing a musical was deceptively difficult, and very few did it well. However, *Swan Song* appealed to her instantly. If she'd learned anything from Margolies about picking a show, it was that you had to go with your gut. If a show grabbed you the first time, even if it was just a musical reading, then there was something there that would also grab your audience. If you didn't have a visceral reaction to at least some aspect of the material that first time, it was unlikely you or your future audiences would ever fall in love with the show. Producing 101.

Scarlett had had to offer the piece to Margolies first, since she had been scouting shows on his dime when she discovered it. But with unknown writers and the particular subject matter, he wasn't interested.

"I've been laying the groundwork with some of my non-profit theater contacts here in the city. I think you're right—we're ready for a production," Scarlett said.

"We could easily do any final tweaks during a rehearsal process; otherwise, it's ready for an audience," Jersey Jeremy said.

"Well, then, I'll start making some calls. Rumor has it that the Manhattan Theatre Workshop may lose their next show if Neil Patrick Harris isn't available to star in it..." Scarlett said.

"Isn't that show supposed to be happening like next month?" asked Buff Jeremy.

"I'll admit, it would be a little insane to pull our show together to go into rehearsals that quickly, but someone's going to get that spot if it opens up. Why not us? We know they loved *Swan Song* when they saw the reading."

"I never thought I'd actually be praying that Neil Patrick Harris *not* come to New York for a show," Jersey Jeremy said with a laugh.

"Don't get your hopes up, guys," Scarlett said. "It's still a long shot, and for all we know they may already have a back up show lined up. But it's definitely worth a try. It would certainly be the perfect next step for the show. High profile but downtown."

Scarlett's role as producer was to continue to find next steps for the development of the show. Musicals could take years to develop. Each reading, workshop, and production that had to happen to make a perfect show took time and money. Scarlett was hoping to get this one produced at a non-profit theater company. At the right theater, it could get both the exposure it needed and the benefit of the theater's own production budget. The alternative—namely, Scarlett producing it by herself—would be a several hundred-thousand-dollar endeavor. That was a less-ideal alternative, considering the producer didn't make a penny until, and unless, the show found success.

"Speaking of which," Buff Jeremy said. "Any news you're at liberty to share about the *Olympus* extravaganza? I read in the paper that the show got a theater."

If there was anything harder on Broadway than raising the many millions of dollars needed for a Broadway show, it was getting a theater.

"And not just any theater," Jersey Jeremy added. "The Jackman, no less. Have you mopped the blood off the floor from the *Thelma & Louise* debacle?" Quintessential theater nerds, Jeremy and Jeremy were always well informed on the latest gossip and rarely able to restrain their cattiness around Scarlett, who loved them just as they were.

Buff Jeremy jumped in. "That reminds me, what's the deal with the Kanter suicide? Do you think he left a suicide note written in letters from cut-up playbills?"

"That's ice cold," Jersey Jeremy said. "More important, do you think Liza Minnelli will be at the funeral?"

"Oooh, or Stephen Sondheim?" Buff Jeremy said. He started singing, "Every day a little death..."

"More like 'He had it comin', he had it comin'...'" sang Jersey Jeremy from the "Cell Block Tango." "Though I suppose that would have been more appropriate if someone had killed him."

"How about 'There's a grief that can't be spoken...empty chairs and empty tables, now the-critic-we-hated is dead and gone...'" sang Buff Jeremy. "I guess that doesn't really work, either."

They both turned to Scarlett at that moment, and Jersey Jeremy said, "If you get invited you have to take us with you! Pretty please?"

Scarlett pursed her lips. "So you two can serenade the mourners with you musical-theater funeral medley? No, thank you! Anyway, there isn't going to be a funeral, according to the paper. And is it too much to ask that you guys show a little respect?"

"Moi? Respect?" Jersey Jeremy said with a dramatic gesture to himself. "I'm sorry, my name is Jeremy, have we met?"

"He's hopeless. You should know better than to try and make him behave," Buff Jeremy said, rolling his eyes at his boyfriend. "But you know how personally he took it, each time Kanter panned any new musical he actually liked."

"Did you read Reilly Mitchell's piece on Kanter this morning?" Jersey Jeremy asked gleefully.

At the mention of Reilly's name, Scarlett felt her cheeks flushing. She hadn't quite been able to get him out of her mind. She knew she was being silly but supposed a little celebrity crush was harmless.

"Well, no point in reveling in Kanter's demise. I'm sure someone just as unpleasant is waiting in line to take Kanter's place. Fortunately, that's not my problem." Scarlett was eager to change the subject away from Reilly's column before they noticed anything unusual. She fished in her purse for her wallet. "Speaking of which, some of us have to get to work."

"And some of us have to finish re-painting the bathroom today..." Buff Jeremy said mock-glaring at Jersey Jeremy. They shared a cute apartment in Chelsea that Jersey Jeremy's father had bought for him in an overboard effort to prove that he loved his musical-theater-inclined gay son. Scarlett often wondered which aspect of Jersey Jeremy caused his father more consternation: the fact that his son was gay or that he had chosen musical theatre as his profession.

"It's not my fault that there was a *Desperate Housewives* marathon last weekend. You couldn't possibly expect me to paint under those circumstances."

"…While I was working my fingers to the bone at the office," Buff Jeremy said in his best woe-is-me voice. He contributed to their finances by working part-time as a dog walker, so he could make money and contribute to his physique.

"Same time and place next week?" Scarlett had to be aggressive to get a word in when those two got started.

"We'll be here with bells on," Jersey Jeremy said.

"Speak for yourself. I'll be here *sans* bells," Buff Jeremy said.

Scarlett made her escape as their banter started up again. It was a pleasant start to her Friday.

Scene 8

Candace ascended the steps to the unmarked door on 46th and entered the elite hot spot that was Bar Centrale. The bar was already crowded, but Candace wasn't looking to rub shoulders. Tonight, her mind was on work.

Her managing editor, Tom, hadn't arrived yet, so she grabbed the last two stools at the bar. A booth would have been better, but on a Friday night at 7:00 p.m., that wasn't going to happen. As she ordered her usual Manhattan, Candace glanced at the young woman on her other side. She didn't particularly want an audience for her upcoming conversation. Luckily her bar neighbor, from the looks of her, was just another pretty enough, dime-a-dozen wannabe actress in a zebra coat. The girl practically blended in with the zebra-print bar stools. How tacky, thought Candace, uncharitably. She caught the eye of her editor and waved him over as he came in through the heavy velvet curtains at the door.

While he ordered a glass of wine, Candace took a few unladylike gulps of her Manhattan.

"Nice to get out of the office. What a week," her editor said as his wine arrived. "Shall we toast our fallen comrade? To Ken Kanter, may he be wielding his poison pen wherever he is."

"Tragic," Candace said, forcing her face into a grim mask as they clinked glasses. She polished off her drink with a nod to the bartender for another.

"So, Candace, you wanted to talk to me about something."

"Yes." Candace perked up. Thank goodness he'd been willing to meet there. She needed some liquid confidence that night. "I've had some thoughts about the replacement for Kanter."

"I assumed we'd promote the junior critic to chief. That's certainly what *he's* bound to assume, though I'm not opposed to discussing alternatives. He's still a little green. Don't we have a short list of candidates in a file somewhere whom we could interview?"

"We could, and we do. But I think this could be an opportunity to generate some new attention around our section. Kanter came in with a whimper and went out with a roar. What if we started with a roar?"

"Okay. I'm intrigued."

Candace had to give Tom credit. For all the pressure he'd been putting on her, he was a good guy and respected the fact that she'd been at the paper twice as long as he had. Of course, that might just be the bourbon speaking. Her second Manhattan had arrived, and Bar Centrale was anything but stingy on their pours.

"What did you have in mind?"

She leaned closer in an attempt to not be overheard. "You know how our reviews are getting diluted by the bloggers and chat rooms?"

Of course he knows, she thought. It's the reason we're having this conversation in the first place. "Anyone with a computer these days thinks they can be a journalist. They love nothing more than to tear apart our reviews and lambast our critic, regardless of what he prints."

Tom nodded and took a sip of his wine. She couldn't understand people who could nurse a drink all night like that.

"Well, what if we let *them* pick our next critic?"

"Go on."

"I'm thinking of it as our version of a reality show. It would work like this: We select, say, five candidates qualified for the job. Then, for the next five high-profile opening nights this season, we give one of them a shot at the review. The bloggers and chat room folks knock themselves out, analyzing the finalist's every word. It would be a reading frenzy. At the end, we put it out to a vote. Let our readers and detractors pick the critic. They'll stand behind whoever it is, because it was their choice!" She finished triumphantly, aware that her voice was getting loud.

"I like it, Candace. We let the people pick the next critic, up our sales in the process, and bring back the respect of our critic's pen," he said. Candace could practically see the wheels turning in his head. "Let me run it up the food chain and check it with legal. I have a feeling they might just bite. Like you said, it smacks of reality TV, and there is no denying that's where the ratings are these days, god knows why."

They discussed the logistics for a few more minutes. Heading into spring, there'd be a lot of shows opening to get in the running for the awards season. The junior critic could pinch-hit for the next couple of reviews, but they'd need to put the plan in action right away to have the first candidates ready to go.

Candace was pleased with herself. She nodded to the bartender for a third Manhattan—a personal celebration of her successful proposal.

"Can I have him bring you another glass of wine?" She batted her eyes at her boss, feeling the weight of the week lifting from her shoulders. Her phone, which she had set on the bar, buzzed. She ignored it.

"No, thanks," he said to the bartender quickly. And to Candace: "I have to get home to my family."

Family. Who needs family? thought Candace derisively as her drink arrived.

"I can have an answer for you next week," he continued. "But feel free to start pulling together a list of candidates. We'll need to get the initial interviews out of the way, and there won't be a lot of time to vet our five finalists."

"That won't be a problem. I can reach out to our colleagues and contacts and have some legitimate resumes on my desk right away. I'm sure it won't surprise you that I've already received several inquiries." Her third drink was hitting the spot. Her phone rang again. "A job opening like this doesn't come along very often."

"Do you need to get that?" He gestured to her phone on the bar. "Sounds like it might be urgent."

Candace squinted down at the name on the caller ID, feeling for her reading glasses, which were never where they should be. Her drink sloshed onto the bar as she set it down abruptly. Her mind was starting to swim a little. Had she eaten that day? She couldn't remember. She had to keep it together for her boss.

"Can you excuse me for just a second?" she said as she ungracefully dismounted from her bar stool, dropping her coat in the process.

"Sure. Are you okay, Candace?" He asked that last question to her back. She had already thrown her coat over her arm and was heading toward the door as she put her phone to her ear.

Scene 9

Scarlett couldn't believe what she was hearing. She felt like she had a front-row seat at the best show in town as she waited for Lawrence to arrive at Bar Centrale. The eavesdropping opportunities at the bar were always promising, but she'd hit the mother lode tonight.

Doing her best to stay inconspicuous, she hung on every word issuing from the ever-more intoxicated middle-aged woman on the stool next to her.

Scarlett waited until she thought the conversation was winding down and slipped out to call Margolies. Though Margolies had a knack for always somehow having the inside scoop, she had a strong feeling that it would be news to him.

She shivered on the front stoop, having left her coat on her bar stool to save her spot.

"Hey, boss, I just got word on the new *Banner* critic."

"I'm listening," Margolies responded into the phone, his voice level.

Scarlett glanced around to make sure she wouldn't be overheard, but the passersby, bundled against the chilly evening, were out of earshot.

She proudly filled him in on the plans she had overheard.

"Who did you hear this from?"

"I sort of overheard it, actually. From some woman at the *Banner*. I think her name was Candace—"

"I have to make a call," he said tersely, and she heard the click that meant he had hung up on her. Classic. But what was she expecting. Praise? A pat on the back?

As she pulled open the large wooden door to get back to the warmth of the inner industry sanctum, the woman she'd just overheard, Candace, was stumbling out the door with her coat thrown over one arm and her cell phone to her ear.

Practically bumping into Scarlett, she slurred into the phone, "Well, look who holds all the cards now!" she cackled as she nearly fell down the stone steps. "And there's nothing you can do about it."

Scarlett waited to make sure the woman made it to the street in one piece, looking on in horror of seeing a train wreck in progress. She almost felt bad for her. Clearly an unhappy person, she thought as she made her way back to the bar.

Lawrence arrived seconds later.

"Hello, Gorgeous. Am I late?" He kissed Scarlett on the cheek. Turning to the, now-solo man from the *Banner* who had been left to settle the not-unsubstantial bill, he asked, "This seat available?" The man nodded, and Lawrence hopped onto the elegant bar stool that the *Banner* woman had recently vacated.

"You're right on time," Scarlett said with a wide grin.

"It looks like someone's had a good day," Lawrence said, picking up on her good mood. "Or are you just happy to see me?"

"I'm always happy to see you," Scarlett said. "And this is the perfect way to end the week."

"I couldn't agree more," Lawrence said, flagging down the bartender and ordering a glass of champagne for each of them.

"Except you do this kind of thing every night," Scarlett said.

"Not with you," said Lawrence with a charming smile.

"Excuse me! Don't you know it's rude to bring up other women?" Scarlett teased. "You're such a cad!"

Lawrence was momentarily taken aback. "Hey! That's not what I meant, and you know it. I was trying to pay you a compliment."

"I know. But I'm allowed to give you a hard time, every once in a while," she said, squeezing his hand good-naturedly. "You know I couldn't care less who you see."

"I'll never understand you... *women*!" Lawrence said in exasperation. "But that's why I love you."

"Cheers!" Scarlett said with a laugh, raising her glass.

"Cheers!" Lawrence echoed.

Scene 10

Reilly slid into a tall chair at a bistro table by the window at the Sardi's second-floor bar, forgoing his normal bar stool. He had told himself that he was going to Sardi's to try to seek out the breakthrough he needed to finish the exposé article that would be above and beyond his normal column material. And yet every flash of a black-and-white coat out the window on the street below caught his eye.

"You brought some work with you today," the bartender said, making friendly conversation in the afternoon quiet of the bar while eyeing the papers in front of Reilly.

"My editor's breathing down my neck." It had been two days since Reilly had met Scarlett, and his initial attempts to discover who she was were unsuccessful. He needed some new gossip, and to get it he needed to keep his nose to the grindstone without being distracted by a beautiful face and witty personality. "I'm hoping to chat with a few friends here later. You expecting a good crowd?"

The bartender raised his eyebrows. "I expect so. You should stick around." The bartender had overheard Reilly eliciting his fair share of gossip, much of which later made an appearance in Reilly's column. Through the unspoken law of bartender-client confidentiality, Reilly knew his sources were safe.

"What'll it be?"

"Will you be disappointed if I start with a club soda?"

"Not at all. This one's on me," he said, filling a tall glass from the bar.

"You're a good man." Reilly smiled as a flash of black and white caught his eye out the window. Not her.

"And you're a good customer." The bartender winked at Reilly before he turned his attention to a couple of well put-together elderly women who were sidling up to the bar in their politically incorrect winter furs.

Reilly forced himself to focus on the pages in front of him on the bistro table—his notebook of unanswered questions. He was still chipping away at his exposé. If he got it right, it could mean a big break for him, and he could potentially rise above the gossip columnist post to a more serious position. He was still working on the proper headline, given Kanter's demise:

"Corrupt Critic Gets His Due." Or maybe "Broadway Bribery Scandal."

Another flash of black and white caught his eye. That time he was sure it was that zebra coat he had been scanning the New York City sidewalk crowds to spot. There she was—Scarlett. She was deep in conversation, threading through the mid-block 44th street traffic, a stack of files in her arms. Reilly was so distracted by the fact that he was finally seeing her that he almost didn't notice who she was walking and talking *with* so intently.

Reilly froze as recognition hit. Margolies. She worked for Margolies. He couldn't believe his luck.

Scene 11

Scarlett took a deep breath. It was going to be a tricky meeting, and the players would arrive at the theater any moment.

The writers of the *Olympus* musical were major celebrities—a rock-star couple who fronted the British pop band Cupid and Psyche. Margolies had convinced them to tackle a musical. Though publicly an "item," their relationship had long ago become a working, if rocky, partnership, rather than a romantic one. Margolies and Scarlett were plenty used to wrangling celebrities through the artistic process of a Broadway musical, but the couple's interpersonal challenges were proving to be particularly difficult.

Cupid and Psyche (real names: Carl and Phoebe) weren't used to taking direction, much less revising their work. Paired with Margolies, a producing genius with a severe deficit in the tact department, Scarlett could already picture the inevitable carnage between now and opening night.

"The talent has arrived, loves!" Cupid said in his thick Liverpool accent, referring to himself, as he made a grand entrance, striding down the aisle into the theater. Scarlett could see Margolies cringe at his over-the-top theatrics. Psyche, close on his heels, just rolled her eyes.

Cupid bounded up onto the stage on skinny, tight-jean clad legs and a t-shirt that appeared to be made out of an actual British flag. He took a seat at the long folding table that had been set up, center stage, for the purpose of that meeting. Normally, meetings and the first few weeks of rehearsals would not be held at the theater. However, the extreme technical requirements of the show had resulted in Margolies' moving the show into the theater for the entire rehearsal period, at no small expense. Scarlett had been present for several of the negotiations with the theater owner to discuss the structural changes that Margolies was making to the inside of the theater to accommodate the unique requirements of the huge show—also not cheap.

Psyche grabbed the furthest seat from Cupid and sullenly picked at her chipped cotton-candy pink nail polish, which was a perfect match to her hair color. They were both in their early thirties, but to look at them you'd think they were eighteen. Personalities aside, Scarlett was the first to admit that they had talent—both musically and at capturing a worldwide fan base that spanned generations. The fact that they were starring in the musical as the married Greek gods, Zeus and Hera, was a major coup for the production. Cupid and Psyche were the show's biggest asset and biggest liability, all at the same time.

Next to jump into the fray were the director and co-writer; the former was a well-known Broadway stalwart, and one of the few who could garner enough respect from Margolies to hold his own with the overbearing producer. He was used to Margolies' exceedingly hands-on producing style that often irked other directors who didn't appreciate Margolies' micro-managing approach to the artistic process.

"Good to see everyone," the director said as he took a seat. He smiled pleasantly, pretending everyone was getting along, though he knew full well that it would be a meeting fraught with tension.

Margolies had yet to utter a word. He simply glowered from the head of the table. Scarlett enjoyed observing Margolies in action at these meetings. It was highly informative to watch his masterful work, every gesture and every word carefully executed to propel each show, from inception to hit status.

As the rest of the meeting's attendees—set and lighting designer, costume designer, stage managers, flying and special effects designers, and other members of the technical team—made their way to the table, Scarlett handed out the revised budgets and schedules that she and the general management team had prepared for the meeting. Margolies had assembled the most innovative and creative designers for *Olympus*. Throughout the development process, Scarlett had continually marveled at what they would be bringing to the live stage for the production.

"Let's begin," Margolies said.

Abruptly, the various conversations that had been going on around the table went silent. Scarlett took her usual seat to Margolies' right.

"You have the revised budgets in front of you. This is the one we're going with. Non-negotiable. If you can't stick to it, I'll find someone else who will." He paused as his eyes swept the table for signs of an argument. Most of the attendees were looking down at the budget. Though each of them had weighed in with their initial budget projections, a show that big was sure to have budget overruns. Scarlett knew it was a testament to Margolies' power that these hugely accomplished creatives would allow him to talk to them that way.

"Moving on. Let's go around the table. Cupid, let's start with you. Where are we on the music?" Cupid was sitting to Scarlett's immediate right.

"The score is done. And I think you'll find that it's absolute perfection," he said arrogantly. Scarlett could tell he was preparing to wax poetic about the music, as he had on many occasions.

"Good. Next," Margolies cut him off.

Next up was the sound designer. "I think we've resolved several of the issues that came up in the last meeting. The new costume adjustments should make it easier for the actor's body microphones to come on and off for the storm scene." He referred to a scene where real water and pyrotechnics would be used to represent Zeus's anger. It would present a challenge for the sound and special-effects people, who had to make it work while allowing for the actors to be heard, and body mics weren't made to get wet. Scarlett had seen amazing storm scenes done with lighting effects to simulate water and lightning, but that time, they were going for the real thing. It was probably unnecessary, but par for the course on the epic show. And Scarlett had to admit, if all went as planned, the effect would be truly spectacular.

They continued around the table. Scarlett was making notes as they went so that she could follow up with the various designers and schedule any additional conversations that needed to happen, based on technical challenges.

She felt a hand squeeze her upper thigh. It wasn't the first time Cupid had tried something like that. Scarlett didn't understand why a man with thousands of screaming fans who would welcome his advances was determined to hit on her, though she gave him zero encouragement. As he began to slide his hand up her thigh, all the while pretending to pay attention to the meeting, she discreetly crossed her legs and slid as far as she could to the edge of her chair away from him.

He glanced sideways at her with a look that said he wasn't giving up that easily. But he took his hand back, like it was all a fun flirtatious game. Scarlett glanced at Margolies to see if he had noticed the interaction, but he was focused on the update from the flying designers. The distraction had taken her focus away from the meeting. They were talking about the first act finale flying sequence when she tuned back in.

"...innovative remote-control technology that requires fewer cables and pullies in the rigging." The designer was gesturing to the tracks and cables that were being installed for the flying sequences that would occur over the audience. He held up a remote-control device. "We should be ready to test it next week."

The stage manager jumped in. "Let me know when you start testing the flying effects. The actors union will need to come through to do their usual safety check, since this is new technology."

Margolies cut in. "I'm counting on the fact that we won't get any pushback from the unions, gentlemen. Do what you need to do to assure we pass the safety inspection." Both men nodded. "I don't want anything to hold up the rehearsal process. We start previews in a couple of weeks, as you well know, and a lot of eyes are on us. No delays. No mistakes."

"Cupid," asked the flight designer, "can you stick around after the meeting today to do a final fitting for the harness?"

"No can do, love," Cupid said. "We've got the photo shoot for *Rolling Stone* this afternoon, I'm afraid. Can't you have the understudy do it?"

Cupid still doesn't get the concept of an understudy, thought Scarlett. He treats his understudy like a film stand-in who does the dirty work so the star can waltz in for the final take. Such was not the case for theater understudies, who usually stayed out of the way during rehearsals and observed, so the star could have the maximum time to settle into their role.

Psyche piped in: "Maybe the understudy should just do the role for you, Cupid."

"He is certainly *doing* something of mine these days."

"Shut your face. At least I haven't heard him complain once about my lyrics, which is a nice change."

"Well, now," Cupid said, "I wonder why that would be." He made a lewd sexual gesture with his hands.

Margolies cut them off. "Enough. We'll meet again next week. Scarlett will be checking in with you in the meantime. " He pushed back from the table, and the rest of the group began collecting their papers. He leaned over to Scarlett. "Go with them to the photo shoot. We can't have them ripping each other's heads off in front of the press."

Scarlett had hoped to make a quick escape back to the office. Instead, she would be babysitting a grown man and his wife.

Cupid leered at her. "My driver's out front. Care for a ride?" he said *ride* in a way that made it clear he wasn't talking about carpooling.

"No, thanks," she said quickly as she got up from the table. She checked her phone. She really didn't have time for his rock-star antics.

A text had come in from the intern: *A delivery came in for you. You back in the office today?*

She shot a text back: *Prob not. Can it wait?*

The response: *Perishable.*

She couldn't imagine what it could be, but she figured if she was quick, she could run back to her office and still get to the photo shoot. She glanced around to see where Margolies had gone. She saw him in the back of the house talking intently to someone. He didn't look like one of the designers. In fact, he wasn't anyone she recognized. Strange, since she knew everyone involved, and they didn't let just anyone into the theater during rehearsals.

On her way out, she walked that way to get a better look. She caught only a second of their whispered conversation.

"...taking your word for it, Margolies," the stranger was saying as he handed Margolies an envelope.

"You won't be disappointed," responded Margolies before Scarlett moved out of earshot.

She ran across the street and up to her office. On her desk was a single red rose and an envelope.

"Who delivered this?" Scarlett asked the intern.

"It was a courier. Looks like you have an admirer," he teased.

She couldn't imagine who it would be from. She opened the note and read its contents.

Headline: "Gossip columnist seen dining with beautiful up-and-coming producer this Friday night at 8:00 p.m."

Scarlett felt her pulse quicken, and a smile played at her lips.

Scene 12

Scarlett didn't have occasion to spend much time in the Murray Hill area of Manhattan. It was just a few blocks southeast of the theater district, and yet, like all Manhattan neighborhoods, it felt like a different world from the hive of theater activity. But maybe that's why Reilly had suggested they meet there. She felt nervous, but not unpleasantly.

The taxi dropped her off at Artisanal Bistro. She had splurged on a cab since she wasn't entirely sure where the restaurant was, and she was wearing new black heels. Though fashion wasn't her forte, she felt good. It had been a while since she had been on a true date, and it was nice to get some *welcome* attention from a man for a change—even if it was a man she probably would be smart to avoid.

She was right on time but was pleased to see he was already waiting for her at the table.

"You look fantastic," he said as he stood and kissed her cheek.

"Thanks." She actually blushed. Why she had turned into a silly school girl that night, she didn't know. She hardly knew him. His columns, though clever and witty, could also be so biting and heartless. They made it hard for her to believe he could really be a good guy. Nice looking, yes, but nice?

They exchanged pleasantries and got the initial ordering out of the way—two glasses of the house champagne and Artisanal's signature cheese fondue.

"I must admit, I was surprised by your invitation," said Scarlett.

"Really? I assumed a girl like you would be turning men away right and left."

She waved off the compliment. "I mean, I sort of gave you a hard time when we met the other day."

"I deserved it. It was nice to have an honest conversation," he said sincerely. "You certainly weren't easy to track down."

"How did you find me, by the way?"

"I never reveal my sources," he said with a wink and then continued, casually, "You didn't mention when we met that you are Margolies' associate producer. That's a big job. I'm impressed."

"I don't like to broadcast my job around industry people. When I do, they either want to give me the script to their new un-produced musical or regale me with horror stories about Margolies. Believe me, I don't need to hear them."

"I'm sure you don't. You probably know him better than anyone these days."

"Unfortunately for me, that's probably true," she said as their champagne arrived.

"Cheers to the girl with the best and worst job on Broadway." He raised his champagne flute.

"And to the columnist with all the dirt." She raised hers in return.

She eyed Reilly over the rim of the glass as she sipped her champagne. It was nice to meet a guy who asked questions and seemed genuinely interested in what she had to say. She figured it was probably due to that fact that he was a journalist and made his living interviewing people for gossip column fodder. A thought suddenly occurred to her.

"Is it safe to assume this evening is strictly off the record?" she asked.

"I never kiss and tell." He was nothing if not charming.

"Seriously, though," she said, "I probably shouldn't even be talking to you, much less having dinner."

"Look—I like you. I'm not going to screw this up by betraying your trust after our first date."

Just then their fondue arrived. It smelled amazing. This evening has the potential to be the perfect date, thought Scarlett.

She changed the subject. "So, did you always want to be a journalist when you grew up?"

"Something like that. I liked writing in school and have always been curious and interested in getting to the bottom of things."

"Well, it's impressive what you've managed to do with your career so far. Your own column. A name in the business."

He seemed pleased by the compliment. "Thanks, but I don't see myself being a 'gossip columnist,' as you say, forever."

"It sounds like a pretty good gig. And you certainly keep the rest of us on our toes."

"It's been fun," Reilly said.

That was an understatement, Scarlett figured. You didn't land a job like his without some major effort and a lot of politics.

He turned the conversation back to her. "Do you see yourself producing with Margolies until he drives you into the ground?"

"Not a chance!" she said, a little too emphatically.

"I see I struck a nerve."

"As producers go, I'm glad I'm learning from the best. No one else has his track record of rave reviews and hits, as I'm sure you know. But as soon as I can get a project of my own off the ground, I'd love to have my own producing office."

Their second round of champagne arrived.

"As you should. Cheers!" They clinked glasses for the second time.

"Rumor has it they're taking applications for the critic position at the *Banner*," Scarlett said. By now, news of the contest had circulated the Broadway backrooms. There was no way Reilly hadn't heard, but she was curious to know his thoughts as a journalist himself.

"Can I be honest with you?" he said.

"I assumed you were," she said with a wry smile.

"You know what I mean," he said. "I haven't told anyone this, but I actually threw my hat in the ring for the position."

"Really?" she said, raising her eyebrows.

"Hey, don't sound so surprised. I've been around the block."

"Oh, don't get me wrong. I'm sure you're more than qualified. It's just that it seems like such a lonely job." She thought about it. "But I guess in your world, it's probably the top spot."

"I'd just love to see some things change. I think it's time Broadway had a less…How shall I put it?…*biased* reviewer. Let the shows stand on their own merits."

She shot him a puzzled look.

He paused, seeming to consider how he'd frame what he was about to say. "Does it ever feel like it's not entirely logical why some shows get panned and others get raves?"

"That's showbiz, I guess," she said. She took a sip of her champagne as he continued to look at her intently. "Wait…are you saying you think it's rigged? That's not possible! Margolies, for one, would have put an end to that."

"Or would he?" Reilly said cryptically.

"What are you implying?" She was getting agitated. She pushed her champagne away.

"Hold on. I'm not implying anything—it's just something I'm looking into."

"The article you mentioned last week…"

"Look, just forget it. It doesn't matter." He seemed suddenly in a hurry to change the subject.

"But the implications…! Reviews can make or break careers and fortunes, put hundreds of people out of work or make people stars. Kanter closed our last musical with his review—"

"I'm sorry I mentioned it. I'm sure it's just me looking for a story where there isn't one." He reached across the table and took her hand. "Now, don't tell me you showed up tonight, looking like that, to talk about work."

Scene 13

Candace walked in the door to her Greenwich Village brownstone where she had lived alone since the divorce. She poured herself a bourbon on the rocks before even taking off her coat. There was a knock on the door. She rarely had company and wasn't expecting anyone that night. She tossed back half her drink before answering the door.

"Well, look what the cat dragged in," she said, leaving the door hanging open and walking back into the small living room to retrieve her drink.

Margolies didn't need an invitation to enter the house he had once called home. He had lived there with Candace a lifetime ago. It had been nearly twenty years since he'd been back, but not much had changed. Candace's drinking certainly hadn't changed, either, he thought, eyeing the drink in her hand. But she had a hardness about her now that was new to him.

"How many have you had?" Margolies asked, holding up the bottle of bourbon to gauge how lucid she'd be that evening. He wondered for the millionth time why he'd ever actually married the pathetic woman.

"Grab a glass for yourself. Oh, that's right. Never touch the stuff. You really should try it sometime."

"Because you make it look like such a good idea." He regretted the insult. He hadn't come there to fight.

Candace sat down heavily on the couch. "What the hell are you doing here? Just wanted to come by and insult me? Thanks, but I'm not in the mood."

She had never been "in the mood" thought Margolies, remembering their frigid marriage. There were exactly two things they had had in common when they'd met—a hunger for power and the ill-advised infatuation of young lust—neither of which made for a happy marriage.

"I just thought I'd check in on you. Figured you've been having a rough time of it," he said, making his best effort to convey sincerity. Candace wasn't fooled.

"Cut the crap. We had a deal. Now Kanter's dead. Game over. I don't need you anymore." She finished off her drink and slammed the glass onto the coffee table.

"You wouldn't even be there if it weren't for me," Margolies said, stepping in front of the bourbon bottle as she got up to pour herself a refill. He could see the web of wrinkles across her once-smooth face. The circles under her eyes not quite disguised by makeup. Her once-thick blonde hair was thinning and flat, these days. She had been so beautiful, he thought.

"And you wouldn't be the Great and Wondrous Margolies," she said sarcastically, "if it weren't for me and that idiot of yours, Kanter. But apparently he couldn't take it anymore. Now, thanks to his grand gesture, I'm practically getting a promotion, and you're screwed."

She pushed past him, grabbed the bourbon off the counter, and took a defiant swig directly from the bottle.

"You say *I'm* screwed?" Margolies turned to face her and pressed her up against the counter. He could see the look of lust that flashed in her eyes. A little late for her to decide she wanted him that way. She always was so easy to manipulate.

He cooed to her, "We've done okay for ourselves these past few years. We've made it to the top like, we always said we would, haven't we, Candy?" She flinched at the nickname that she had banned as she ascended the ranks at the paper.

"We've talked more in the past few days than we have in twenty years," she said, tilting her head back to look him in the eye. She was tall but he was taller.

"I think it's time we discussed a new deal." He returned her gaze.

The moment passed, and she slid out from the counter and got a fresh glass before taking the bottle back to the couch.

"Why should I do anything for you?" she asked. "I could ruin you. I'm sure more than a few people would love to know that you were paying off Kanter." She smiled just a little. "Now it looks like I'm the only one in the world who knows your dirty little secret."

"*Our* dirty little secret, you mean. I see you have a selective memory these days, Candace. Must be the booze. If I hadn't pulled strings at the *Banner*, you'd still be a two-bit assistant editor. And it was *you*, need I remind you, Ms. Arts and Culture Editor, who's on record for hiring Kanter."

"We had a deal then. I don't need you this time around. No blackmail. No pay offs. This time the public gets to pick the theater critic."

Margolies changed tactics. She was so damned combative, and he desperately needed to get her to cooperate.

"I actually think your critic contest is a great idea, Candace. You did good."

She stared at him, slacked jawed. Already through her second drink. Her bourbon-soaked brain was unable to process the compliment. She narrowed her eyes. "You're joking."

"Not at all. You'll get public support of your guy. The new critic will take back the power of that position."

"What's the catch?" she asked suspiciously.

He went over to the couch and sat down facing her. He was getting somewhere now. So close, the smell of bourbon on her breath disgusted him. "You can still make sure the right guy gets the gig."

She started to protest. He refilled her glass.

"I've done well these past few years. I can cut *you* in this time. Think about it. Put it away for retirement. Maybe get a place in Florida."

He could see her considering the proposal.

"I don't see how it could work. The public will vote."

He always *did* have to spell things out for her. How she held onto her editor position, he had no idea—sheer force of will with a healthy dose of longevity, he imagined. The spark and drive she once had was now dulled by years of drinking.

"But who is selecting the top candidates?"

"I am."

"And who is collecting the votes?"

"Me and my staff."

He could see that his point was finally sinking in. "Bingo."

She stood up and paced the room.

"I don't know. It doesn't seem right."

"*Now* you have a conscience? This is a win-win, Candace." He stood up, set her drink on the coffee table, and took both her hands. He needed to convince her. He hadn't sacrificed everything to get where he was only to have it all fall apart now. "Just do this one last thing for me, and I'll take care of you for the rest of your life. Don't you want that?"

She hesitated, but she seemed to be seriously considering his plan. He hadn't lost his touch.

She wrapped her arms around him and he stroked her hair as he calculated exactly how long he'd have to stick around.

Scene 14

The Margolies office was quiet the next morning. Scarlett had arrived later than usual, but Margolies wasn't in yet. She vaguely remembered that the intern had taken the day off.

Margolies was likely over at the theater across the street. Rehearsals for *Olympus* were starting to get intense and Margolies was spending more and more time there, terrorizing the cast and crew in an effort to make sure his ambitious visions for the show were fully realized, as well as ensuring the already-astronomical costs didn't get further out of hand.

Scarlett was supposed to be finalizing invites for the media event/investor reception she was organizing for the next month, a sort of "go team" event designed to build even more buzz around *Olympus*. But her thoughts kept straying to her date last Friday. If she wasn't careful, she could fall hard for Reilly. They had unmistakable chemistry and had practically closed down the restaurant.

Remembering their goodnight kiss, or more accurately, good night kisses, as he put her in a cab home, was enough to stir the butterflies in her stomach again. Scarlett had been accused by more than one potential suitor in the past that her love affair with Broadway didn't leave room for a boyfriend. For better or worse, when it came down to it, her career had always come first. There was no arguing with the fact that Broadway was an all-consuming, twenty-four-hour-a-day lifestyle choice.

With Reilly, however, it was different. He had the same passion for showbiz that she did. Instead of putting them at odds with each other, it was clear after one date that their mutual devotion to theater only brought them closer together. The only thing stopping her from falling into pure bliss was the nagging suspicion that there was more to the rigged review story than Reilly had revealed. Could he have been fishing for information that she might have? Or was she simply becoming cynical?

It had certainly been news to her that those rumors were floating around. But maybe he was just being an overzealous reporter.

Margolies wouldn't stand for rigged reviews. He had too much money on the line. He *is* Broadway, she thought. Unless...

Her boss's ethics left much to be desired, but bribing critics seemed a step too far, even for him. That would mean his entire career was built on corruption. He'd employed thousands of people on Broadway stages and was one of the single largest drivers of the largest economic tourist engine in New York. It just couldn't be true.

Her phone buzzed. It was a text from Reilly: *When can I see you again?*

Her stomach fluttered again, but she forced herself to turn her mind back to the matter at hand. Could Reilly really be on to something? If it were true that Margolies had been bribing Kanter all along, she was probably the one person in the whole world who could find out. She stood up abruptly. There was only one way to know for sure, short of confronting Margolies directly.

She walked into Margolies' empty office to have a look. If he had an organizational system besides Scarlett herself, it was unclear. She made it her habit every couple of weeks to sit down with him and the intern to sort through the piles and get everything filed away neatly in the row of filing cabinets lining his office wall.

At the moment, his imposing desk was littered with papers: the usual collection of file folders, sales reports, contract drafts, and ad comps that Scarlett had handed off to him in the prior days and weeks. The only uncluttered space in the whole office was a long shelf with Margolies' pristine collection of Tony Awards.

Feeling guilty already, she walked around to his side of the desk. It was uncharted territory for her. And she couldn't resist sitting in his chair. So this is how the world looks to Broadway's biggest producer, she thought. I could get used to this. She eyed the file drawers under the desk. She couldn't guess what he kept in there, since she managed the filing system. She gently pulled open the large file drawer.

Her phone buzzed on her desk in the other room and made her jump. Reilly again?

Not deterred from her mission, however, she started thumbing through the documents in his desk drawer. They appeared to be bank statements . A quick scan revealed nothing out of the ordinary. They looked like several years of monthly statements.

While the theaters collected the money from the Broadway box offices for distribution, Scarlett knew that Margolies kept several accounts for investor funds as well as development funds for future shows. Banking wasn't in her job description. Scarlett helped manage the budgets, but Margolies handled the money himself.

Out of curiosity, she pulled out the file of statements from the past year and thumbed through for the months in which they'd had Broadway openings. There had been three openings from the Margolies office during the past year—an ambitious number. Two had received raves and were still playing successfully, and the third, *Thelma & Louise*, had come and gone.

She ran her finger down the list of deposits. Nothing raised any red flags in her mind. A quick glance at the withdrawals seemed in line as well. She turned to the next month with an opening night. Similarly uneventful, except... During the opening week of both shows, there had been a $10,000 cash withdrawal. Scarlett knew the opening-week budgets well. Any show expenses wouldn't be coming from these accounts. She checked the third show month and found the same withdrawal. She quickly paged through the other non-show months. No sign of the withdrawal.

It can't be, she thought. And, anyway, if they were payouts, why did the third show get panned? It didn't make sense. She wondered how she could ask Margolies without revealing that she had been snooping. She closed the file and quickly put it back, feeling disloyal to the man who was making her career and the careers of so many others.

On her way out of his office, she pushed closed one of the file drawers along the wall that had been ajar. It bounced back open. She paused to see what the problem was. It was a file cabinet that she maintained. It had files for every investor over the years, with current show investors in front and past years' investors in the back. It was records of their contracts, checks, and correspondence.

She saw Lawrence's file, one of the thickest, alongside all the other investors', most of whom she knew well by now. Many of them had thick files of their own, since Margolies' Midas touch brought them back, show after show. More than a few stalwarts had been faint of heart about *Olympus*, however, worried that the unprecedented costs were just too risky an investment. Still, they had convinced several of the regulars to invest.

An unmarked file caught her eye. It was sticking up, keeping the cabinet from closing. That's strange, she thought. Maybe the intern got lazy. She pulled it out to see what was inside.

It contained copies of checks made out to *Olympus, LLC*. That wasn't unusual. Every file around it contained the same thing. But every file would *not* contain three checks for $3,000,000.00 each. The name on the check, M____ Corporation, was a company she didn't recognize. A new $9 million investor seemed like something she would have heard about. How strange.

Just then she heard the front door of the office open. Not sure what she had just found, she slid it back into the file cabinet and closed the drawer firmly.

"Is it filing day already?" Margolies asked, coming up behind her.

Is it my imagination, thought Scarlett, or does he sound suspicious?

"Uh, no, I was just double-checking an investor's address for the reception invites," she lied.

"Did you find it?" he asked. His eyes were boring into hers.

Does he always look at me this way? she wondered. All of a sudden, she couldn't remember.

"Yes."

"Where is it?"

"Where is what?"

"The address you said you were looking for!" he responded with frustration.

Her hands were empty. She felt her cheeks flush.

"I was just, uh, confirming the address. I had it right after all. Just wanted to make sure we didn't miss anyone. The reception is shaping up to be one of the biggest events of the season, boss."

"Thanks for the news flash," he said sarcastically as he sat down behind his desk. "Close the door behind you."

She needed to get her wits about her.

She checked her phone to see who had called earlier. It had been Margolies. No message. She turned her focus back to the event preparations. Half an hour later, Margolies strode out of the office without a glance her way and with what she was sure was the unmarked file folder under his arm.

She breathed a sigh of relief. She hadn't realized until then that she had been so tense. She decided to go out to grab coffee. Get some fresh air. Think. At the door she paused, turned back to Margolies' office, and grabbed the file of the past year's bank statements. She quickly ran them through the rickety copy machine (the bane of each new intern's existence) and stashed the copies in her laptop bag before re-filing the originals in his desk. With that, she walked out the door.

Scene 15

Reilly opened the pizza box on his kitchen table with a flourish.

"Voila! Dinner is served."

It had already been a busy week so far for both of them, so they had mutually decided to forego another formal date in favor of a quiet evening at Reilly's midtown apartment.

"I see you slaved in the kitchen all day," she said with a smile.

Reilly loved that smile. He had been thinking of little else since their last date.

"So it seems we have reason to celebrate tonight. I saw the article on playbill.com that *Swan Song* got picked up by the Manhattan Theatre Workshop. How'd you swing that, Madam Producer Extraordinaire? That's a pretty major deal."

"Why, thank you!" she said, looking pleased with herself. "They heard about the show when it was being developed up at the Pinter Theater Center, and a last-minute spot opened up in their season. We got lucky."

"You're being modest. I'm sure they had a million shows that could have gone into that spot."

"Well, I'd gotten to know the artistic director, and he and I have been talking about the show for a few months now. He fell in love with the it, like the rest of us. The timing worked out for us. We start auditions next week, if you can believe it. It's all happening so fast! I can't wait for you to see it."

"From everything I've heard it's amazing."

"Let's just say I'm very proud. And thrilled for the Jeremys."

"It's certainly a great way to kick off your solo producing career."

"Speaking of careers. You've had some big news, too. Are you ready for your interview at the *Banner*?"

"Ready as I'll ever be. Try me!" he said, unwilling to fully admit how desperately he wanted—no, needed—the chief critic job.

"So tell me, Mr. Mitchell." Scarlett imitated a formal interviewer voice. "Why do you want to be the theater critic at our hallowed institution?" She continued but started to giggle. "Do you have a death wish or simply a penchant for being truly evil?"

"It didn't say anything in the job description about being evil."

"Oh, come on. Or were you planning to go from lethal gossip columnist to 'Reilly the Friendly Critic'? Please."

"Are you going to let me answer the question?"

"By all means. Continue."

"Well, Candace... Or should I call her 'Ms. Gold'?"

"Better keep it formal."

"Well, Ms. Gold, it has come to my attention that the critic's role has devolved over the years to the point where it's not about the art but about how vicious the criticism can be of any given show. As the *Banner's* critic, my goal would be to bring a fresh, unbiased voice to the table. Let the shows stand on their own merit."

"Isn't that what's already happening? Hey, are you still thinking there's something fishy going on with rigged reviews?" The subject hadn't come up in any of their phone conversations during the week. "Ms. Gold may not like what you're implying."

Reilly refilled their glasses of wine and went over to the couch. Scarlett followed. The cold rain on the window blurred the city lights outside Reilly's one-bedroom apartment, but inside it was cozy. Scarlett curled up on the couch.

"It's nice to be here with you like this," he said, their interview prep forgotten for the moment. "But I promise I'll take you out on the town next time."

"Do you hear me complaining? This is perfect. I feel like I know you better already." She gestured to the crowded shelves of books lining the walls.

Reilly loved reading almost as much as he loved writing. He was pleased that she had read several of his favorites, although his taste was more eclectic than most: theater books, history, fiction, philosophy, travel.

"This is me. The mask comes off," he joked.

"I like what I see."

"So do I," he said as he leaned over and kissed her. She moved closer to him and their kiss deepened. He pulled her to his side on the couch, and she rested her head on his shoulder.

"I could get used to this," she said.

He smiled and kissed the top of her head. He had all but forgotten that he had originally asked her out to get information on her boss. Since getting to know her, that hadn't seemed nearly as important as figuring out how to keep her right there, by his side, for as long as possible. He hadn't been looking for it, and yet it felt like what he'd always wanted.

Scene 16

Candace spun her chair away from her desk and gazed out the window, rubbing her temples with her fingers. Interviews could be exhausting, and she'd had a full day of them. Even weeding out all but the best resumes, there had still been a long list of candidates. Her editor had taken on several of the interviews, since they needed to move quickly, but she had handled the bulk of them.

There was a tap on the door, and she reluctantly turned back to her desk.

"Any keepers today?" her boss asked. "This woman seemed like finalist material." He tossed one resume onto her desk and dropped a larger stack on the floor along the wall with other similar stacks of resumes.

"What's her story?"

"Fashion critic. She's been bureau chief in Paris for the past few years. Sounds like she could bring a unique voice. We've never had a major female critic here."

"I remember reading her resume. Let's add her to the mix."

"Where does that put us as far as finalists?"

"Well, we have our junior critic, that's one. This woman, two. That blogger we liked could be three, and the guy from Chicago. That leaves one last spot." The thought that the interviews would be coming to an end was cheering her up.

"Let's hope we find our last finalist in next week's group," said her editor, looping his thumbs through his suspenders. "I can't tell you how excited the higher ups are. This should buy us at least two months of bonus publicity as we roll out the candidate reviews. The readers are going crazy for the idea."

"So are the producers, I'm afraid," she said sarcastically. "And not in a good way."

"Well, despite what they seem to think, we don't write for producers, we write for readers," he said, quoting their office mantra.

If only that were true, thought Candace. At least it would be from now on. Despite Margolies' best efforts, she hadn't fallen for his tricks that time around. She didn't need anything from him, and he'd get nothing, much less another corrupt critic, from her this time.

Scene 17

Scarlett decided to walk home from the office. She needed to clear her head. To think. The crisp, dry air was refreshing, and New Yorkers were clearly beginning to come out of their winter hibernation.

Her week had been going so well. She'd had another amazing date with Reilly. The investor reception was ready to go. Margolies was in a better mood than usual. But what she'd found - or rather, hadn't found - in her Google search at the end of the day had left her spooked.

She had forgotten until that afternoon, when she saw Margolies leaving the office with that same unmarked file, that she had meant to look up the M____ Corporation, to find out just who it was that was coming in as their major investor. The company hadn't come up in her reception invites, and she had a hunch that asking Margolies directly might not be the best first step.

What she'd discovered on Google made her wonder what Margolies had gotten himself into. She thought about calling Reilly as she made her way on foot past the sparkling Time Warner center, but she knew she couldn't. Though she trusted Reilly, she was careful to keep the proprietary details of her work life separate from their relationship. Her suspicions were exactly the kind of thing that Reilly would want to run with in his column.

She found herself on the steps of Lincoln Center, looking toward Lawrence's penthouse. She hadn't seen him since their fun evening a few weeks back, yet she suddenly realized that he was exactly who she could talk to that night.

She sent a quick text: *Can I come up?* It wouldn't be the first time she'd made an impromptu visit to his place for a chat or a bite on her way home.

An immediate reply. He always had the latest and greatest gadgets: *Course! Just finishing a mtg.*

She crossed the busy intersection, weaving through the crowds that were making their way to the opera and ballet at the Met. Lawrence's white-gloved doorman waved her through the lavish, chandelier-lit lobby as she trod the familiar path to his elevator—which was practically the same size as her entire apartment. Oh, to be that rich, thought Scarlett.

Lawrence greeted her at the door with a kiss on the cheek and his customary "Hello, Gorgeous!" He flashed her his great smile. She could only imagine how hard it must have been to get where he was, yet he always seemed so upbeat and care free. He had the enviable air of someone who had nothing to prove to anyone. She loved that about him. He took her coat from her and offered her a drink.

"To what do I owe this pleasant surprise?"

"I was in the neighborhood and haven't seen you in a while."

"Is this a social call? Or are you here on business?" he asked with a wink. "It seems to be Lawrence Day in the Margolies office."

Scarlett wasn't sure what he meant by that. "Mostly social, though I do actually have something I wanted to ask you about. What do you know about the *Olympus* investor pool?"

Lawrence, as one of their largest investors, liked to keep tabs on who else was financially involved in any given show. He claimed it was so that he would know if the investor parties would be any good, but she knew it was also so he could keep an eye on whom he would be doing business with. He made big business look so effortless.

"Aren't you the keeper of the investment pool? I know how we can get some answers to whatever questions you have," Lawrence said.

Scarlett heard the bathroom door open down the hall. To her disappointment, out walked Margolies.

"Well, well, well, I didn't know you made house calls, Scarlett."

While her relationship with Lawrence, such as it was, wasn't a secret, she hadn't gone out of her way to tell Margolies. It wasn't like they sat around discussing their personal lives. She'd always gotten the impression that he wouldn't be pleased, and it looked like she was right. Margolies was glaring at her. Lawrence jumped in, rescuing her from Margolies' unwavering gaze.

"Margolies and I were just finishing up."

That's right, she thought, he did say he was in a meeting. He could have told her it was with her boss. It occurred to her that maybe Lawrence was showing off just a little. Lawrence was well aware of Margolies' advances on Scarlett and her constant refusal. Guys could be so territorial—and she didn't appreciate that it was at her expense this time.

Lawrence continued. "Pleasure doing business with you, good sir! *Olympus* will be your greatest achievement yet!"

"I appreciate your help with the funding. It's been a tricky one, but we got there, thanks to your *creativity,"* Margolies said with emphasis on the last word.

Suddenly Scarlett felt uneasy. She had been planning to tell Lawrence about her suspicions that a big portion of the funding was coming from some shady sources. She'd seen enough TV crime-drama episodes where dubious financial firms and outside-the-law investment entities figured in to sense when things weren't adding up. Large checks. Unlabeled files. A company that didn't seem to do anything and had absolutely zero web presence. She had been so hoping that Lawrence could help her get some answers.

"Glad I could help. I'll bring a check to the reception."

Scarlett began to wonder if Lawrence might actually be involved. Was that what Margolies meant by 'creativity?'

"Good night, Lawrence," Margolies said, picking up the unmarked file folder from the table in the entry hall. With a disapproving nod in her direction, he added, "Scarlett." And with that he was gone.

"So." Lawrence turned his attention to Scarlett. "Shall we make a night of it? A friend of mine's having a little soiree at his new loft in Tribeca tonight. Should be a good time."

"Not tonight. I should go."

"But you just got here!" He put his arm around her and tried to usher her further into his grand living room.

"What did Margolies mean by your 'creativity' in getting the extra funding?"

"Is that what you came here to find out? I roped in a few friends for this one. First-time investors, but it's about time they ponied up. They owe me."

Scarlett's mind was spinning. What could those people owe Lawrence? The pieces were falling into place, and Scarlett was beginning to feel like she didn't know Lawrence anymore.

"I really have to go."

"But, Gorgeous, what's the matter? Stay!"

"I can't. I'm seeing someone now, anyway."

She could see that stung him, but she didn't care. She just needed to get away. It was way too much for her to compute. The only person she had thought she could tell was most likely in on it.

"What? Just because you have a boyfriend doesn't mean you can't come to a party with me!" he said, practically chasing after her as she walked back through the foyer to the door.

She kept walking the last few blocks to her apartment in the dark and didn't turn back. She felt very alone.

Scene 18

The unease Scarlett felt didn't dissipate over the next two days. When she woke up Thursday morning, she felt grateful that she had asked Margolies for the next two days off. She had originally felt guilty about taking time off to work on her own musical, when things were so busy at the office. Bad timing that *Swan Song* got its big break just as *Olympus* was throwing the Margolies office into overdrive. When it rains it pours, she thought. Though, unlike *Olympus*, her show would forego the real rain on stage.

She had been honest with Margolies the week before, when she'd told him that she'd need a couple of personal days to spend some key time on her own project. He hadn't seemed to care. She hadn't felt the need to lie to him about it, and he'd be hard pressed to find fault with the work she'd been doing during her particularly long hours at the office.

He had been so distracted lately. Recently she'd found herself playing back their conversations, trying to figure out if there really were shady dealings going on that she should be worried about, or if she was simply being paranoid. She had certainly been under a lot of stress during the past week. *Olympus*, *Swan Song*, her new relationship with Reilly. Maybe she was imagining things.

She forced herself to push all thoughts of Margolies out of her head and focus on the day at hand. She got dressed and made her way to Pearl Studios, where callbacks were underway for *Swan Song*.

The Jeremys smiled as she took a seat behind the table in the rehearsal studio they were using for auditions. The company's artistic director, casting director, and the show's director were huddled around a table, discussing which scenes they'd have the actors read for the audition in addition to their prepared songs.

"Have you seen the updated callback list?" Jersey Jeremy asked with excitement. "It's a musical theater nerd's wet dream."

"Don't be crude," Buff Jeremy said, but he was smiling. "Though he's not wrong."

Scarlett had seen the list and was thrilled that so many of Broadway's top actors and actresses were interested in their show. It was a good sign that buzz of their work had already infiltrated the artistic circles. That boded well for the show's future. Getting one or two big Broadway names onboard would be a huge plus for the show.

"Try to be objective, guys," Scarlett said. "We're casting a show, not putting together an all-star concert."

"Would it be unprofessional to ask for autographs?" Jersey Jeremy asked. Scarlett and Buff Jeremy opened their mouths to object, but he cut them off. "Only kidding, only kidding." Under his breath he added, "Sort of..."

Scarlett smiled. It was refreshing to work with people who were genuinely excited about every step of the process. It was a nice change from the jaded and entitled team at the top of *Olympus*. Days like the one she was having, and people like the Jeremys, were the reason she got involved in theater in the first place. She vowed to not lose sight of moments like those.

She reached out and squeezed their hands. "Can you believe we're doing this?"

"Next stop, Broadway!" Buff Jeremy said.

"In our dreams," Jersey Jeremy said.

"Let's just take it one step at a time, shall we?" Scarlett said, not wanting to ruin the moment with pipe dreams. Though Broadway was obviously their final goal, she didn't want to jinx their current success by getting ahead of themselves. It was an amazing step in the right direction. But she knew how many shows fell off the map, even after great productions at places like that. "We never thought we'd be this far this quickly. Let's enjoy what we have now."

"Amen, sister," Buff Jeremy said.

The accompanist arrived at that point, and everyone settled in behind the audition table as the first group of singers arrived. At this stage of the game, everyone who walked in the room was exceptionally talented. Scarlett was glad to have a great director and casting director involved to start honing in on the final candidates. As producer, she didn't need to be involved in the nitty-gritty of casting, just the final approvals. But she was enjoying the process. Plus, Margolies had always gotten the best results by being as hands on as possible.

At the first break, Scarlett and the Jeremys went to the little snack bar near the elevators to get coffee. On their way through the hallway, they passed rows of benches filled with Broadway hopefuls auditioning for their shows and others. In the various other rehearsal rooms, Broadway and off-Broadway shows were rehearsing. She could hear a brilliantly sung rendition of one of her favorites, "Taylor the Latte Boy," wafting from one audition room, while a less-successful rendition of "Defying Gravity" was tormenting those inside (and outside) another rehearsal room.

There was a great energy of expectation and possibility in a place like this.

"So, drinks at our place later to debrief?" Buff Jeremy asked, sipping coffee out of a paper cup.

"Wish I could, but I have date," Scarlett said casually.

Both Jeremys snapped to attention. That was the kind of dirt they thrived on.

"Pray tell, has our Scarlett been holding out on us?" Jersey Jeremy asked.

"Don't tell us it's with that hot but too-old-for-you sugar daddy of yours. That's old news," Buff Jeremy continued.

"He's not my sugar daddy. We're just friends," Scarlett said.

"With benefits!" Buff Jeremy interrupted.

"It's not with him, anyway," Scarlett said.

"Well then, spill it before we die of suspense."

"You're not going to like this, but I actually can't tell you who it is." It occurred to her that she should probably keep her relationship on the down-low, at least for the time being. While she was probably just being overly cautious, she didn't like the idea of word getting out that she was dating the famous gossip columnist. At least not right away.

"You're such a tease!" Jersey Jeremy shrieked.

"Maybe she wants us to guess!" Buff Jeremy suggested. And that set them off.

"Is it someone we know?"

"Someone famous?"

"Someone married?"

"An actor?"

"That rock star dude from Cupid and Psyche?"

"Eew, gross!" Scarlett said. "And don't bother guessing, I'm not going to tell you. I shouldn't have brought it up." But she couldn't keep a beaming smile off her face.

"Scarlett's in love," Buff Jeremy said in a sing song voice, drawing out the last word.

"Oh, stop!" Scarlett said, blushing as she turned away to head back into the auditions, the Jeremys following hot on her heels as they continued to make ever-more outrageous guesses about who it might be.

Scene 19

Scarlett spotted Reilly at a coveted back-corner table at the bustling midtown coffee shop. Snagging any table at all in a midtown coffee shop in the middle of a chilly afternoon was no small feat. She greeted him with a kiss on the cheek. They were still careful about displaying their relationship publicly, though anyone looking on would be hard pressed to miss the romantic sparks that crackled between them.

Reilly flipped his laptop closed and slid a latte toward her as she took a seat.

"Fancy meeting you here," Scarlett said with a smile. "Out of all the coffee shops in Manhattan, you just happened to find yourself at the one next door to our audition studio?"

"Guilty as charged. Does that make me pathetic?" he said, giving her a puppy-dog look.

"That makes you very sweet," Scarlett replied. "I was thrilled to get your text. Sorry I've been so busy."

"It's a good thing. All my interview prep has put me behind on my column. Not to mention a certain someone who's been occupying a few too many of my thoughts," he said with a flirtatious glint in his eye.

"I can't imagine who you mean." She batted her eyes with faux innocence.

"Of course you can't," he said with a laugh.

"Speaking of which, what misdeeds and dirty dealings are you exposing in your column today?"

"Nothing nefarious to report this week. I'm doing my annual roundup of original musicals on deck for Broadway this spring."

"That should be a pretty short article. There aren't very many original musicals slated to open before the Tony Award deadline."

"And why might that be?" Reilly said, accusingly.

"Yeah, yeah. I know," she said. It was common industry knowledge that most producers were holding off on bringing in new shows that Broadway season for fear that they'd be hopelessly overshadowed by the *Olympus* behemoth, come Tony Awards time. Scarlett checked the time on her phone.

"Am I keeping you from the *Swan Song* auditions?" Reilly asked.

"They can spare me for a few more minutes," she said and took a sip of her latte. "I have a new respect for casting directors. Every person who's come through the door today has been ridiculously talented."

"Who's on the short list to play the lead 'swans'?" he asked casually.

"Nice try," she said with a pointed look at his laptop. "But my lips are sealed."

"You know I won't print anything you tell me not to." He held up his hands. "But I'd love to do whatever I can to help you. A little free publicity might be a good thing for *Swan Song*."

"You have a point there." It had crossed her mind that her relationship with a celebrity gossip columnist could have some added fringe benefits. But she was wary about blurring those lines. "Let me think about it."

"Why don't you come over later and let me talk you into it," he said with a provocative smile as he brushed his hand across her knee under the table, setting off the butterflies in her stomach.

"So that's how you get all the dirt for your column! You seduce unsuspecting sources at your apartment?" she said teasingly, jabbing her finger at his chest across the table.

"Only one particularly difficult source..." he said with a wink.

"I bet that's what you tell all your sources."

"You're so right." He leaned back in his chair, sipping his coffee. "In fact, I have another one showing up in five minutes, so could you please drink up?"

"Hey! Don't be mean!" She started to get up.

"Don't pretend to be mad. I have to maintain some air of mystery," he said. "I can't have the whole world knowing that New York's highest and mightiest theater columnist has been relegated to skulking around coffee shops on the off chance that he can snag a few blissful minutes with his super-busy and important Broadway-producer girlfriend."

She tried to conceal a wide smile but knew she wasn't succeeding at hiding the joy his words brought her. "So I'm your girlfriend, now, am I?"

Reilly actually blushed. "Would that be such a terrible thing?"

"I must admit, it has a nice ring to it," she said, reaching across the table and briefly squeezing his hand. It took every ounce of will power she had not to lean over and kiss him right there in the middle of the coffee shop. "But that doesn't mean I'll spill the beans on *Swan Song* casting!" she said with an impish laugh.

Scene 20

"Nice to meet you in person, Mr. Mitchell," Candace said from behind her desk. "I've read your column. Please have a seat."

Reilly glanced at his surroundings as he took a seat for his interview at the *Banner*. He had done as much research as he could about Candace Gold, but he hadn't found much. He was hoping a scan of her office decor would give him some clues about her personality, some hints on how he should play it. What he found was generic decor, a tidy office, and not a single photo.

"I appreciate the opportunity to be here. I know you must have seen a lot of people for this job."

"It's been a busy few days," she said, her tone clipped and professional. "Shall we begin?" She picked up her pen and made a note on a hard copy of his resume that she had in her hand.

He held up the pen in his hand. "Looks like we have something in common." They both had Montblanc pens. At several hundred dollars, you didn't see them every day, and they usually came with a back story. Finally, he thought, something to go on. "My parents gave me this when I got my first job at the paper," he explained. "They told me a pen could have a lot of power, so I shouldn't use it lightly."

"Sounds like your parents are smart people. It's important not to forget the weight our words can carry. My first Montblanc was a gift from my husband." She looked wistful. "Been using Montblancs ever since." She paused, deep in thought.

A husband, thought Reilly. She wasn't wearing a ring, and he hadn't come across a husband in any of his research.

Candace's tone became professional, "So, let's get right down to it. Why are you interested in the position of chief critic?"

The interview commenced in earnest. Half an hour in, Reilly knew he had nailed it. After the initial interview questions, they had fallen into a discussion of the future of theatrical criticism in light of social media's threat to its existence.

"It's been a pleasure. Nice to talk shop with a kindred spirit," he said, hoping he sounded like a colleague and not like he was sucking up to the woman who he hoped would be his future boss. She lapped up his every word. He was grateful he'd spent so much time preparing for it.

He couldn't help himself from fishing just a little for fodder for his exposé, though it occurred to him that he probably wouldn't publish it if he did in fact become a finalist. Oh, well, he thought, my year of research will be a small price to pay.

"It's nice to meet someone who values journalistic integrity as much as I do," he said.

He saw something flash in her eyes at his words, only for a brief second. A hint of confirmation of his theories, perhaps? He paused to see if she'd say anything, but there was only awkward silence. He jumped in. "So, can you tell me when I might hear something?"

"We'll be notifying the five finalists in the next day or two," she said, all business. Then she softened and met his eyes. "I don't want to speak out of turn, but you should stay by your phone."

Reilly tried to look nonchalant, but inside he was beaming. "Great. What's the process going to look like, if I might ask?"

"The finalists will be introduced to the public in a spread in the Sunday Arts section this weekend. Then each finalist will get one shot to review an upcoming show. An audition, as it were, with the *Banner's* readers as the judges." Reilly nodded as she continued, "Can you hold on a minute? I'd like you to meet our managing editor who's working with me on the finalist selection."

Reilly was thrilled. He couldn't remember ever having had a better interview in his life—and for this, of all jobs. Candace got up and walked down the hall. Reilly glanced at the neatly stacked papers on her tidy desk, trying to glean any hint as to who the other finalists might be—or any clue that could work to his advantage.

He quickly looked back down at his own notebook as Candace's assistant walked in and laid out a couple of phone message slips on the desk.

As Candace came back to the office, he caught a brief look at the first message. He wasn't sure. He only got a quick look before Candace swept the messages into her top drawer, but he could have sworn he saw the name *Margolies*.

Scene 21

Scarlett was on cloud nine after two fantastic days of auditions for *Swan Song* and another perfect date with Reilly to celebrate his selection as a finalist at the *Banner*. She wasn't looking forward to how behind she'd be at work, but it would be worth it.

She walked into the office to hear Margolies screaming into his phone. Despite the closed door, she could hear him clearly.

"I'm warning you... You don't know who you're messing with this time... I promised I would take care of you, but I could ruin you just as fast... I'd like to see you try!... This is not the end of this conversation... Don't you dare hang up on me. Don't you dare—"

Scarlett heard his fist slam into the desk. "Damn it," he said, presumably to himself, since it sounded like whoever he was talking to had hung up on him. She could think of any number of people he might have been talking to, though his tone had been particularly intense. She couldn't remember him ever resorting to explicit threats in the past. The stress of *Olympus* must be getting to him, she thought.

Just then his door flew open. He seemed surprised to see her there.

"Well, look who decided to show up to work today."

"You gave me the time off."

"Well, I take it back. No more days off, no more weekends, no nothing until *Olympus* opens."

So much for my good mood, she thought. "I'm sorry, but that's unacceptable," she said in frustration, trying to stay professional. Her own show was starting rehearsals that week, and she needed to be there. She was already disappointed that she would be on site for so little of the process, but to miss the weekends would be devastating.

"Your personal life is unimportant, Scarlett. We are making history here." He pounded his fist on her desk. "In this office." He pounded his fist down again. "With *Olympus*! Do you want to be a real producer or not?"

She didn't respond. There was no sense trying to reason with him when he was in such a rage. She wished he wasn't taking it out on her. Given the fact that he hadn't taken the time to so much as read *Swan Song* or ask about the latest developments, his words cut her to the bone.

Don't cry, she thought to herself, gritting her teeth. She took a deep breath. He continued to stand over her desk.

"I'm here now," she said, keeping her voice level. "What do you need?"

"I need you to know that your job is on the line."

"With all due respect," she said as she forced herself to hold back tears, "I've never missed a deadline, the production schedules are running on time, and the investor event is ready to go." A tear escaped and rolled down her cheek.

"Are you crying, Scarlett?" he said with a sneer. "Maybe this business is too tough for you." She stared down at her boots, biting the insides of her cheeks so hard she could taste blood. He continued, "Believe me, I didn't get where I am by crying. You better get a thicker skin, little girl."

She turned around abruptly, grabbed her coat and her computer bag, which she hadn't unpacked yet, and ran out the door. As the elevator opened, she could already feel hot tears streaming down her face. It was too much. It was just too much. At that moment, she didn't care if he fired her. She just needed to get away from him.

Coming out of the elevator as she went in was the same well-dressed but vaguely menacing man she had seen Margolies talking with at the production meeting the week before. She didn't know why, but just looking at him made her skin crawl.

As the elevator let her out, she already had her phone to her ear. "Reilly? Are you home right now? …I need to see you."

Scene 22

"Oh, my god!" Reilly said when he opened his apartment door to Scarlett's tear-stained face and wild eyes. "What happened?" He grabbed her hands and pulled her into the apartment.

"I can't tell you. But I need to know something."

"Okay," he said uncertainly. He took her bag off her shoulder and slipped off her coat. "Can I get you some water or something? Some tea? I was just making some for myself." It was a writing day for him, so he was still in his sweat pants and hadn't been planning to leave the house all day. He had just been finishing his latest juicy column for the week when she'd appeared on his doorstep.

She ignored his attempts to make her comfortable. "Do you really think there was something going on with rigged reviews at the *Banner*?"

"Why do you ask now?" he said, hedging for time. He felt torn. On one hand, he wanted to come clean, to tell her what he'd found and enlist her to help him. Yet he worried she'd think he had only been interested in her because of her job all along. And while that may have been partly true in the beginning, their relationship had since become very real to him. He put his arm around her slender shoulders and gently steered her over to the couch. He pulled her down on the couch next to him.

"Please," she said, turning her teary eyes to him, "just tell me if you really think the reviews are being rigged. I need to know."

"Well, it's complicated."

Now that he was a finalist for the critic job, he had put his exposé on the back burner. His editor was mad at him, anyway, since the article about the five finalists had disclosed to the world the fact that he was looking for another job. He had to admit to himself that he hadn't fully thought through the short-term ramifications when he'd applied for the job at the *Banner*. He had been so focused on nailing the interview. Now he was likely to lose his old job before he even found out about the *Banner*. He needed to get the *Banner* job that much more.

"Do you have something or don't you?" she said impatiently.

What got into her? wondered Reilly. Has she found some proof? If she has, it could really change things for him. For them. But he needed her to trust him. And though they had an unmistakable attraction, he needed to be able to trust her.

He got up and walked over to the window and gazed out on midtown, not sure where to start. "What do you know about Margolies' marriage?" He turned to look at Scarlett.

"As far as I know, he was married and divorced years ago. What does that have to do with anything?"

"Potentially a lot. Do you know who the former Mrs. Margolies was?"

"Not a clue. Frankly I can't imagine any woman being willing to tie the knot with him."

He sat back down next to Scarlett and pushed a stray lock of dark hair off her face. He decided to risk disclosing what he'd found out that very morning in his research. "Well, what if I told you it was Candace Gold?"

"The Arts and Culture editor at the *Banner*? *That* Candace Gold? It can't be."

"It can be and it is. Or I should say, *was*. They were married very briefly and got divorced years ago. And no one seems to remember that they were ever together."

"Well, that's certainly good gossip," Scarlett said.

Reilly realized she hadn't yet connected the dots. "It's more than good gossip," he said. "I've been looking into the circumstances surrounding Kanter's hiring. It was way before my time, and yours, but I've been doing research, and he basically appeared on the scene out of nowhere. There was some throw-away article about his journalistic history, but he was just sort of there one day, reviewing shows. A nobody, as far as I could tell."

"And you think Margolies and Candace had something to do with all that?" she asked, cocking her head. He could see that she was starting to understand.

"Well, he was hired right after Candace was promoted to Arts and Culture editor. In fact, he was her first hire. Margolies had done a few shows at that point, but he hadn't really hit his stride. That's when his reviews started to get better. Not every single one. But I did some quick statistics, and since Candace's hiring, Margolies' shows have gotten *significantly* more good and great reviews than any other producer on Broadway."

"He also produces more shows than any other producer on Broadway," she countered.

"True, but wouldn't you, if you knew you would get a stamp of approval 90 percent of the time from the *Banner*?"

Reilly had actually expected Scarlett to be shocked, considering how she reacted when the subject came up at their first dinner. Maybe it wasn't news to her after all.

"Do you have proof?" she asked.

"I'm working on it." He paused and then decided to just go for it. "Do you?"

She stood up and glared down at him. "Is that why you asked me out in the first place? To get dirt on my boss?"

He hoped with every fiber of his body that his face didn't betray his guilt at the truth of her statement. He couldn't bear for her to think that about him now. She started to go for her coat.

"No, Scarlett, wait!" He grabbed her arm and she wheeled around to face him.

"Why would I have proof?"

It wasn't going well. "Please just sit down and let's talk about this."

"I'm done with this conversation." She jerked her arm out of his grip.

"Just hear me out, and if you want to leave after that, you're free to leave." He took her hand and she flinched. "I know you're angry, but please stay. Give me five minutes."

She sighed again. "Fine." She left him to sit on the couch alone and took a seat in his favorite reading chair across from him.

"Thank you. Now let me finish before you storm off again." She continued to glare at him. "I believe that Candace and Margolies worked together to get Kanter the job and that they paid him off for good reviews. I've been putting this together for a year now in bits and pieces, and that's the only conclusion that makes sense."

"But you're a finalist for that job. Are you hoping to pad your paychecks from Margolies' bank account, too?"

"No," he said, stung by her accusation. "I want the job specifically so that I can ensure that no one is getting paid off for anything. Do you realize how long this has been going on? How long it's been since Broadway has had unbiased, honest journalism?"

"Do you think others are doing this, too?"

"From what I can tell, it's just Margolies and it's just the *Banner*. But they're the biggest players in the biz."

"But Kanter panned Margolies' last show."

"He couldn't make all the reviews good. That would be a giveaway."

"This could certainly explain why Kanter might have chosen suicide. Being a nasty critic is one thing, but being a nasty corrupt critic is a lot to live with."

"More important at this moment is that Margolies and Candace have a lot to lose from Kanter's death. They're just lucky he didn't seem to have left a note."

"Why should I help you?" She got up abruptly and went over to stare out the window.

"Because..." He got up and stood behind her, gently placing his hands on her shoulders, hoping she wouldn't pull away that time. He whispered in her ear, "Margolies' job could be yours."

She turned to face him with an icy gaze, and he took a step back. "I think you've seen *All About Eve* a few too many times."

"Think about it for a second. You could pick up all his shows. I know you're doing most of the work already. It would be so easy. This is your chance to have what you've always wanted."

She stared at him in stony silence.

"He built his career on a lie," Reilly continued, reaching for her hands, trying to coax her over to the couch.

She still wasn't convinced. "His shows run for years," she said, batting away his hands. "He may be bribing critics, but a lot of those reviews were well deserved. People flock to his shows in the millions. He's made Broadway what it is today. That's true regardless of one critic's reviews."

"I can't believe you're defending him!" It was Reilly's turn to be angry. He began pacing around his tiny living room. His cards were on the table, and he honestly didn't know what she'd do with that information. All of a sudden, he felt extremely vulnerable. What a disaster, he thought.

She watched him pace for a moment and then said slowly, "So, let me get this straight. You're going to run this exposé article, I get to take over for Margolies...and despite the scandal, the *Banner* hires you as their new critic?" She shook her head in disbelief. "To be honest, it sounds fairly unlikely."

She was right, he thought. It was pretty far-fetched when he looked at it that way. However, during the conversation, another thought had occurred to him. If he had proof about the rigged reviews, he could turn it around on Candace and Margolies. After all, they might already be scheming about how to ensure that the next chief critic was equally corruptible.

Reilly simply couldn't let that happen—and he realized that the best way to ensure honest journalism would be to get the job himself.

He was warming to the idea in his head. If Candace and Margolies were determined to play dirty, maybe Reilly just needed to beat them at their own game. Candace would certainly be interested to know what he knew—and interested in keeping his mouth shut. He could forego his exposé article and, instead, use what he knew of their fraud to force them to hand him the chief critic position on his terms—reader votes or not.

If he could only get some real proof. But he couldn't tell Scarlett, not until he'd worked out the details. He worried that his new plan would make him sound opportunistic and out for his own career advancement. And yet he firmly believed that the situation was much bigger than just his career. He knew the integrity of the *Banner* was at stake, and he realized that he was quite possibly the only person who could restore it.

He couldn't risk Scarlett misunderstanding his motives, although that didn't lessen the fact that he still needed her help. He wondered again what had made her so upset before she came over. Margolies must have pissed her off. That was good for his own cause, though he hated seeing her so unhappy.

"Are you in?" he said, carefully grasping her shoulders and meeting her eyes, willing her to go with it.

"Why should I trust you?" she said, meeting his gaze.

"Because I just told you what I've never told anyone. You of all people, who could so easily run to Margolies and tell him everything." Reilly pulled Scarlett over to the couch and she allowed him, that time. He put his arm around her shoulders and took in the scent of her hair. Her recent misery at the hands of Margolies only intensified his desire to bring her boss down. "Who knows what he'd do to me if this got back to him before I have a chance to get it published."

She tilted her head to glance at him. He could tell from her look that she had already thought of that. He continued. "I'm trusting you. I'm at your mercy." He kissed her temple. "But this could be a win-win for both our careers."

At that, she stood up and looked at him for a minute. He could see she had made a decision in that moment. She went over to her computer bag and took out a stack of what looked like copies of bank statements. "What kind of proof would you need?"

Scene 23

Early the next morning, Scarlett got back to her apartment. She dropped her computer bag heavily on the floor and leaned against the door. The past twelve hours had made her head spin.

Her eyes burned. A combination of yesterday's crying—she really needed to get a thicker skin—and getting very few hours of sleep at Reilly's apartment. By the time they had finished combing through the bank statements, it had been way too late to go home.

The excitement of their first real fight combined with their discoveries about Margolies had proved to be an irresistibly provocative cocktail. She worried that they were moving too fast, yet she had to admit, it had been wonderful to spend the night with Reilly. The evening's earlier drama had been stressful and fraught with all kinds of moral and emotional implications. And yet she felt like, if anything, all the drama was pushing them closer together.

Waking up in Reilly's arms had felt fantastic. In fact, her impulse was to turn right back around to his apartment and climb back into his inviting bed. She knew, however, that it wouldn't be prudent to give in to infatuation. She was determined to play it safe where her heart was concerned, though she had a sneaking suspicion that it was way too late for her to turn back.

A few weeks earlier, she never would have guessed that she'd fall for Reilly Mitchell, of all people. Or that, by all appearances, he had fallen for her as well. It crossed her mind that in an ironic way, she and Reilly were mirroring a young Candace and Margolies. The aspiring producer and ambitious journalist. It would be an appropriate bookend, Scarlett told herself, for the two of them to make right what Candace and Margolies had set into motion decades before.

That morning, the reality of what she had potentially done to Margolies—as well as the reality of what Margolies had been doing all those years—began to sink in. She could hardly comprehend the turn her life and career seemed to be taking.

Though she should have been getting changed and heading into the office, she couldn't get motivated quite yet. She hoped a hot shower would clear her mind.

As she stood under the faucet, a wave of mixed emotions washed over her. On one hand, she felt incredibly guilty for not only stealing Margolies' bank statements but also proceeding to share them with a journalist. On the other hand, she was horrified that all evidence pointed to the fact that Margolies very likely had been bribing Kanter to guarantee good reviews for years.

On top of all that, she wondered what would happen when Reilly's exposé hit the presses. Would she really be in a position—and capable of—picking up the pieces of Margolies' producing career? Maybe it would blow over and nothing would happen. After all, hadn't Margolies told her that she was in over her head? Maybe such was the way the world worked at that level. Her mind felt like a broken record, replaying her conversations with Margolies, and later, with Reilly the night before.

She wrapped a towel around her wet hair and grabbed her threadbare robe off the hook on the back of the bathroom door. Her brother had bought her a new robe when she moved to NYC, but she had yet to find the right occasion to lounge in its purple satin, fur-cuffed "fabulousness." She liked the fact that her brother, though he knew better, insisted on picturing her lounging in her Broadway apartment in the elegant satin robe, eating bonbons and smoking a cigarette from a long holder—though he also knew she'd never smoked anything in her life. In reality, there was another reason she hadn't let go of her old cozy robe. It was a daily reminder of how far she'd come. It was the same robe she'd had since high school. It seemed like much longer than the ten years it had actually been since she had sat in the school's "cafetorium," dreaming of being exactly where she was.

That day, however, she felt nostalgic for her life back home. The stress of her high-school theater world which had kept her awake many a night at the time now seemed ridiculously petty compared to what was giving her sleepless nights now. She couldn't bring herself to call her parents. They'd probably have good advice. High school teachers and lawyers tended to have an answer for everything. But she wasn't in the mood to rehash her week. Plus, it would be really early in the morning their time. Though they claimed she should call anytime, day or night, she knew they would be very worried if they saw her number on caller ID at such an unusual time

Unwilling to face the day, she shot off a quick text to the Jeremys: *Let me know how it goes today. I'm there in spirit.* It was the first day of rehearsal, and it broke Scarlett's heart to be missing it.

She felt tempted to text Reilly as well but resisted the urge. She reminded herself that she needed to take things slowly, even after the night they'd spent together.

Reluctantly, Scarlett got dressed and made her way into the office with palpable dread.

Scene 24

The elegant gallery of the Metropolitan Museum of Art was packed as Scarlett squeezed her way through the impeccably dressed guests. *In my next life, I'll come back as a wealthy theater investor,* she thought. *They got to have all the fun and glittering glory of showbiz and none of the late nights and heart-attack-inducing crises that made up her daily existence.* The ritzy guests had their own daily stresses, she assumed, but their brush with Broadway, at least when the Margolies production team had anything to do with it, was always impressive and memorable.

The night was a perfect example. She was pleased that the *Olympus* investor reception that she'd been working so hard on had such a good turnout. After wracking her brain, she'd found just the right venue—opulent enough for the upscale guests, yet creatively Broadway. As she took in the view of the Greek and Roman galleries of the hallowed Upper East Side institution, she felt gratified to see the perfectly coifed and sculpted investors drinking and laughing animatedly under the unblinking gaze of the gallery's ancient marble inhabitants.

Between her huge effort to forego another run-in with Margolies and her attempts at avoiding Lawrence, she also had to make sure the event went off without a hitch.

"So glad you could be here," she greeted a member of the press who had just arrived. "Have you met our director?"

She wound her way through the imposing Roman columns. The soft art museum lighting set off the bejeweled silver-haired men and women who were financing the Margolies machine. Scarlett greeted various investors and members of the media, making introductions to the creative team where she could. These extravagant events were one of Margolies' key strategies for getting and keeping investors. On so risky a show, the funders really needed to be onboard. Regardless of her frustration with Margolies, it was to her benefit that she appear professional in the crowd. Someday she'd need them for her own productions.

Lawrence caught her arm. "Scarlett, you look stunning."

His eyes swept over her dress—a playful, white, one-shoulder dress draping over her slight frame, hinting at a Greek-goddess—and strappy heels. She had bought the wardrobe combo during a holiday shopping spree with her brother, Colin, who served as her unofficial stylist. She was pleased with her evening attire, but was in no mood for compliments from Lawrence.

"Thanks." She gave him an obligatory smile and attempted to continue toward the entrance.

"Are you mad at me? You haven't answered any of my calls."

"No, just busy," she said, too brightly, and made a quick escape.

"I need to talk to you!" she heard him say to her back.

The truth was, she *had* been avoiding him. She still didn't entirely know what was going on but she wanted to stay out of it as much as possible, despite feeling thrust into the middle of it by the very nature of her job.

She touched base with the check-in table. The last few guests were trickling in, which meant she could give the cue to start the brief presentation. Margolies would be speaking, followed by Cupid and Psyche performing a duet from the show and backed by their own band. They were off in a closed side gallery, waiting to make their grand entrance.

Scarlett glanced at the list that the intern was keeping at the door. It was a good sign that there were surprisingly few no-shows, a rarity in New York, where people were perpetually overbooked.

At the bottom of the list were a few handwritten names. That was not unusual, as people sometimes arrived with extra guests or unexpected members of the media dropped in. One name caught her eye: *Candace Gold*. Scarlett glanced over her shoulder, looking for the woman who she had seen only at the bar one night but never actually met. Scarlett spotted her over by the bar and couldn't resist the impulse to talk to the woman who had been married to her boss and was also part of Reilly's alleged scandal.

"Excuse me," she said as she held her hand out to Candace, "I don't think we've met. I'm Scarlett, Mr. Margolies' associate producer."

Candace looked her up and down before extending her hand, none too warmly. "Scarlett? That's quite a name. Candace Gold. *New York Banner.* "

"My mom watched *Gone with the Wind* four times while she was in labor with me." Scarlett recited her standard explanation. People asked about her striking name upon almost every introduction. "Thank you for being here!" She was curious to get a sense of the woman.

Candace seemed to be ignoring her entirely, downing her drink in one long gulp.

Scarlett tried again to start a conversation. "Are you familiar with our project, *Olympus*?"

"Very," Candace responded tersely before turning back to the bar to order another drink.

"Right, of course," Scarlett said to Candace's back. "There have been several articles about it in the *Banner*..." She trailed off.

Candace was apparently done with the conversation, and it was time for the presentation, anyway. Scarlett scanned the crowd for Margolies. Lawrence had pulled him aside and was talking to him intently. Scarlett caught Margolies' eye and signaled to him that it was time. She saw Margolies excuse himself. Lawrence tried to wave Scarlett over. She ignored him and started weaving her way to the side gallery to give Cupid and Psyche a heads-up that they were on in five minutes.

The crowd hushed as Margolies stepped onto the small platform they were using as a stage. At times like those, he reminded Scarlett of a circus ringmaster. In his impeccably tailored black pinstriped suit, he expertly commanded his own three-ring circus: the investors, the press, and the stars.

"Welcome, brave and fearless gods and goddesses of New York," he began. He was the consummate showman when he needed to be. "We are in this room tonight among the celestial beings of the past making our very own theatrical history. Each and every one of you is joining us for something unprecedented that will change the face of Broadway!" That statement was greeted with enthusiastic applause from the guests. Margolies continued, but Scarlett couldn't hear him as she poked her head into the room where Cupid and Psyche were supposedly warming up. She encountered a chilly scene.

Cupid was in one corner, Psyche in the other and their band members looked bored with it all. The band wasn't exactly thrilled that their leaders were going to be tied up on Broadway, leaving them unable to tour or record albums for the unforeseeable future. They had all been offered jobs in the show's orchestra, but it wasn't exactly the rock-and-roll lifestyle to which they had grown accustomed. But the pay was good.

"You're on in five," Scarlett said. No one acknowledged her. "See you out there," she said as she closed the door behind her.

Margolies was mid-speech. "A show of this magnitude has never been attempted on Broadway. With a budget of over $50 million, we are creating an epic of unimaginable proportions. I am standing here tonight to say that, thanks to all of you and our incredible creative team, we are going to give Broadway something it's never seen before. It is my promise to all of you here tonight that you will be rewarded for joining us in this endeavor."

Scarlett noticed Candace Gold standing a few feet away with a grim look on her face. It suddenly occurred to Scarlett that if Margolies and his ex-wife really had been bribing the critic, then Margolies would be at the mercy of a real critic for the first time. No wonder he's been in such a state recently. It isn't just *Olympus* that has him on edge--it's losing his ace in the hole. Scarlett didn't have time to think it through just then. She needed to get through the evening.

Margolies started wrapping up his presentation. "Audiences and critics alike will have no choice but to adore what they see. Storms of Zeus's wrath!" The crowd *oohhed*. "Fire!" The crowd *aahhed*. "The gods will literally take flight, like you've never seen before in live theater!" Another round of applause. The investors were helpless to resist the intoxicating combination of champagne and Margolies' words.

"And now, without further ado, it is my pleasure to introduce the real stars of the evening." Despite his modest words, not a single person in the room was fooled by Margolies' feigned humility. "Our very own divine royalty, straight from *Olympus*. The love birds of legend, both in our time and in the storybooks. Dare I say the most talented artists of our day, as proven by their worldwide acclaim, will reach new heights, literally, as the stars of our show. I give you Cupid and Psyche!"

The crowd went crazy as Cupid and Psyche bounded up onto the stage. Cupid pulled Psyche into a deep kiss. The genteel, well-bred crowd was eating it up.

Oh, please, thought Scarlett. She could see why so many veterans of Broadway ended up jaded and burned out after spending time with the Cupids and Margolies of the world. Ultimately, she craved the *real* people she had been working with on *Swan Song*. Would they all turn out like that, too? Would they too eventually create public personas as a facade to disguise miserable, unhappy personal lives? Scarlett fervently hoped not.

Lawrence was by her side again. He whispered urgently in here ear. "Please, I really need to talk to you." He was more serious than Scarlett had ever seen him. But the band started, making all conversation impossible.

"I can't hear you," she mouthed to him, gesturing to her ears and the band. "Sorry."

Scene 25

Margolies stepped off the platform, relieved to see Cupid and Psyche taking the stage. The "lovebirds'" relationship was so tense these days that Margolies half-expected them to strangle each other before opening night arrived. The project was turning into a total nightmare, but it was too late to turn back now.

He still didn't know how it could have happened. He had made sure that everything had been in place for his crowning Broadway achievement. A fool-proof show. The money. The critic.

His pep-talk minutes before might have gotten the crowd fired up, but it had left him feeling worse. Everything single thing was going wrong.

The critic. His critic was dead, and Candace wasn't cooperating. And to think she had the nerve to show up. He had always known Kanter was weak; that's what had made him such a malleable pawn for Margolies. But he hadn't thought the pressure of the critic's job would push Kanter to the brink. He gritted his teeth in anger before remembering that he was at a party. He regained his mask of composure, a major effort under the circumstances.

A fool-proof show. Sure, it had been a good idea, but with impossible stars and technical effects that pushed the creative team to its limits, he was beginning to have doubts. OSHA and the safety inspectors were breathing down his neck, and the theater owners weren't helping much with the structural renovations to the space. Where had everyone's artistic vision gone? Couldn't they see that he was making Broadway history? They needed to stop breaking his balls over this or that wireless remote flying track or pyrotechnic.

The money. He had always had a cordial relationship with certain "money people" but hadn't needed to resort to working with them, despite their increasing attention as he proved that he could turn a Broadway gamble into a financial win. He'd never wanted to mix with that contingent, having seen what happened to people who get on the wrong side of that crowd. Now, not only had he been forced to go to them by *Olympus'* Olympian budgets, but it was costing him legitimate investors. Lawrence had somehow found out and pulled out his own investment just that evening. It was a lot of money that Margolies couldn't afford to lose. But how could Lawrence have known about the source of the other money...?

Scarlett. That bitch must have told Lawrence. He already knew that he needed to fire her. Unfortunately, he needed her too much at the office to throw her out right away. The perfectly executed event that evening was just another example of how good she was at her job. But he should have known better than to let her get so deeply entrenched in his work, despite the fact that she made his life easier. He couldn't trust her. As soon as *Olympus* opened, he could focus on getting rid of her and finding a replacement. He just needed to make sure she didn't do something stupid and get herself mixed up in all that. If his new business associates knew that she knew, getting fired would be the least of her worries. And he needed her in one piece right now.

Cupid and Psyche were finishing their second and final song. Margolies steeled himself to put on a smile for a room full of people who were depending on him. He smoothed the lapels of his expensive suit. He might not feel like the "king of Broadway" at that moment, but he'd defy anyone to say he didn't look the part. Through the cheering crowd, he saw Candace making a beeline in his direction—or as much of a beeline as she could make, being unsteady on her high heels. Before she got to him, however, he was enveloped by a crowd of electrified investors.

Scene 26

The room was positively bursting at the seams with excitement. Despite her personal challenges, Scarlett felt immensely proud of her work that evening. Everyone was thrilled. Well, everyone except Lawrence.

She supposed she should hear whatever it was Lawrence had been wanting to talk to her about all night. She had lost him in the crowd, but she didn't have time to worry about it at the moment. She still had several investors to schmooze. Her evening's work was far from done.

She pushed her way back into the crowd, chatting with people along the way and keeping an eye out for Lawrence. Out of the corner of her eye she saw Candace talking to Margolies. Candace was leaning against the wall for support. Margolies didn't look happy. She couldn't picture the two of them married. Then again, many things about Margolies surprised her these days.

Making her way to the back of the room, she could feel the crowd starting to thin out as people left for their evening plans. Suddenly, she felt arms wrap around her from behind. She was frozen in shock for a moment that anyone would be so forward. A brief glance down at the thin hands adorned with gaudy rings and arrow tattooed forearms confirmed her fear—it was Cupid.

"You look positively good enough to eat," he whispered in her ear, his arms tight around her. She could feel him pressing his hips against her back. She felt *positively* disgusted.

"Get your hands off me," she said, none too politely. She had developed a high tolerance for sexual harassment during the past few years of working in theater, but that was way over the line.

"I'm just having a little fun." He licked her neck as she pried his hands off her waist.

"I'm not interested." She wiped his spit off her neck. Disgusting! "I have a boyfriend."

"Perhaps he'd like to watch," Cupid said, as Scarlett tried to get away. She found herself trapped in the corner of the room. She turned toward him and scanned the crowd over his shoulder, trying to catch the eye of someone who might rescue her from his unwanted advances. Unfortunately, the shadowy corner was protected from easy view by a headless Adonis-like statue atop a pedestal.

Cupid ran his fingers down the side of Scarlett's face and along her breasts. "The more you resist, the more I want you." The smell of his breath and his sweat so close made her want to retch. She could see traces of white powder under his nose. He had told Margolies that he had kicked his drug habit. Apparently not.

"I just want one little kiss, love." He brought his face close to hers. She turned her head and tried to push him away when they were interrupted by a voice behind them.

"Don't you two make a pretty little couple?" Psyche hissed in her over-emphasized cockney accent, glaring at them under her hot pink bangs. "Husband, darling, leave Margolies' little slut for a minute and pretend like you don't hate my guts as much as I hate yours. We have a public to greet."

Scarlett was relieved to see that she might have been rescued, despite Psyche's insults. She couldn't wait to get home and get in the shower. There was something almost lizard-like about Cupid. She couldn't help but feel like he'd left a film of reptilian slime on her skin; probably just sweat. Unfortunately, Cupid wasn't done having a little fun with her.

"You can spare me for a few more minutes, wife. You've been doing fine without me for years." He gave her a sickeningly sweet smile. "Buh-bye." He waved as Psyche stormed off. He turned back to Scarlett, who had been trying to quietly slide out of the corner.

"Not so fast." Cupid gripped her arm tightly. Too tightly. Scarlett felt herself starting to panic. With his other hand he reached around her back and pressed her hips onto his, grinding their bodies together.

Scarlett wanted to scream, but she didn't want to cause a scene. The last thing she wanted was for the investors and the media to see her like that. And yet why wasn't anyone paying attention? She pushed Cupid away with all her might. For such a skinny man, he was unexpectedly strong.

Suddenly stronger hands than hers pulled Cupid away.

"What the...?" Cupid wheeled around to see who would dare interrupt them yet again.

"Get away from her," Lawrence demanded, towering over Cupid. Cupid started to protest, but Lawrence cut in. "Now!"

"Screw you, man," Cupid said. To Scarlett he added, "You'll come around, love. Let me know when you're ready for a real man." He shot Lawrence a contemptuous look before smoothing his greasy black hair and strutting toward his wife. Psyche was making an unlikely tableau, chatting with a retired banker and his wife. Before Cupid got to her, he turned to Lawrence, his face contorted with anger, and yelled, "I want you off my show!"

"Done," Lawrence said. "*Buh-bye.*"

"Thank you," Scarlett said, eyeing the red welts on her arm left by Cupid's fingers.

"Are you okay?"

"I guess. Good thing you got here when you did."

"I'm always watching out for you, Gorgeous." He smiled, and her heart softened toward him.

Scarlett felt exhausted. She glanced around the room. The party was winding down. She didn't see any sign of Margolies.

"Are you really off the show?" she asked. "Cupid can't do that to you. He's an idiot."

"I know. I was already off the show."

"What are you talking about? Are you serious?" That was a major deal. Losing a $3 million investor would be a huge blow to Margolies.

"This is what I've been trying to tell you." Lawrence whispered. "After you acted so strangely at my apartment the other night I did some poking around into the Olympus financials. I couldn't get all the details but there were enough red flags to convince me that there are some seriously shady backers involved. The last thing I want is to have my money tied to potentially illegal dealings. Life's too short to deal with the devil. Margolies must be desperate on this one."

"After I ran into Margolies at your place that night, I was afraid you were somehow mixed up in it too," Scarlett said apologetically.

Lawrence looked hurt. "I thought you knew me better than that."

"I do. I was just so confused..." Scarlett trailed off, suddenly feeling overwhelmed with exhaustion.

"Can we get out of here?" Lawrence asked.

Scarlett gave herself permission to be done with the event for the night. "Yes, please."

Scene 27

Reilly woke up early, threw his coat on over his sweat pants and t-shirt, and slipped into the tennis shoes he kept by the door. Not his best look, but he was only going to the corner newsstand to buy the day's *Banner*.

He brought the paper back to the apartment and dropped it onto a table already covered in newspaper clippings. He'd been busy the past week. After the full-page spread had come out announcing the finalists, he had made it his mission to learn everything he could about his competition. Each candidate had been given 500 words to introduce themselves, and he was pleased with what he'd come up with for himself. However, his attention had been primarily focused lately on what the other finalist did—and didn't—have to say about themselves.

Reilly was obsessed with his speculation that Margolies and Candace would be working together again, all these years later, to plant a new corrupt critic. Could it be one of the finalists? Or would each finalist's integrity be tested in some way as part of the process? His mind had been racing with conspiracy theories.

He flipped on the pot of coffee he had prepped the night before and opened the *Banner* to the day's Arts and Culture section. The first finalist's review had come out that day.

In Reilly's analysis of his competitors he found only two really viable threats, from a writer's perspective. The junior critic was one, since he'd been at the *Banner* for several years and knew how to write for their readers. Plus, he was a familiar name to them already and was not unpopular.

The other strong competitor was the woman. The *Banner* had never had a female critic, and that one was imminently qualified for the job with her journalism background as a bureau chief in Paris, and before that, in the States.

The other two candidates were an active theater blogger whom Reilly discovered had a solid, but probably too niche-y, following; and a critic from Chicago who could probably do well at the job but wouldn't get through the competition, as the readers would likely penalize him for not being "New York" enough.

It was the Chicago candidate who had been tapped to go first. His assignment had been to review the previous night's opening of a new musical called *Evening Madness* at the Public Playhouse. It was customary those days for critics to see a show a night or two before opening so as to have time to write a thoughtful review and still hit the print deadline. Back in the days when critics attended opening nights, they could often be seen sprinting up the aisle as the curtain fell, trying frantically to get their scathing or revelatory thoughts on paper and turned in. But that rarely happened anymore.

Reilly had made a point to see *Evening Madness* the week before, so he could practice and compare notes with whatever his opponents came up with. He briefly wondered what the Public Playhouse thought about having one of the critic candidates review that particular piece. They had an impressive track record of moving new shows onto Broadway—a boon both financially and for their reputation for discovering the best new talent in the country. But a Broadway transfer for that particular show would require a rave review.

As Reilly took in the review, he knew the Public Playhouse would be pleased. The Chicago candidate, likely in an attempt to prove to New Yorkers that he loved their town as much as his own, had written what the industry called a "love letter" to the show. He praised the theater, the piece, and the author. Reilly closed the paper and smiled smugly.

It wasn't that he disagreed with the sentiments. *Evening Madness* was an excellent show. However, the candidate had made a huge mistake. Reilly knew from the success of his own column that even when writing praise, readers need an undercurrent of dirt, wit, criticism—writers were *critics* after all. A straight-across-the-board rave was boring. It provided no fodder for the water coolers and dressing rooms around town, which meant, in that case, no buzz for the finalist.

Reilly got up and poured himself a cup of coffee, still smiling. One down, three to go. Reilly wondered if he had been deliberately selected as the last to audition, or if it was just the fact that he had been the last finalist to be selected. Either way, he was pleased with his position.

By his calculations, it would be a month before he was up to the plate. His attempts to determine which show he might review had been only somewhat successful. There were two Broadway openings coming up—a play and musical—but they were likely opening too soon to fall to him and would go to the other two finalists.

Reviewing a Broadway show would have been good. But he felt a non-Broadway opening would give him more leeway to make a splash. The high-profile, non-Broadway openings a month out, however, were too hard to predict. There had not yet been enough buzz around any of them to indicate which would be singled out for him.

He picked up his cell phone and called Scarlett, eager to share his good mood. He knew she would have read the review. He could imagine how much fun they'd have dissecting it and discussing it. Maybe she would even read the practice version he had written and confirm his belief that his version would have been better.

No answer on her phone. That dampened his elation for a moment. It had been two days since they had talked, and he was shocked to realize how much he had been missing her. He'd always prided himself on his independence, especially where women were concerned, and he had all but given up on the idea of an actual relationship. He always had plenty of women willing to keep him company. Now he only thought of one woman. He knew he shouldn't be concerned. It was still too early in their relationship for a routine. But they had been talking more frequently up until that point.

The only other thorn in an otherwise-rosy weekend was his upcoming lunch with his editor on Monday. Not surprisingly, his own paper was less than thrilled that their columnist was so visibly looking for work at the *Banner*. Then again, it made for good gossip. If they were smart, he thought, they'd use it to their advantage. He was planning to pitch to them that if he *didn't* get the job, he'd use any additional dirt he got on the *Banner* in his much-anticipated and now very overdue exposé and make it that much better.

His eyes drifted over to the bank statements Scarlett had left with him. She had gone way out on a limb for him, and he wanted to do right by her. Maybe it was best that they weren't talking for a few days. It would make it easier for him to do what he needed to do without getting her more involved than she already was. She could thank him on the other side, when everything worked out.

He took a deep breath and thought about the best way to approach Candace with what he knew. Could he really pull it off? Fight fire with fire, he kept telling himself. So what if on the surface it looked like he was blackmailing Candace for his own benefit? He was convinced that it was for a larger cause. He'd come clean later, after he'd brought integrity back to the *Banner*.

Reilly sipped the hot coffee and walked over to the window. He could see people scurrying to work, some stopping at the newsstand that he could just see from sixteen stories up. Some of them may be buying a paper that held his column. Even from up here, he knew that most of them would be reading the *Banner,* and in a few weeks, they'd all be reading him.

Scene 28

"Don't be nervous," Scarlett said to the Jeremys, as they came out of the subway station at 66th Street.

"I'm not nervous," Jersey Jeremy said, passing his stack of sheet music from one arm to the other for the hundredth time.

"He doesn't like having to play and sing his own work in public," Buff Jeremy reminded Scarlett. Then turning to Jersey Jeremy, he said, "I'm sure Scarlett's boyfriend will love our show, despite your attempts to mangle it with your singing voice."

"Gee, thanks for that. I don't see you getting up there to sing with me!" Jersey Jeremy said.

"Have I ever told you how much I loved your singing voice?" Buff Jeremy said to Jersey Jeremy with chagrin.

"You better stop with that whole *boyfriend* business, too," Scarlett said as they crossed the street to Lawrence's building. "Lawrence is *not* and never has been my boyfriend,"

"Right, of course. I meant to say *boy toy*," Buff Jeremy said to Scarlett. Then, considering Lawrence's more than several years on Scarlett, he added, "Or *man toy*? Which do you think he'd prefer?"

In response, she punched his shoulder playfully as they waited at the light.

"You still dating mystery man?" Jersey Jeremy asked. "We're beginning to think he doesn't exist!"

"You'll meet him soon, I promise," she said, knowing that she needed to call Reilly. After their impromptu sleepover, he'd be wondering by now why she hadn't called. She was pleased with herself for having the will power to get some distance, in light of everything that was happening, and despite her desire to call or see him every minute. Apparently, absence was only making her heart grow fonder.

The *Swan Song* trio walked through the sparkling revolving doors into the grand lobby of Lawrence's building.

"Is there a dress code I should know about?" Jersey Jeremy said, eyeing the white-gloved, uniformed doormen, fresh flower arrangements, and endless gold leaf.

"Yes," Scarlett said. "A Rolex, some Armani, and a few million dollars in your wallet."

"Damn, I left my Rolex in my limo," Buff Jeremy said sarcastically.

"Don't worry, honey, I'm sure Lawrence has fifteen or twenty to spare," Jersey Jeremy said.

"Behave yourselves!" Scarlett said, smiling. "We're here on business. I've told Lawrence how great you are. Don't let me down."

They all stepped into the elevator.

"We'll be perfect angels," Buff Jeremy said, fluttering his eye lashes and putting his hands together as if he were praying, which showed his pecs off to best advantage.

"Now you're pushing it." Scarlett laughed, as the elevator opened.

The doorman had let Lawrence know they were on their way up, and he was waiting for them.

"Welcome! Come in, come in!" Lawrence said grandly. "You must be the famous Jeremys that Scarlett's told me so much about!"

Scarlett enjoyed watching the Jeremys' eyes widen as they entered the main room and took in the view of Lincoln Center and Julliard. It was not often Scarlett saw them speechless. It is fun to have friends in high places—literally and figuratively, thought Scarlett. The Jeremys took in the early evening view, watching the city's lights twinkle on one by one. Scarlett wondered how long it would be before they realized that, with the binoculars perched on the window sill, they could actually watch ballet rehearsals going on through the windows across the way. It was one of Lawrence's favorite past times.

Lawrence gave Scarlett a hug and a kiss on the cheek. "How are you holding up, Gorgeous?"

"I'm good. Thanks for meeting with us."

"The pleasure's all mine." He turned to the guys. "Can I get you a drink?"

"No, thanks," both Jeremys said. They were standing forlornly in the middle of the living room, clearly not sure where to park themselves among the sleek black and chrome bachelor-pad furniture. Jersey Jeremy was eyeing the grand piano.

Scarlett jumped in to rescue them. "Shall we get down to the business at hand?" She had no doubt that they would all hit it off, once they got to know each other. She was eager to get past the awkward getting-to-know you phase.

"Please sit," Lawrence said with a flash of his charming smile. The Jeremys sat on the black leather couch directly behind them. "I've heard so much about you from your lovely and brilliant producer, here." He gestured to Scarlett, who had taken a seat in the black leather Barcelona chair near the piano.

Lawrence perched casually on the other couch that was littered with tech magazines and the intimidating master remote that Scarlett learned operated everything in the apartment from the lights to the music to the blinds. Lawrence could be such a tech geek. She wouldn't be surprised if one button ordered take-out and another made the bed.

"Um, thanks," Jersey Jeremy said. She had never seen the Jeremys so nervous.

Eager to put them at ease, she said to Lawrence, "I've told them a bit about our conversation. But why don't you tell them why we're here?"

"Of course!" Lawrence said with enthusiasm. "Well, as Scarlett has probably told you, I've been investing in several Margolies' shows over the years and have been having a blast. However, due to some recent events"—his eyes met Scarlett's for a moment—"I've decided it's time to broaden my portfolio, so to speak. From a financial perspective, it really doesn't make sense to throw in my whole lot with Margolies. I've decided to diversify, and, it seems our Scarlett here has had a project up her sleeve all along."

Despite her close relationship with Lawrence, Scarlett had kept quiet about her own producing projects. She hadn't wanted to come across as poaching Margolies' investors—a big no-no, even though it happened among producers all the time. All that changed, though, when she learned that Lawrence had discovered the source of the additional *Olympus* money and had pulled out.

"I've told him about our success at Pinter and the fact that we got slotted into this season at the Manhattan Theatre Workshop," Scarlett said. "I've invited him to come to rehearsals next week, of course. In the meantime, I want him to meet you guys and learn more about our plans."

"I'd love to hear what you have, if you don't mind," Lawrence said to the Jeremys. "Scarlett said you'd be nice enough to give me a sneak peek. How'd you come up with the idea, anyway?"

That was the right question. The Jeremys' eyes lit up and they launched into the story Scarlett had heard a million times about the genesis of their musical project—Jersey Jeremy's love of *Swan Lake* as the first ballet he ever saw, one magical night in Manhattan during his childhood. Buff Jeremy's obsession with *Black Swan*, Darren Aronofsky's recent film with a dark take on the same story. The combination had inspired their own contemporary version of the *Swan Lake* story. Lawrence had gotten the basics from Scarlett, but hearing the Jeremys' compelling description was clearly thrilling for him.

The ice broken, the three men gathered around the piano, where the Jeremys walked Lawrence through the show.

"Do you know the original *Swan Lake* story?" Buff Jeremy asked.

"I've seen the ballet a few...hundred times, give or take," Lawrence said with a smile, gesturing out his window to Lincoln Center, home of the New York City Ballet. "A Russian prince who is looking for a wife comes across a lake made from the tears of swans that were once women but have been transformed by an evil sorcerer. He falls in love with one of them—"

"Odette. The white swan," Jersey Jeremy prompted.

"Right. But the sorcerer somehow tricks him with a different woman—"

"The sorcerer's daughter, Odile. The black swan. He tries to trick the prince into marrying her instead," Jersey Jeremy said.

"Does that about cover the plot?" Lawrence asked.

"Basically, other than the fact that the prince eventually figures out he's been tricked and he and Odette are reunited, where upon they promptly drown themselves in the swans' lake."

"...And they all live unhappily ever after," Scarlett finished.

Jersey Jeremy jumped in and started playing the introduction to the opening number on the piano. "Now put all of that in the back of your mind, because this is *Swan Song*." He kept playing, underscoring his narration. He adopted a lilting Southern accent. "Let us take you to Louisiana. 1952. Simple set, small but brilliant cast, lush orchestra. A small-town sheriff's deputy we call Prince. A powerful, and, might we suggest, evil sheriff. And the beautiful girl Prince loves, Odette." He continued through the opening number, singing through all the parts as the characters were introduced and the exposition was set up.

"With us so far?" Buff Jeremy asked Lawrence.

"Absolutely! Did I hear a little hint of gospel in that opening number?"

"You caught that?" Jersey Jeremy beamed. Then picking up his accent again, he continued: "Why, yes, sir, you did. Did we happen to mention that the lovely Odette is African American?"

"Does that make her the black swan?" Lawrence asked Buff Jeremy.

"Not exactly! In our version, the white swan is black, and the black swan—"

"...the sheriff's beautiful blonde Southern-belle daughter—" Scarlett inserted.

"...is white," Buff Jeremy finished.

They continued through the show that way with the Jeremys trading off on narration and singing through a few of the songs, portraying all the different characters.

At "intermission," Lawrence ran to his wine cellar (if you could call it a *cellar* in a penthouse) and popped open a bottle of Moet & Chandon.

"To *Swan Song*," Lawrence said, raising his crystal champagne flute.

"You haven't heard the rest of it," Jersey Jeremy said.

"You're right!" Lawrence smiled. "Get back to work! Intermission is over."

"Yes, sir," Jersey Jeremy said flirtatiously. Both Jeremys were now obviously, if harmlessly, enamored of Lawrence. He had that effect on everyone, including Scarlett.

Scarlett was pleased to see them all so excited. She'd had no doubt they would hit it off, but their enthusiasm was incredible to experience and so exactly mirrored her own. As they wrapped up the Act Two synopsis, Lawrence applauded loudly.

"I'm in!" he announced. "Though I'm disappointed in you, Scarlett," he said in mock anger.

"What did I do?" Scarlett asked, enjoying the cozy feeling of warmth that came from sharing a nice champagne buzz with great friends—feelings she had been sorely missing of late.

"You've had this gem of a show for a year now, and yet, till tonight, you left me floundering in Margolies' *Olympus* schlock! Imagine, a musical that doesn't rely on spectacle to be successful. I really have been drinking the Margolies Kool-Aid for too long."

"Well, better late than never," Scarlett said.

"Where do we go from here?" Lawrence asked the question on everyone's mind. All eyes turned to Scarlett.

"Well, we start previews at the Manhattan Theatre Workshop in three weeks. Opening night is the following week. If we get good reviews, we'll have some options."

"Are you thinking Broadway?" Lawrence asked.

"That's certainly an option," Scarlett responded. "A lot would have to fall into place to make that a reality, in addition to a rave review—which is never a guarantee." Except when it is, she thought bitterly. "Even finding a Broadway theater to rent would be tough. Experienced producers cultivate those relationships for years."

"Can't Margolies help with that?" Buff Jeremy asked. "He owes you that much, after all you've done for him."

Scarlett hadn't mentioned the current drama in her personal life to them. They needed to keep their focus on *Swan Song*. "I think I want to branch out. Find a producing partner who doesn't think of me as his Girl Friday, for one."

"Plus, Margolies will be pretty busy with *Olympus*," Jersey Jeremy said.

"Well, there's no way we can come in this season anyway," Scarlett said.

"Why not?" Lawrence asked. "That's exactly what *Rent* did. Look how that turned out! Don't we want to jump on the momentum from downtown?"

"Just because a show's a hit downtown doesn't mean it's right for a Broadway transfer. *Rent* is the exception, not the rule. Though, you're not entirely wrong. Other shows have pulled it off. But it's a long shot. And coming in the same Tony Award season with *Olympus* would be risky."

"*Olympus* is exactly why we *need* a show like this. This is what theater is supposed to be. Beautiful music, real heart, raw talent up on the stage," Lawrence said.

"Let's not forget, we'd also need about $5 million for Broadway. Maybe more."

Lawrence's eyes twinkled. "Well, I did just save $3 million on *Olympus*. My investor friends are pulling out, too. Why don't you leave the money part to me."

Throughout the conversation, the Jeremys were exchanging excited glances and finally could no longer contain themselves. They practically tackled Scarlett and Lawrence in a group hug.

"I can't believe this is happening!" they squealed together.

Scarlett couldn't believe it, either. The odds of taking her first show to Broadway had been so remote a few days ago. And now, it was a distinct possibility. She felt nervous, excited, and so very grateful for those wonderful people piled together with her in a tangled mess on a $30,000 couch in a penthouse in Manhattan.

Scene 29

Candace poured a shot of bourbon into the coffee mug on her desk. It's after 5:00 p.m., after all, she thought to herself. So what if I need to let my hair down a bit? She had every right to be pleased with herself. The first two candidates' reviews had come out, and the readership numbers were through the roof. On top of that, the story was getting picked up by other news sources, and those damned chat rooms were driving people to the *Banner* website by the thousands. How nice, thought Candace, that they are actually working to my benefit for once.

Today's review by the latest candidate was open on her computer screen, allowing her to watch, in live time, as reader comments came in. Though she was determined not to play favorites in the competition, she felt secretly pleased that the second candidate to audition, the one lone female of the finalist pool, was getting such a positive response.

Candace had assigned her a Broadway opening to review and was not disappointed to see that the candidate had nailed it. The readers clearly agreed.

Her desk phone rang and she flinched. For several weeks she hadn't been able to shake a feeling of dread every time the phone rang. She took a sip from her mug. "Hello?"

"Hi, Ms. Gold, er, Candace, please."

"This is she."

"Hi, this is Reilly Mitchell. One of the critic finalists."

He sounded nervous. She wondered if the competition was getting to him. That would surprise her, since he was a strong candidate and must have a lot of nerve to write his usual column.

"Ah, yes, Reilly," she said, warming up. Reilly was actually her other favorite in the competition, if she had to be honest. She liked his freshness and integrity, and it didn't hurt that he was cute and younger than the other candidates by a few years. "What can I do for you?"

"I was hoping to come by and talk to you."

"Is this regarding the competition? I'm keeping my distance from the candidates. Can't be seen as giving anyone an unfair advantage. I'm sure you understand. If you have logistical questions, I can put you through to my assistant who is handling those things."

"Well..." He hesitated. "I really need to talk to *you*. It's, uh, important."

She paused, not sure what to do. She wanted to stick to the competition rules, which she and the *Banner's* legal team had so carefully crafted. But what harm could it possibly do to meet with him? He said it was important.

"Hello...?" Reilly said into the silence on the other end of the line.

"Sorry, I was just..." She supposed it would be okay, particularly if they were discreet. "Alright, we can meet. But not here."

She racked her brain for an out-of-the-way spot. Both she and Reilly were well-known enough that they needed to steer clear of the theater district. "Can you meet me in an hour at the lobby bar in the Bowery Hotel?"

"Yes! Thank you!" Reilly said into the phone.

An hour later, Reilly waved Candace over as she walked through the door of the Bowery Hotel. He didn't spend much time in the East Village neighborhood and had never been to that bar before, but he could immediately see why Candace had suggested it.

Still March, it was dark outside, and almost as dark in the bar. The rich oak paneling, dim lighting, and profusion of nooks and crannies housing deep wingback chairs all provided the perfect setting for clandestine conversations. He had been browsing the impressive cocktail menu while he waited, but decided he'd better stick with water. He needed his wits about him.

He knew it was irrational, but his imagination was running wild with the whole scenario—secret meetings in a shadowy bar, an older blonde, blackmail, suicide. He snapped out of it as she took a seat in the wingback chair opposite his. She glanced around the room briefly, but he knew it was unlikely that they would be noticed, tucked away as they were.

"I really appreciate your meeting with me," he began, but she held up a manicured finger for him to wait, flagging down the waiter with her other hand.

"Manhattan. Rocks."

"What kind of bourbon would you prefer? We have..." He began with a plethora of brands, but she clearly didn't have the patience for it. She cut him off immediately.

"Blantons. Thanks." She turned back to Reilly. "What are you having?

"Oh, nothing for me," Reilly said, half to Candace and half to the waiter who was still hovering, waiting for his order.

"Bring him the same," she said to the waiter with a gesture indicating that she wouldn't tolerate any argument. The waiter took the cue and made his way to the long bar in the back.

"Thanks. I don't think I've ever had that kind."

"It's the best," she said.

Reilly made a mental note. It would be good information to know about his future editor.

"Well, you shouldn't have to drink alone," he said with a smile as the waiter returned almost immediately with the drinks.

"You're such a gentleman," she said with a hint of sarcasm. "Cheers."

The ice glittered in the candlelight as they clinked glasses, lending ever more ambiance to the film noir fantasy playing out in Reilly's head.

She took a deep sip of her bourbon and leaned back in her chair. "So, you wanted to talk to me."

He felt his mouth go dry. He was suddenly grateful she'd insisted he have a drink. Though he had planned exactly what he was going to say, he was having trouble keeping the lines he'd rehearsed in his head.

"Uh..." He stole another quick sip of bourbon. "Well, first I wanted to thank you again for selecting me as a finalist. I am confident that we will work very well together. I have so much respect for you and for the *Banner*, and I'm eager to join the team."

"You said as much in your interview," she said, looking at him over the rim of her glass. "If you think you can bribe me with good bourbon and flattery, you are mistaken."

Her words sounded severe, but her tone of voice almost gave him the impression she was flirting with him. She had given him the opening he needed.

"Interesting that you should mention bribery."

Her eyes went wide but she remained silent.

Reilly took a breath and leaned toward her. This is it, he thought. He spoke quietly but urgently. "I have proof that you were in on a scheme to plant Kanter in the chief critic spot to guarantee good reviews for your ex-husband, Margolies. And I'm prepared to make this information public if I don't get the job."

He felt a wave of relief at having said it. He had been worried for days that he wouldn't follow through with the blackmail. It felt good to have gotten it out. His relief was short lived, however, when he took in the look of unadulterated wrath on Candace's face.

She leaned close to him and hissed, *"How dare you threaten me?"* Having gulped down the rest of her drink, she snatched his off the tiny table between them and nearly finished it off as well. "You know nothing."

He had expected that, but faced with her anger, he felt agitated himself. She was a business woman, after all, and he'd expected her to treat it like a business deal. Instead, she was clearly in a rage. He could see her hands shaking in anger.

He tried to keep his voice calm. "I can prove it and I will. But I don't want to have to do that. I believe I am the right person for the critic job, and you have the power to give it to me. Though, as the new chief critic I will adhere to the highest standards of integrity. There will be no more bribery or rigged reviews."

"So let me get this straight." Her eyes were slits as she glared at him. "You're blackmailing me to get the job, and yet you plan to bring—what was it you said?—the 'highest standards of integrity?'" She rolled her eyes. "You'll understand if I don't buy a word you're saying. Even if you could prove it, this is a contest. Readers are voting."

Reilly let out an exasperated sigh. "As if you're really going to leave it up to the readers. I wasn't born yesterday, and neither were you." Now he was angry. It felt good to say whatever he wanted to say. He was certain that his accusations were true and it gave him confidence.

"Then prove it. Right now." She slammed her glass on the table.

If looks could kill... he thought. "I'm not going to do that."

"That's because you're bluffing."

"Do you really want to find out?"

Reilly was all-in now. His lunch with his editor—ex-editor— hadn't gone well. They planned to cut him loose since he had so publicly thrown his lot in with the *Banner*. He knew it was all or nothing for him.

She glared at him through narrowed eyes for a long second and finally said, "This is not the end of this conversation."

But it clearly was for that evening. She grabbed her coat and purse and stalked out of the bar.

Reilly slumped in his chair. He was sweating even though it wasn't warm. As he settled up the tab, he reflected on the conversation. He had said what he needed to say, and she hadn't said no. He hadn't needed to show his proof, and there was no record of their conversation. He was pretty sure he was safe. He just hoped she'd say yes.

He made his way out of the bar and into the cold, clear evening. It was still early, and, as usual these days, he found himself wondering what Scarlett was up to. He didn't have to wonder for long because, to his surprise, she appeared just up the street.

"Scarlett!" He waved to her.

She spun around at the sound of his voice and rushed toward him with a huge grin. "Reilly? What are you doing all the way down here?"

"I could ask you the same thing."

"I have *Swan Song* rehearsal." She looked at him as if he should have known. Which, of course, he should have.

"Right, of course." He slapped his forehead. The Manhattan Theatre Workshop was a block from where they were. "Things still going well at rehearsal?"

"Totally amazing," she said, with a look of pure bliss. "Hey! Why don't you come and watch for a bit?"

A full moon shone in the sky, and Scarlett looked radiant—the perfectly cast femme fatale to complete his cinematic reverie.

"Love to. Lead on." He laced his fingers with hers, and they headed down the street. He had miraculously managed to avoid telling her the reason for his presence there. Thankfully, she was too consumed with her work to care.

They were both too consumed to notice Candace watching them from under the shadow of an awning across the street.

Scene 30

Margolies stalked through the doors of the Angus McIndoe restaurant and headed up to the third floor. The meeting was the last thing he needed that night, but it was not the time to lose sight of his competition. The old boys club comprised of top Broadway producers and theater owners had been meeting once a month for years, to scheme, commiserate, and otherwise keep a close eye on each other.

He was the last to arrive. The group had migrated to the third-floor bar at Angus a few years back, when the producer-friendly restaurant had been opened by Angus himself in 2001 with the help of several celebrity investors. Later in the evening, it would be filled with cast members from nearby shows, seeking a post-show nightcap. For now, they had the quiet upstairs space to themselves for as long they needed it.

"The man of the hour!" Mr. Erlander said as Margolies came around the corner, gesturing toward large windows that provided an eye-level view of the massive *Olympus* marquee, illuminated on the theater across the street.

"Just keeping up with the Jones's," Margolies replied with a nod to Erlander's own marquee, the corner of which was also visible through the window. It was dwarfed by *Olympus*.

"That show will be the death of me," Erlander said of his own show. The most senior member of the group at eighty years old, he had survived a career in the industry despite – or maybe because of – his perpetual doomsday demeanor. Crotchety and battle scarred, he never missed a gathering of his cronies.

Margolies took a seat at the round table with his back to the window. He didn't want to face his marquee just then, though he could feel the glow of it beating down on the back of his neck.

To Margolies' left was Mr. Stewart, severe-looking man born into fortune as heir to one of two theater-owning families who, in essence, controlled Broadway by means of real estate. Those families could arbitrarily decide whether or not to give a producer a particular theater—and securing the right theater for any given show could make or break the show's chance for success. For years, Margolies had always gotten his first-choice theater from both families because he was a tried-and-true cash cow. Between weekly theater rent and box-office commissions, the theater owners were all too happy to have their hands in as many of his successful productions as possible.

To Margolies' right was Mr. Rubin, one-time Broadway wunderkind, by then just as much of a fixture as the rest of them. He was short and stocky, and his once-dark hair was shot through with gray.

Mr. Franklin was next to Rubin. Franklin was a serial producer. He always had a string of shows lined up, turning them out like a factory. While Margolies respected Franklin's fundraising prowess and the success he'd had with his "shotgun approach," Margolies preferred to be more strategic in his own show choices.

He glanced around the table at the other familiar faces— another theater owner, a few other producers. He knew each of their strengths, each of their flaws. They were his enemies and his brothers. How had they all gotten so old? It seemed like yesterday they were the pioneers of Broadway; now they were the old guard. There hadn't been a new addition to their circle in a decade, though they'd lost a few members in recent years.

A leggy young waitress came out from behind the bar to take their drink orders. All conversation ceased as each man undressed her with their eyes. They are about as subtle as a Times Square billboard, thought Margolies. He caught himself eyeing the coltish brunette along with the rest of them and felt foolish. Is this what we have all become?

Even before walking into the restaurant, he'd known how the evening would go because it was always the same. They'd rib the theater owners for the recent rent hike, they'd lament the latest union disagreements, they'd discuss legislative issues, and they'd curse this or that reviewer or upstart producer who threatened to infringe on their ivory tower. Margolies was tired of it all.

Rubin turned to Margolies. "I hear you've got the actor's union breathing down your neck with that new wireless remote fly system?"

"Nothing I can't handle," Margolies said, a little too sharply. He reminded himself not to get defensive about the overwhelming challenges he was facing on *Olympus*. The group could smell fear.

Erlander leaned over. "What's your capitalization these days? I've heard it's up over fifty mil." He whistled through his teeth. "Brought in some big guns for this one, huh?"

Interesting choice of words, thought Margolies. These guys had no idea what he had gotten himself into in order to fund the Herculean endeavor. Eager to change the subject, Margolies asked Rubin, "How'd things go in Washington, DC? Any luck with the FCC?"

Broadway had come late to the table in building relationships with the government, and their negligence was catching up with them. The film industry had great tax incentives for investors that had been on the books for nearly a century, and Broadway was finally fighting for equal treatment.

The biggest issue that had them all concerned, however, was "white space"—a technical issue that made Margolies' head hurt but would be key to the future of the industry. With the rise of wireless *everything,* the bandwidth that shows needed to operate wireless mics, headsets, and equipment was threatened by smart phones and handheld supercomputers that were becoming all too common.

"I think we made some headway," Rubin said, "but we still have work to do with the FCC. Did you hear about the stunt that Stewart pulled last week?"

Of course Margolies had, but that didn't stop Rubin from sharing the story again. Margolies had to admit it was a good one.

"Get this," Rubin said. "So you know how the latest word from the FCC is that we'd still have the bandwidth we need, we'd just have deal with an occasional, brief interruption if one of our patrons walks by with a powerful smart phone or laptop?"

The news was met with nods and grunts.

"Well," he continued, "we brought the FCC to *Phantom* last week before a show. We started up a production number, big song, all that…and half way through, we cut the wireless for thirty seconds." He paused.

Everyone at the table knew exactly what that meant. The famous falling chandelier would halt in midair, the actors and orchestra microphones would become silent, making it impossible to hear anything, the cues for lights and sets would not go through. Basically the show would fall apart instantly if there was even thirty seconds of interruption in the wireless systems.

Margolies shivered. He hadn't had time to focus on the legislative issues, but he was glad that his colleagues were on top of it. That could be a nightmare, particularly for the new technology that was the cornerstone of *Olympus*.

"You have to beat this, Stewart," Franklin said.

"I'm working on it. You know you're all welcome to join me in Washington," Stewart said grimly. And around the table, the men who drove one of New York's biggest economic engines nodded in agreement.

Margolies leaned over to Rubin. "Anything new since last month? What's on your radar?"

Rubin had an eye for off-beat new musicals. He'd transferred several unlikely musicals from hole-in-the-wall theaters, and turned an impressive majority of them into commercial hits, but he hadn't done much in the past few years.

"I could ask you the same thing," Rubin replied. "Don't tell me you've had your nose so deep in your rock-star extravaganza that you've missed what's happening in your very own office."

Rubin eyed Franklin and Erlander with a sly smile. They returned his looks, well aware of exactly where Rubin was going.

"What the hell are you talking about?" Margolies wanted to punch someone but kept his calm. Not that a burst of his temper would surprise anyone at that table.

Franklin clapped Margolies on the back with his withered hand and said, "You're losing your touch, old man."

Erlander let out a little giggle. "This is too good."

"I'm glad you're enjoying yourselves at my expense, gentlemen," Margolies said as the waitress came around with their drinks. Scotch, scotch, martini, water for Margolies. As she leaned over his shoulder, he felt her lean in just a little too close and catch his eye when he turned his head. That cheered him up for a second. Clearly an actress, the waitress knew power when she saw it. He raked his fingers through his still thick silver hair, grateful that he could attract a girl like that even at his age. Something his colleagues couldn't say for themselves.

"Does a little show called *Swan Song* sound familiar?" Rubin asked.

It *did* sound familiar, but Margolies couldn't place it. "Sure..." He was noncommittal. "Why?"

"You mean *Swanee Song*, more like," Franklin said, waving his fingers in a non-politically correct minstrel show reference.

"Have you asked your hot little associate what she's been doing on her evenings and weekends?"

It suddenly dawned on him. *Swan Song*. Scarlett's pet project. She had mentioned it a couple of times, but he hadn't paid any attention.

"Right. Scarlett's project. How do you know about it?" Margolies asked.

The men passed wide-eyed glances between themselves.

"Everyone knows about it, old man," Franklin said.

"My sources at the Manhattan Theatre Workshop tell me it's brilliant. And can you believe it was a last-minute substitute? Crazy business," Rubin said. "I tried to option it myself, but your little

Scarlett is keeping it to herself. Apparently there's money there. Who knew?"

Margolies mind was spinning. What was going on? How could Scarlett's little nothing of a project have caught the attention of Rubin and Franklin and Erlander. The world didn't work that way. At least, his world didn't.

"Excuse me. I have someplace to be." He abruptly shoved his chair away from the table.

That was met with laughter. He didn't care. Maybe it is time I quit the group anyway, he thought. What good are they? As he turned the corner to the stairs, he could see them all enjoying a laugh at his expense, under the glow of his *Olympus* marquee.

Scene 31

"What took you so long?" Candace snapped as she met him at the door of her brownstone. She had called Margolies before she even left the Bowery Hotel bar.

"Producer's Association meeting at the Angus. I got here as soon as I could," Margolies replied, taking off his coat and throwing it over the back of the couch. He took a seat in the cushy leather arm chair. He remembered the day they bought that particular chair, all those years ago. He had been overloaded with new musical submissions and had wanted the perfect chair to set up shop in the living room and weed through the scripts, searching for the perfect shows that would allow him to launch his producing career.

He couldn't remember the last time he'd read a script. Scarlett did that for him, and his other projects came through connections and commissions. They were stunt casting, star vehicles like *Olympus*. There had been some good scripts, back in the day. He wondered what ever happened to those scripts, those writers.

His reminiscing was cut short by Candace, who had resumed her pacing. Watching her agitation made him tired.

"Ok, Candy, what's going on?"

"I have bad news and worse news. Which do you want first?"

Margolies sighed. "Just tell me."

"Our secret's out."

Margolies sat up. "What are you talking about?" He wondered if Candace was just being overdramatic. When they first put their plan into place all those years back, any little thing could spook her. She was constantly paranoid they'd be found out. It was part of what had led to the demise of their relationship.

"You heard me. One of my finalists, Reilly Mitchell..."

"That gossip columnist kid?"

"That's the one."

"He knows something?"

"Evidently. He cornered me in the bar tonight and claimed he had proof. Said that I needed to give him the job or he'd go public."

This is for real, thought Margolies. The wheels starting to turn in his head. First the news about *Swan Song,* and now this. This is turning into a really bad night. He narrowed his eyes. "What proof?"

"He didn't say." She was pacing like a mad woman. She hadn't even touched the drink she'd poured for herself. "What the hell are we going to do?"

"You're going to calm down, and we're going to work this out."

"Calm down? Calm *down*? My career is on the line. Your career is on the line. Our reputations..." She was starting get shrill.

Margolies got up and took her by the shoulders. "Candace, we'll figure this out, but you have got to calm down." He guided her over to the couch.

"I knew this was going to happen!" she said with wild eyes. "I told you. I knew it!" Margolies put her drink in her hand.

"We'll figure this out, Candy. Haven't I always figured it out before?" he said, trying to calm her. In the meantime, his mind was racing.

He knew he should be as worried as Candace was, but he just couldn't believe that some quasi-celebrity columnist like Reilly with no skin in the game could really bring him down. Margolies was way beyond that. Blackmail seemed petty in the face of his *Olympus* problems. Nonetheless, it would have to be dealt with.

Candace picked up her drink and watched him expectantly. He considered the situation.

"So we're being blackmailed," he said aloud. Now it was his turn to pace. "Blackmailed by some two-bit journalist who wants the top critic job. A nobody—"

"He's not exactly a nobody—"

"A *nobody*! And he thinks he can beat us at our own game."

He suddenly had an idea. It was their game, his game. And no one played it better than him. He smiled.

"You've either had a great idea or you're losing your mind. How can you be smiling?" asked Candace, observing the look on his face.

It was good, really good. He went back to his chair and looked at Candace over his steepled fingers, feeling almost giddy.

"Let's think about this, shall we?" he said. She looked at him blankly. "This guy wants the job, and he's willing to stoop to blackmail to get it." He paused as she nodded. "We want a critic we can keep under our thumb. Someone who won't mind operating just outside of the truth. Someone who understands things like, say, blackmail. It seems we've found our guy!" he ended triumphantly.

"But this is a contest. It's supposed to be fair."

"It was never going to be fair, Candace. We talked about this," he snapped, registering the fact that she had actually thought she could get away with not rigging the contest. He'd deal with that later. It didn't matter now that events had turned in his favor again.

"Right. Okay." She actually squirmed.

"Let's meet with this Reilly Mitchell. It just may be his lucky day." And mine, thought Margolies. Reilly had no idea who he was messing with. But, that would be Reilly's problem. Funny how things worked out. "Not this week, though. Make him sweat a little. The ball's in our court." A thought occurred to him. "Was that the bad news, or the worse news?"

"Right, I almost forgot. Don't you wonder at all where he got his so-called proof?"

"He's a journalist. Those idiots—no offense, Candy— sometimes get lucky and uncover something."

"Or get lucky under the covers is more like it," she said.

"What are you talking about?"

"Let's just say I had the pleasure of meeting your little office girl at the reception last week." Her voice dripped with sarcasm. She was clearly enjoying it.

"Scarlett."

"Whatever. I had just assumed she was keeping *your* bed warm," she said. He glared at her. "But it seems she has another boyfriend."

"Get to the point." He stood up.

"Reilly Mitchell."

Scarlett and Reilly Mitchell? Margolies saw red.

Scene 32

Scarlett checked the time. She had been in the Jackman Theater for ten straight hours, for the third day in a row. And yet they had barely gotten through three scenes that night. She flexed her aching fingers, tired from the copious notes she'd been taking about everything from scene transitions to costume adjustments to dramaturgical fixes. Scaling Mount Olympus would be easier than mounting this show, thought Scarlett.

At least she hadn't needed to worry about Cupid. Since he'd spent the majority of the day strapped into a remote-controlled harness, flying around the theater, his flirtations with Scarlett had been relegated to leers and lewd gestures from above, which she could safely avoid, sitting in the darkened audience well below his grasp.

The show was really starting to come together. Though Scarlett preferred her musicals with a little more heart and a little less spectacle, she couldn't fault Margolies' vision of *Olympus*. Even with only piano accompaniment—the orchestra wouldn't be called in until later in the week—the songs were stunning. The choreography performed by the top-notch cast, in dazzling costumes, was truly breathtaking.

Scarlett had miraculously managed to avoid unnecessary run-ins with Margolies as well. The activity at the theater had reached a fever pitch. Margolies and Scarlett were more or less taking turns running between the theater and the office, conveniently ensuring, as a result, that they were rarely in the same place at the same time, other than for production meetings with various other players. That suited Scarlett just fine, as she had neither the time nor inclination to get any more humiliating beratings from her boss.

It had been the toughest two weeks of her life at work. Luckily, a couple of late night dinners with Reilly—when she could get away from the theater—as well as constant update texts from the Jeremys and Lawrence, who were deep in rehearsals downtown, were getting her through.

"Doughnut?" the intern whispered, coming down the aisle of the theater. He squeezed into the theater seat next to her. She had to give the kid credit, though he really should lay off the doughnuts. He'd been tireless in the past couple of weeks, bringing her food, apprising her of Margolies' whereabouts, making her laugh when things got particularly stressful. Maybe the intern would do okay after all.

"No, thanks."

"Is it alright if I head home? It's after ten," he said.

"Oh!" Time went by so quickly. "Sure, of course. I had no idea it was so late."

"That's okay. I had a lot to do at the office," he said. She'd been dumping work off on him like it was going out of style. "You were the one who was here all weekend."

"Look, I really appreciate everything you're doing. You really are a lifesaver."

The intern had pretty much taken the reigns of the extensive press and marketing activities, in partnership with the ad agency. In true Margolies style, the boss was keeping a close eye on everything that was being done, but the extensive day-to-day management that usually fell to Scarlett had landed squarely on the interns shoulders.

The intern craned his head to look at the remote-controlled flying contraption that now held Cupid's understudy. Cupid had left hours before to make an appearance at some glamorous party. The remote-control technology they were pioneering was almost perfect. And the effect was breathtaking.

"We're making history here, right?" the intern said with a sense of awe. "I'm just glad to be part of it. Are you sure you don't want a doughnut?"

"I'm sure." She was grateful that she wasn't a stress eater. At times like those, she had to force herself to remember to eat anything at all. At least all the drama was good for her waist line. "Did you close up the office?"

"The boss is still there."

"I thought he left for the night."

"Nope. Been there all evening. Looked like he was having some meetings."

"With whom? Everyone's here," Scarlett said, gesturing around to all the designers, actors, and directors who were scurrying around the darkened theater. At that moment, they were busy resetting the stage to re-rehearse the scene they had just run ten times already. It was the tricky Act One finale. All the gods took flight while Cupid, as Zeus, had his triumphant Act One finale song, a spotlight-lit rock-and-roll crowd pleaser sung from the flying contraption above the audience. They had almost gotten it right. The next day they'd rehearse the rain scene with the lightning pyrotechnics. It felt more like what Scarlett imagined a movie set would feel like, rather than a Broadway show. But there was no doubt that they were blazing new territory. Audiences would be wowed, that was for sure.

"I think they were money people," the intern said in answer to her question, licking powdered sugar off his fingers. "Not sure, since they kept the door closed. One of them was that guy who's been hanging around a lot. I've never caught his name. Black hair. Fancy suite. Kinda creepy."

Why did the hair on the back of Scarlett's neck stand up every time she saw or thought about that guy? "Sure. I know the one." Not wanting to share her discomfort with the intern, she pasted on a smile.

"Well, I guess that's it for the night," she said, giving him permission to go home. During the conversation, he had finished off the doughnuts he had brought for her.

"How much longer are you sticking around?" he asked her.

Now it was her turn to take in her surroundings. Rehearsal was still in full swing. "It'll be a while." She had been hoping to see Reilly, but the night was ticking away. Ah, well. The show started previews in three days.

Scene 33

"Do you really need me here tonight?" Reilly asked Scarlett as they walked arm in arm out the door of his building, huddled together under an umbrella. They were on their way to a dinner party at the Jeremys' apartment in Chelsea. Scarlett was thrilled to have a night off, but Reilly seemed jumpy and irritable. He'd been distant all week.

"Yes! Everyone's dying to get to know you," she said, squeezing his arm and giving him an encouraging smile. She was eager for her good mood to rub off on him.

"Do you think it was a good idea to tell all of them about us?" Reilly asked, frowning.

"It would have to come out sooner or later. And, anyway, that's one bonus of you losing your job. At least I'm not dating New York's nastiest gossip columnist."

"Don't rub it in."

"I meant it as a compliment." Scarlett kissed his cheek as they made their way through Times Square, the umbrella only keeping them somewhat dry. "And, anyway, you'll soon be re-employed!"

Scarlett could see Reilly trying to muster a smile for her benefit. Clearly his heart wasn't in it. He claimed he hadn't been sleeping well. It seemed that losing his columnist job had really shaken his confidence.

"Don't you see how quickly someone can go from being somebody in this town to just another nobody on the streets of New York City?" He gestured to the throngs of tourists brushing by them. The busily flashing Times Square billboards promoting *Mamma Mia*, *Jersey Boys* and *The Lion King* were splashing a collage of colors onto the wet sidewalks.

"Oh come on, you saw the review this week! The junior critic blew it," she said. She was trying so hard to cheer him up. They had dissected the most recent audition review earlier that day on the phone and confirmed that it wasn't good for the junior critic, but was very good for Reilly.

"The world is waiting for you, Reilly." Scarlett forced Reilly to stop and face her under the umbrella. "I know you're nervous, but this is everything you've always wanted." She kissed him on the lips. "Look at us! At the center of the world!" She held her arms out wide.

Reilly's eyes locked on the massive *Olympus* billboard that dominated a two-story high space over her shoulder, dwarfing the *Wicked* and *Phantom of the Opera* ads. Scarlett could see his spirits sinking again. She gently placed her hands on either side of his face and gazed into his eyes. "You are poised to get your dream job, Reilly. And, my show starts previews next week. Let's enjoy this. How many people get where we are? This is Broadway."

Reilly just stared back at her with a bleak expression. She kissed him again, but there was no passion in his return kiss. She could feel her good mood starting to ebb. She held his gaze for a few moments longer. Her heart was eager to make the relationship work. Their mutual attraction was undeniable. And yet, it had only been a few weeks since they'd met and it felt like they were on a constant emotional rollercoaster.

Reilly shivered and pulled his coat around him with one hand, re-angling the umbrella with the other. "I'm sorry, Scarlett. I'm in a weird mood tonight. I don't want to bring down the group. Why don't I head home?"

"We don't have to stay long, but you *have* to make an appearance. Please. I promise they'll all love you as much as I do." She looked at him pleadingly.

Reilly sighed. "Ok. I'm sure you're right." He kissed her forehead. "Lead on." He crooked his elbow for her to take. As they strode through the center of Times Square arm in arm, she desperately hoped that an evening with friends would rehabilitate his mood.

Scene 34

They were the last to arrive at the Jeremys, where they were met by a lively group lounging on couches and on the floor of the living room. Scarlett had been looking forward to the evening all week. It had been a while since she'd carved out an entire evening for a non-work related event.

"Doth mine eyes deceive me?" Jersey Jeremy asked, greeting them at the apartment door with two glasses of wine. "Or is the one and only Reilly Mitchell in my humble abode?"

Scarlett cast a wary glance at Reilly. She could see that Jeremy's flattery was perking him up already.

"And I'm chopped liver? Is that any way to greet your producer?" Scarlett teased.

"The red carpet is at the dry cleaners," Jersey Jeremy said as he took their coats.

Scarlett fished a bottle of wine out of her purse and added it to the other guests' alcoholic offerings on the kitchen counter, just to the right of the front door. The Jeremys' apartment was three times bigger than Scarlett's, but that wasn't saying much. Still, the cozy group of friends that had gathered for the evening fit just fine.

"Scarlett, you know everyone here, but have they met Reilly?" Buff Jeremy asked, sliding from the couch onto the floor to let Scarlett and Reilly share the small plush loveseat.

"We all know you!" said an impeccably dressed young guy in an argyle sweater and jeans.

Scarlett made introductions starting there. "Reilly, meet Rob. He does what I do in Erlander's office."

"Head slave, at your service," Rob said, leaning across the low coffee table laden with fancy cheeses and crackers to shake Reilly's hand.

"This is Mara and her husband David."

"Of course," Reilly said to Mara. "Didn't you write that Oscar Wilde bio-musical that made it to Broadway last season? It was good!"

"Thanks." Mara beamed.

"And David is an entertainment lawyer," Scarlett continued.

"Broadway power couple," Reilly said with a wink.

Scarlett continued around the room, pointing out the various friendly faces draped over the furniture and on the floor of the living room, ending with Andrew, an up-and-coming independent Broadway producer who, like Scarlett, was hoping to someday be a major player. Lounging on his lap due to lack of any other available surface was his girlfriend Cat, a talented singer/dancer.

The group quickly devoured the cheese and crackers and more than a few bottles of wine amid lively conversation and theater gossip. Scarlett stole a look at Reilly, deep in conversation with Andrew, who was regaling him with the sordid details of his current projects. He was probably hoping to get a mention in Reilly's column, Scarlett thought. No one knew yet that Reilly was no longer at the *Journal*. She was pleased to see him getting along so well with her nearest and dearest friends in New York. They all appeared to be more than willing to accept Reilly into their circle despite his public profile as a snarky columnist.

"So, Reilly," Jersey Jeremy began, "when do you get your turn in the *Banner's* critic competition?"

"I'm last," Reilly said.

"They're clearly saving the best for last," Scarlett said, kissing Reilly on the cheek.

"We'll see," Reilly said modestly.

"Any idea what show you'll be assigned to review?" Buff Jeremy asked.

"I should find out in the next week or two," Reilly said.

"Well, we're all rooting for you, man," Jersey Jeremy said. "Anyone who can capture the heart of our lovely Scarlett must be a good guy."

Reilly suddenly looked uncomfortable, but the conversation quickly shifted to the usual topics. Mara and David began debating loudly with Andrew about whether Patti LuPone or Bernadette Peters was the greatest diva currently working on Broadway, while Cat and Scarlett attempted to help the Jeremys finish up in the tiny kitchen.

Half an hour later, the group squeezed around the Jeremys' dining room table and dished up heaping portions of truffle mac and cheese, cranberry walnut salad, and lemon chicken, their version of gourmet comfort food, and the perfect menu for a rainy New York night.

As the Jeremys took their seats, Scarlett tapped her fork on her glass to get everyone's attention. "I'd like to toast our fabulous hosts! Chefs par excellence, soon to be the brightest stars off-Broadway!"

"Here, here!" "Cheers!" echoed the group.

As the happy crowd dug into their meals, David, the entertainment lawyer sitting across from Scarlett, leaned in and asked her the inevitable questions: "So, how's *Olympus*?"

The clattering of silverware hushed as everyone waited for her response.

"Don't make her talk about work!" Jersey Jeremy said— somewhat selfishly, since, having heard more than his fair share about *Olympus* during his daily conversations with Scarlett about *Swan Song*, he already knew the dirt.

"I don't mind, really," Scarlett said. "It's going well, actually. The new flying technology is working and looks pretty cool. The rain and pyro still have some kinks, but we'll get it together."

"That's all well and good," Mara said, "but we could have read that in the *Banner*. There've been editorials almost every day. Margolies sure has the PR racket in his court. We want to know what's *really* going on."

"I invoke the cone of silence," Buff Jeremy said. "Nothing said here leaves the table."

"In that case, it's actually just more of the usual," Scarlett said. "Crazy leading couple. Cupid is a total disaster. He's not untalented, but he's driving the music director crazy. He rewrites his and everyone else's songs weekly, even though we are technically working off of the final draft…which probably explains why he never remembers his lines. And his lovely wife and the understudy were caught 'in the act' between acts, in the orchestra pit, while the musicians were on dinner break."

"Is it going to be any good?" Andrew asked.

"Depends on how you define *good*," Scarlett said candidly. "The script isn't much to write home about, but the visuals are going to be spectacular, that's for sure. And the music has a few high points. It's not really my idea of true musical theater, but the tourists will probably like it."

"I hope you're getting combat pay for this," Andrew said.

"If only," Scarlett said. "The best compensation I'm getting on this show is that I haven't had to spend as much time alone with Margolies as usual. I should complain about how crazy busy we've been, running between meetings and rehearsals, but it's really a blessing. Not that there haven't been the requisite Margolies meltdowns."

"You deserve a trophy for working with that man," Rob said, raising his glass.

"I could say the same to you, working for Erlander," Scarlett replied, clinking glasses across the table with Rob.

"Margolies, Erlander... Aren't there any nice people in this business?" David asked.

"You're looking at them," Buff Jeremy said, gesturing to the people gathered around the table.

"If we do say so ourselves," Andrew said with a wry smile. "I don't disagree. But we're the next generation. I'm talking about our role models. Several of us here want to get to the top echelons of this biz. Don't you find it discouraging when you look at how nasty so many of the handful of top producers have turned out to be?"

Scarlett and Andrew had had that conversation many times before, commiserating over drinks.

"They can't all be like that," said David.

"Name one top Broadway producer who's known for being nice," Andrew challenged. "Margolies is a tyrant. Erlander is a royal jerk."

"Well, what about that Michael guy who headed up the *Hello Dolly* revival last season?" Mara asked. "He's interested in producing my next show, and he seems nice."

"Michael. Yeah, I've heard he's pleasant, but he's only done one or two Broadway shows," Andrew said. "I'm talking about the producers at the very tip top. That crowd of cronies that skulk around the Angus McIndoe."

The table fell silent.

"Franklin?" Rob ventured a suggestion.

"Ick," Cat said. "He felt me up at the *Mamma Mia* anniversary party."

"God, this is depressing. These are our role models?" Scarlett said. "Do you think they started out being assholes? Or does something happen to them along the way?"

"Maybe the backstabbing and competition just wears them down over the years," Rob said. "I know Erlander doesn't trust anyone in showbiz, and that can make you cynical and hard pretty damn fast."

"Rumor has it the theater-owning Stewart family keeps extensive *files* on every player in the business. Probably waiting to screw anyone who crosses them," said Andrew.

"I've heard that the generation before these guys was even worse. We've all heard the David Merrick stories, right?" Jersey Jeremy said. "Maybe they're just doing to us what was done to them."

"Are you saying that gives them permission to be like that?" Buff Jeremy asked.

"Of course not, but it could explain a lot. They had to suffer so we have to suffer. And a few bad apples like Margolies can ruin the whole barrel," Jersey Jeremy replied with a shrug.

"Can I just say right here and right now that I will never be like that," Scarlett said. "I have every intention of getting to the top"—she glanced at the Jeremys—"but I vow to stay nice, honest, and uncynical."

"Cheers to that," Jersey Jeremy said as everyone raised their glasses. "May we all prove that nice guys...*and* gals," he added, nodding to Scarlett, Mara, and Cat, "*can* win in this crazy business we call show."

"Amen!"

"Cheers."

Reilly pushed his chair back abruptly, almost knocking it over. Only Scarlett noticed. "Are you okay?" she whispered. He looked a little ashen.

"Fine. I just need some air."

"I'll come with you," she said, concerned.

"No. I'll be fine." He sprinted toward the front door, leaving his coat and his girlfriend behind.

His dramatic exit did not go unnoticed.

"Is he okay?" Buff Jeremy asked.

"He's had a rough week," Scarlett said apologetically, her mind racing at Reilly's strange behavior. That wasn't like him. "Sorry about that. I don't know what came over him."

"For a gossip columnist, he seemed awfully quiet tonight," Jersey Jeremy said.

"I better see if he's okay," Scarlett said, despite Reilly's telling her not to. "Excuse me. I'll be right back."

"Take your time, darling. I'm sure you'll find a way to cheer him up," Jersey Jeremy said with a devilish grin.

Scene 35

Scarlett waited in line at one of the many Times Square Starbucks, in desperate need of a late afternoon pick-me-up. She had been burning the candle at both ends. There were tech rehearsals for *Swan Song* every evening that week until the wee hours, and then early mornings at the office to get some work done before spending the day putting out fires, literally and figuratively, at *Olympus* rehearsals. Early previews of *Olympus* were going relatively well, but the technical challenges required hours of extra rehearsals during the day before each evening's performance. The cast and crew must be seriously exhausted, thought Scarlett.

Swan Song would start its week and a half of previews the coming weekend. *Olympus* was doing a full month of previews, the standard for Broadway. Preview performances had become nearly as important in the industry as real performances because the chat-room regulars and bloggers came early and often to see the show first and expose the scoop, before institutional reviewers like the *Banner* were allowed to show up. The full-priced tickets for previews gave audiences the impression that there was no difference between a preview and a post-opening production—which often there wasn't.

It blew her mind that her little show, just a producing pipe-dream a year ago, was going to open off-Broadway, even before *Olympus*. True, it was way downtown, but based on the feedback she was getting from her trusted theater friends on the quality of the show, combined with the possible funding from Lawrence, a Broadway transfer was a realistic possibility.

She shot a quick text to Reilly while she waited: *Thinking about you.*

She had been worried about him. After he had fled the Jeremys' apartment the other night, she had found him slumped on the front steps of the building, looking like he was going to cry. She had made polite excuses to the Jeremys and taken him back to his

144

apartment. He'd perked up during the weekend but still didn't seem like his old self. Her schedule hadn't allowed her to spend as much time as she'd like to with him either. It was unfortunate that her life would get especially hectic just as he was temporarily unemployed, and clearly going stir crazy.

A text came back almost immediately…but not from Reilly. It was Margolies: *Need you at the theater.*

She groaned. She hadn't left the theater for five minutes all day, and of course, he'd need her back just as she was taking a short break. Well, he could wait five more minutes. She needed coffee.

A few minutes and a few sips of her latte later, she headed back through the stage door at the theater.

"Have you seen Margolies?" she asked the stage-door security guard.

"He showed up a few minutes ago," he said.

She ventured further into the backstage maze riddled with dressing rooms filled with costumers, dressers, and cast members. Margolies' greasy, black-haired goon slid by her in the narrow hall. Scarlett avoided his eyes. That guy creeped her out, big time.

"Is Margolies back here?" she asked an assistant stage manager, who answered with a grim look and pointed to the half-opened door of one of the dressing rooms.

Scarlett poked her head in the door. "Sir?"

"Come in," Margolies said, not looking up. He was thumbing through a pile of papers that he had spread out across the narrow makeup table. After walking down the dim hallway, the bright round bulbs that surrounded the large mirror made Scarlett squint.

"Shut the door," he continued.

She complied and stood awkwardly with her back to the door, not sure where she should stand. A rack of costumes lined one wall of the tiny room. That particular dressing room was small, meant for one person and maybe a dressing assistant. Margolies filled the space physically and emotionally.

Without turning around, he finally raised his eyes and met hers in the mirror. She realized it was the first time in weeks that she'd been alone with him. He spoke slowly and deliberately. "So, it looks like you have a hit on your hands?"

"We certainly do!" she said, too brightly. "*Olympus* is going to take Broadway by storm." She realized too late that she was quoting the slogan that the advertising firm had created for the show. It had been the first thing to come into her mind, which was reeling under his withering gaze, reflected in the mirror.

"Not *our* show. *Your show.*"

For a second she didn't know what he was talking about. Then she realized he meant her own show.

"Oh, you mean *Swan Song*?"

His eyes drilled into hers, unblinking.

"Um..." she continued. "I guess it's going well. Remember, I told you about it several months ago when I first found it. You weren't interested, so I decided to take it on. You said you didn't mind. It's not interfering with work at all..." She trailed off. She had been babbling.

"Do I get to see this little project of yours?"

"I'd love that. We're in tech, but if you want to come this week, or for a preview, just let me know and I'll get you a comp." She felt surprised that he was interested in her show but flattered all the same.

"Thanks for the invitation," he said sarcastically.

"Sure," she said, unsure about what was going on. Was that why he needed to see her?

"Of course, you're wasting your time."

"Sir?" she said.

"You're little piece-of-crap show downtown has no chance," he said, his voice dripping with anger. "Just because you've watched me work for four years doesn't mean you can play with the big boys. Just remember that."

"Okay..." She could feel her face getting red.

"I need you to focus on your *job* right now!" he said.

"I am!" said Scarlett defensively.

"Not possible. Between your little show and your little boyfriend..." He paused. "How can I count on you?"

"I've done everything you've told me to do," she said.

"It's not *what* you're doing that I'm worried about. It's *who* you're doing," he leered.

"What are you talking about?" she said. It was completely inappropriate.

She couldn't control her temper anymore. After four years of tireless work, she didn't deserve this, even from him.

"Well, then, I need to know what's going on, too!" She stood up and faced him. "What is M____ Corporation, and why have I never heard of them, even though they've apparently given us $9 million! And who is that guy who doesn't leave your side but who you never introduce to anyone?"

He stood up, knocking over his chair, and spun to face her. "What do you know about that?"

"I know that I can't do my job if I don't know what's going on around here anymore." She couldn't believe she had just talked to him that way. Then again, if her job was already on the line, she figured she didn't have all that much to lose.

"M____ Corporation is none of your business. I'll pretend I didn't hear that from you, for your sake…and your safety, I might add. You better keep your mouth shut. You have no idea what you're dealing with. Am I making myself clear?" He took a step toward her.

"I understand," she said, craning her neck to meet his eyes. He was scaring her, but she'd seen his temper before.

"Or have you already told someone? Perhaps I should have a talk with your boyfriend."

"I don't know what you mean."

"I really thought I could trust you, Scarlett."

"You can, sir." Did he know about the bank statements? She felt a pang of guilt to add to her fear.

"Unfortunately, it seems that I can't. You're fired," he said, then turned away abruptly.

"I'm fired?"

Her mind went blank. She knew things had gotten tense, but she hadn't expected that. Her mind raced. "But what about *Olympus*? I'm in the middle of several projects," she stammered.

"You can be replaced," he said, though he didn't sound convinced. "I'll have someone escort you to the office to collect your things. Now."

He turned toward her, and she moved away from the door so he could open it. He gestured to his goon who was hovering, as always.

"Take Scarlett back to the office and make sure she gets *home*."

She followed the silent goon across the street, up the elevator, and into the office. She didn't have much there. A few photos and a souvenir coffee mug from *Sweet Charity,* which she didn't bother to take. The rest she slid into her purse. She eyed the laptop. It belonged to Margolies. She'd be computer-less for a while without it…not to mention without an income.

Her escort didn't say a word as they returned to the elevator. She was in shock. She felt emotionally empty. It was so unexpected! She remembered that Margolies had asked the creep to take her home. But the last thing she wanted was to show him where she lived, although he could probably find out. Better not to try it.

She ducked into Sardi's and he didn't follow. She made her way up to the second-floor bar and sank into a bench seat along the wall, not wanting to see anyone. She needed to think. To sort through the wave of mixed emotions flashing through her mind faster than she could deal with them.

She buried her face in her hands and took a series of deep breaths. She'd been fired! His words were echoing through her brain. She didn't know how, but she'd get through it. She knew she'd need to find a way. She'd come too far and worked too hard to have all her dreams come crashing down.

Scene 36

Margolies leaned back in his chair and looked out the hotel window. His glance was greeted with a view of unobstructed sky. He had purposely picked as isolated a hotel room as he could find. He had chosen the out-of-the way hotel for his meeting with Candace and Reilly for two reasons: First and most important, no one would know of their meeting; second, it gave just enough menacing ambience to accentuate his point.

He was looking forward to the meeting. For the first time in months, things were starting to look up. He was feeling like he was regaining some control.

Olympus was coming together. Although the intern's best efforts couldn't hold a candle to Scarlett's, he and the production crew were picking up the slack of her departure. He should never have trusted her. Too ambitious.

At least she'd learn her lesson soon, thought Margolies. She needed to see how the world—*his* world—really worked, sooner or later. He might even be doing her a favor by giving her a much-needed reality check.

He heard a card key in the door. Candace walked in wearing a trench coat and sunglasses.

"I see you came in costume," he said, eyeing her outfit.

"Shut up," she snapped. "There's a reason people dress like this. I didn't want to be seen. I don't even want to be here."

"What? You'd miss all this?" He gestured around the unimpressive room. He'd booked a suite so they could meet around a table.

"You're enjoying yourself, aren't you? Very cloak and dagger. This isn't one of your musicals, you know," she said, making a bee line to the mini bar.

"It's 11:00 a.m., Candace."

She ignored him, removed several of the tiny bottles, and set them on the round table in front of the chair she'd claimed next to Margolies. He'd need to remember to settle up the additional bill after they'd left, since he'd paid for the room in cash.

They both turned when they heard a knock on the door.

"It's show time," said Margolies, standing up and smoothing his black suit. If there was one thing he'd learned early, it was that intimidation was all about putting on a show, and at that, he was the best.

He paused before opening the door, guessing Reilly would be quaking in his boots on the other side. After a beat, he swung open the door dramatically. Sure enough, he was greeted by a wide-eyed Reilly.

"Come in," Margolies said grandly.

"Thanks," Reilly said, walking into the room stiffly.

"Have a seat." Margolies saw Reilly square his shoulders as he sat down, clearly trying to steel himself for their "business dealings." Candace was already on her second baby bottle of booze. She's not wasting any time, thought Margolies.

"Drink?" she offered.

"Uh...no," Reilly replied, probably surprised, as most people would be, by the offer at that hour of the morning.

"Shall we cut to the chase?" Margolies said, taking his seat and leaning toward Reilly.

Reilly shrank back in his chair then corrected himself and leaned forward to meet Margolies' gaze.

"My business was with Candace. It seems you're involved as well," Reilly said.

"Don't bullshit me. You knew I was involved. I intend to find out how you knew, but we'll get to that later," Margolies said. "It seems that you intend to blackmail Candace and me in order to secure the position of chief critic. Do I understand that correctly?"

Reilly nodded. Margolies could see beads of sweat on his temples. This is fun, thought Margolies. Candace went to open a third bottle, and Margolies reached out his hand to stop her. He didn't need a drunk Candace straying from the script that day.

"I'll start by saying that we're not entirely opposed to that idea." He gauged the look on Reilly's face. A glimmer of hope, perhaps. Maybe relief.

"It seems only fair, however, that you do something for us."

"What did you have in mind?" Reilly asked.

"I'll tell you. But first, I need to know that you're really serious about this job."

"I am dead serious," Reilly said, swallowing hard.

"That's good, because it's very important to me who gets this job."

"I'm not going to take bribes from you, if that's what you're suggesting," Reilly said in a rush of words.

"Oh, really?" Margolies said, raising his eyebrows. "I thought I just heard you say you *wanted* the job."

Margolies knew he was pushing it, but it didn't really matter. I can bring Reilly around once he has the job, he thought. Anyone who would resort to blackmail to get a job had the kind of flexible ethics that Margolies could work with. It was all part of the script.

"I do," Reilly said again, a hint of defiance appearing in his eyes. "But I think the public deserves unbiased theater reviews."

"Oh, you do, do you? Because you think *you*, a gossip columnist..." He paused, not bothering to hide the disdain in his voice. "*You* would be able to be completely objective?" Margolies realized that Reilly truly didn't get it. "*No one* is unbiased." Margolies sighed. "I'm going to explain something to you."

Margolies leaned forward and steepled his fingers. "Broadway is big business. We're not talking about drama club, here. I'll create a show that costs, say, $10 million. I'll employ hundreds of people and bring in thousands of tourists to the city who will go out to dinner, keep theaters operating, stay in hotels. But only *if* I have a hit. Of which I've had many." He glanced at Candace, who seemed to be paying attention. She needed to hear that, too. He wasn't the villain everyone made him out to be. "Tell me this: Why should the petty opinion of one person, a person like *you*, who's never created anything, never employed anyone, tear down my shows, put people out work, and take money from the hotels, restaurants, taxi drivers? If I left myself open to that kind of risk, that would simply be bad business. I owe it to my investors, casts, crew workers, designers, audiences, and the rest of the Broadway driven economy to curb the risk in every way possible. That includes controlling the critic."

He could see Reilly processing it. Margolies had never articulated his reasons quite so clearly, because it had been a secret for so long. Saying it out loud merely confirmed his resolution. I'm not a corrupt producer, he thought; I'm a goddamned saint. Ahead of my time is what they'll say someday.

"I see your point," Reilly said quietly. "But the way you're getting around this is dishonest. It's not fair."

"You are so naive!" Margolies said, slamming his fist on the table. Had the kid heard nothing he had just said? "I'm offering you the chance to do something big. Really make a difference. You should thank me."

Reilly wasn't meeting his eyes anymore.

Margolies wondered why he wasted his breath on people like that. He continued. "But if you don't want the job, get out." He pointed toward the door.

"I do want the job," Reilly said, his eyes darting to Candace and then quickly glancing to Margolies' outstretched arm pointing toward the door.

Margolies lowered his arm and leaned back in his chair. "In fact, you could say you *need* this job," he said with a devilish grin. "Did I hear you've recently become unemployed?" He saw Reilly flinch before collecting himself. It was almost too easy. "You have a lot on the line right now. Let's think about this. You could become the *New York Banner* chief critic, or—" He paused for effect—"The has-been gossip columnist who was fired from his job, couldn't land the *Banner* spot, and offended so many people with his column that he'll be covering community theater in his hometown of nowheres-ville for the next fifty years."

Reilly just stared at him.

"Did I get that right?" Margolies said with an ill-concealed smirk.

Reilly snapped to attention. "Don't forget, if I don't get this job, I'm going to expose you and I'm going to expose her." He pointed to Candace, mid-swig on her third bottle. Margolies swept his hand across the table and sent the bottles flying.

"And you think anyone will believe you?" Margolies snarled.

"I have proof," Reilly said, sitting up straighter.

"Don't be so sure," Margolies said quietly and was rewarded with an uncertain look that flashed across Reilly's face for a split second.

As they were meeting, Margolies had his "shadow" paying a visit to Reilly's apartment. It hadn't been hard to find where Reilly lived. His man had simply followed Scarlett there one night and asked a few questions of the accommodating and apparently underpaid doorman. Any proof Reilly had in his apartment would be found and destroyed. For as much trouble as his new business associates might be, they certainly had their advantages. Margolies could get used to doing business their way.

"So, back to the deal at hand." Margolies leaned forward. "We are prepared to offer you the job right here, right now, and all we ask is one little thing. Just to prove to us that you're for real. That you are capable of the job. It will be easy. Nothing, really...or I should say nothing, Reilly."

Reilly held his breath.

"It's your turn next week for your *Banner* review audition. We have and extra special assignment for you. Have you heard of a little downtown show called *Swan Song*?"

Scene 37

Scarlett rolled over and looked at the clock. 10:00 a.m. on a Monday morning, and she had no place to be. She had spent a miserable weekend trying to sort out her thoughts on what she'd do next, wallowing in her shame at being fired. Fired! The only bright spot in an otherwise depressing weekend had been the sublime first few previews of *Swan Song*. She had allowed herself to forget the prior week's drama, her lack of income, and scary unknown future, for two hours each night, to enjoy the beautiful show that she had helped to bring to life.

It was made easier by the fact that she hadn't told anyone at *Swan Song* that she'd been fired. She didn't want to take away from the amazing momentum and excitement around the show.

She sat up in bed and dug around the sheets to find her phone. Two missed calls from her parents. They must have tried to reach her before they'd left for work that morning. They'd been so concerned about her that they had offered to come to New York or fly her home to Oakland. Of course, she couldn't leave with her show in previews and opening the next week. Plus, she didn't want to. Margolies might have brought her down, but she just couldn't see herself giving up yet.

A text buzzed. She smiled as she read what her brother had to say, a show tune, of course: *The sun'll come out tomorrow!*

She dragged herself out of bed, humming the *Annie* showstopper and starting a pot of coffee and a to-do list. She needed a plan for getting back on track. She'd been unemployed in New York before, she thought—although then it had been because she'd just arrived.

She thought about going back to the producing offices where she had unsuccessfully interviewed four years earlier. She had a ton of experience now, but the thought of going from the Margolies office to more of the same just made her head hurt. Plus, Margolies was chummy with all those guys, and he'd probably make sure she didn't get hired, anyway.

Her cell phone rang.

"Hello?"

"Scarlett, it's Jeremy."

"And Jeremy!"

She held the phone away from her ear. They were practically squealing into the phone.

"Hi, guys."

"Sorry to bother you at work," Jersey Jeremy said. She felt bad for not having told them yet. They'd be upset with her later.

"What's up?" she asked, walking into the bathroom and looking at her disheveled self in the mirror. Her hair looked like someone had taken an electric mixer to it.

"Have you seen broadwayworld.com or All That Chat today?" Buff Jeremy said.

"Or the bloggers roundup?" Jersey Jeremy said. They were speaking over each other in their excitement.

"Um...not yet," Scarlett said. Without a computer she felt like she was missing an appendage.

"Well, then, you are just going to *die!*"

"Read her some of them!"

"Which one?"

"Just pick one!"

"Okay, Scarlett, listen to this...'*Swan Song* is the best new musical to hit New York.' Do you hear that? Not off-Broadway or whatever, but *New York*! Here's another: '*Swan Song* is the best new musical to hit New York this year.'"

"Wow, that's great, guys," she said, trying to muster real enthusiasm. It was always a coup to get some compliments on the usually snarky online chat room boards, but those were just random people.

"Shall I read her more?"

"Scarlett, there are hundreds of them. Each better than the next."

"Really? I mean, of course they're great, but wow!" She couldn't remember the last time a show had gotten such an overwhelming response from the online community. One or two compliments was to be expected, but hundreds—that was a big deal.

"Read her another one."

"Okay, listen to this one: 'This show could be a dark horse for the Tony Award if its producers do the right thing and bring it to Broadway right away.'"

"Don't you love that, Scar?"

"I love their confidence in us," Scarlett said.

"Oooh, read her that one!"

"Not if she's at work."

"Just read it!"

"Okay, you'll like this: '*Swan Song* is what theater should be. Not an overblown, bloated spectacle like this season's upcoming *Olympus*. *Swan Song* could be the David to overtake the *Olympus* Goliath.'" They positively giggled with glee at that one.

"They love us, they love us, they love us!" the Jeremys chanted in unison.

Scarlett's mood was quickly turning around. Her phone beeped with another call coming in.

"Hold on, guys, I have another call. Just a sec."

She clicked over. "Hello?" It was the executive director of the Manhattan Theatre Workshop.

"Are you sitting down?"

"Sure," Scarlett said. She did sit down. So much was happening all at once.

"Our box office just opened." He paused for dramatic effect. "You are not going to believe how many ticket orders came in for *Swan Song* overnight!"

Scarlett took a deep breath. Maybe my job search will have to wait, thought Scarlett happily. She even let herself cautiously dare to hope that her new job could actually be as a real Broadway producer in her own right. Can my lifelong dream really be within my reach?

Scene 38

Reilly fidgeted in his seat at the Manhattan Theatre Workshop. Scarlett put her hand on his thigh to stop the constant bouncing of his knee. He looked over at her face, illuminated by the lights from the stage, and his heart lurched. Despite losing her job a week before, she seemed so happy just then, at that moment, in the theater. *Swan Song* makes her so happy, thought Reilly.

He had been avoiding Scarlett all week since his meeting with Margolies and Candace. He had finally run out of excuses not to see a preview of her show. He knew he was hurting her feelings by putting her off, and that was the last thing he wanted to do.

He tried to focus on the stage. They were in Act Two, and the actors were giving stellar performances. The audience members around them were rapt. He felt sick to his stomach. What was he going to do about the mess he'd gotten himself into? The only options on the table were to kill her show or kill his own career. The quandary was tearing him up. He squeezed Scarlett's hand, and she smiled at him. He'd just have to get through it. He'd need to talk to Scarlett that night. It was mortifying to admit that he'd gotten himself into the situation in the first place, but Scarlett knew Margolies better than anyone. Maybe she could help him find a way out of it.

The crowd leapt to their feet during the curtain call, and Reilly was right there with them. Scarlett looked so incredibly proud. On their way to the lobby, he congratulated the Jeremys, whom Scarlett said had finally started to relax after spending the first week of previews tearing out their hair at the back of the theater. They were finally willing to believe that their show was a hit.

"Can we grab a drink?" Reilly asked.

"Good idea. Let me see if the guys want to join us."

"Wait." He grabbed her arm before she could flag down the Jeremys and Lawrence. "I'd rather it be just us."

"Oooh, okay!" she said with a wink. "It's been a while since we've had a date night."

"Why don't I grab us a table at the pub across the street, and you can join me when you're done here?" Reilly suggested, eager to get away. Seeing all the proud, hopeful faces of everyone involved in *Swan Song* made him feel like the lowest of the low. He held their fate in his hands. That must have been how the late critic Kanter felt, every time he went to the theater. No wonder he had killed himself.

Reilly had thought of himself as having thick skin after years of flack for his gossip column. It was a whole different league.

"Sure. I'll just be a few minutes," Scarlett said, turning away to greet someone whom Lawrence wanted her to meet.

Half an hour later, Reilly looked up to see Scarlett making her way to the back corner booth he'd snagged. She looked radiant and confident.

"Sorry to keep you waiting," she said as she pulled off her coat and slid into the booth across from him.

"No worries." He leaned over to give her a kiss across the table, and they both almost knocked their heads on the low-hanging lamp providing a warm, intimate circle of light on the table. It would be romantic if it weren't for the inevitable subject matter, thought Reilly. "I ordered you a glass of wine."

"Perfect," she said as the waiter dropped off two glasses of wine. "Did you see that guy with Lawrence? He's really interested in investing in the show, if we transfer to Broadway. It's pretty exciting! Wow, I feel like I've hardly seen you all week!"

"I know. Sorry about that. Things have been...crazy."

"So..." She paused, her eyes glittering.

"So..." he echoed. He didn't pick up the hint.

"What did you think of the show? I've been dying to hear your thoughts!"

"Of course! Sorry, I don't know where my mind's been." He reached across the table and took her hands in his. "I loved it. I absolutely loved it."

"You mean it?"

He looked into her eyes. "Absolutely. You should be so proud. It's exactly what a great musical should be. It has heart, great songs, a compelling story, and a knock-out cast."

She smiled widely. "You sound like you're writing a review! Hey, soon you *will* be writing reviews. Too bad you can't do ours. Wouldn't that have been too perfect?"

Reilly's eyes darted around the small bar. He had purposely chosen a seat facing the door so he could make sure no one from the theater could interrupt or overhear what he was about to say.

He let go of her hands and took a sip of his wine. "Scarlett. We need to talk about something."

Her face fell. "Are you breaking up with me? I wondered, when I hadn't seen you all week, I—"

"No! Not at all. Never."

"Phew." She sat back. "I'm so relieved. I really wasn't sure what has been going on with you this week—you were MIA all of sudden. You know, I even thought that maybe it was because I had lost my job and couldn't give you any more dirt on Margolies for your articles. I feel bad for even letting that thought cross my mind."

He hadn't thought he could feel any worse. Apparently, he could.

"Hey, are you okay?" she asked with a concerned look. "You look pale."

"Scarlett. I'm not breaking up with you. I think you know how I feel about you. But there's something serious that I need to tell you, and you're not going to like it."

"Okay," she said, her face suddenly serious.

"It's about my review for the *Banner*."

"Your turn is next week, right?"

"Right. But I need to tell you a secret. For all our sakes, you can't tell anyone. Not a soul. I shouldn't even be telling you. But I needed you to know."

"The suspense is killing me, Reilly. Just tell me." Her cheeks were flushed.

He took a deep breath. "Well, I guess you could say I've been offered the critic job."

She gave him a confused look. "Go on."

His eyes kept darting around to ensure they weren't being overheard. "It's complicated. Margolies and Candace offered me the job if I review *Swan Song* next week..." This is the hard part. "And give it a terrible review."

Scarlett stared at him. Speechless.

"What are you talking about? And what does Margolies have to do with any of this?" she asked, baffled.

"I guess you could say we were right about Margolies rigging reviews," he said in an attempt to turn the conversation around.

"What exactly did Margolies say to you?" she asked, her voice ice cold.

"Well, they said if I proved myself by panning *Swan Song*, they'd rig the public vote so that I'd get the gig," he explained.

"So you'd be working for Margolies?"

"No, it wouldn't be like that. Once I got the gig, I could write honest reviews."

"I guess you've thought all this through," Scarlett said, her voice shaking with anger. "You get your dream job, and all you have to do is kill the dreams of your girlfriend and all her friends. We're just collateral damage in your path to the top. Is that it?"

"No, you're missing the point. And anyway, I would never kill your show."

"But didn't you just tell Margolies you would?" Scarlett asked.

"I didn't exactly say that I would."

She cut him off. "But you didn't say you wouldn't?"

"Of course, I won't. But he put me on the spot, Scarlett. I didn't know what to say in the moment. I really want the job."

"So, what's your plan? To just tell him, 'Never mind, I think I'll give *Swan Song* the good review it deserves after all,' and he'll just leave you alone and give you the job anyway? Let you off the hook? You're a fool if you think you won't become a pawn, just like Kanter was!"

"He said he was testing me. Just making sure I had what it takes to be a tough critic," he said. He was getting flustered. She wasn't taking this well. "I'm telling you this because I need your help figuring out what to do."

"Oh, give me a break! You want my permission to royally screw me?" Scarlett exclaimed. "And I suppose it's just a coincidence that he picked *my* show for you to kill? Wasn't your whole point in *getting* this job not to be a tough critic but to be an *honest* one?"

"I am honest. I told you, I will find a way out." He needed to fix this. But he was feeling monumentally stuck. It was either get that job or disappear into obscurity. At thirty-five, he couldn't accept that as his fate.

"I don't believe you. You're just as bad as the rest of them!" she fumed.

Suddenly he was angry, too. "Wake up, Scarlett. This is how the world works these days. Look at Margolies. Look at the rest of them. They didn't get to where they are by playing nice. I thought you wanted this for me and for yourself."

"What I wanted was to get to the top without having to be corrupt and mean and petty. And I thought that's what you wanted, too!" Her voice was rising.

"I do! But maybe we were both being unrealistic. If I don't get this job, they'll just put someone else in that they can manipulate. Better the devil you know, right?"

"I thought I put devils behind me when I was fired." She sank back in her seat, dejected. "I don't know what to say to you, Reilly."

"Help me fix this, Scarlett. I would never hurt you," he said, trying to turn the conversation around.

"You don't know Margolies like I do." Her eyes were dull and she looked tired.

"I'm definitely getting the idea. I haven't even told you the best part," he said with a mirthless laugh. "If I don't do what they say, he and Candace are prepared to run a column saying that they've knocked me out of the running, claiming I tried to cheat the contest. My reputation will be shot. Career over."

She leaned in abruptly. "Wait, there may be a way out of this. What about the proof you have? The bank statements." She was starting to get excited. "Can't you go to your old editor and see if she'd run the exposé now? If you discredited Margolies and Candace preemptively, they couldn't hold you to their deal."

"If only." If only Scarlett wasn't so smart, he thought. "I didn't want to scare you, but Scarlett, they broke into my apartment. They stole the bank statements, my laptop, my notes."

Her face went pale. "I can't believe they would do that. Are you sure?"

"Of course I'm sure. It happened while I was meeting with them. They were clearly sending me a message and tying my hands all at the same time. I don't suppose you kept extra copies of those bank statements."

Scarlett put her head in her hands and shook her head. Reilly finished the rest of his wine in one swallow.

"What am I going to do?" she said quietly.

Reilly asked himself the same question. At least he had told her and they could fix it together. He reached out and patted her head, still buried in her hands. "Let's go home."

She batted his hand away and looked up at him, her eyes blazing again.

"Wait a second. How did they know about your article? How did they know you would have documents in your apartment?"

His heart sank. He was hoping he wouldn't have to go into his part, how he'd actually started the whole mess.

"Well…" he began sheepishly. "I may have let Candace know that I had an inkling of what was going on with Kanter."

"This all makes so much sense now." A chilly smile played at her lips. "You tried to blackmail them, and they beat you at your own game. You are just like them, Reilly Mitchell. I should have known."

She slid out of the booth in a hurry, knocking over her untouched glass of wine and grabbing her coat. He reached for her hand.

"Don't touch me," she snapped. "Don't ever touch me again."

"It's not what you think."

"It's exactly what I think." She was crying. "I can't believe I ever trusted you, Reilly."

"Let me at least make sure you get home safely."

Ever since the break-in at his apartment, he'd been paranoid and looking over his shoulder. He had managed to avoid mentioning anything about Scarlett's involvement to Margolies, but the man was bound to know. It was probably the real reason she was fired, he thought.

"Oh, so one minute you're killing my show and destroying my career, and the next minute you're worried about me?" she said sarcastically.

"I told you, I'd fix this. Just…please don't tell anyone," he said lamely.

"You're pathetic!" she said, turning on her heel and disappearing out the door.

Reilly put his head down on the table, ignoring the puddle of wine left from her spilled drink. He had never felt more deplorable and miserable in his life. There had to be a way out of it. At the moment, however, he had absolutely no idea how.

Scene 39

Candace pushed through the revolving doors of her office building toward the street. She was glad to be through with another long day. Her work hours had become consumed with working with her staff on prepping the online mechanism they'd use to solicit and collect votes. The vote would happen the week after next, once the final finalist, Reilly, had taken his turn. It was annoying that she'd need to go through the motions for another week, putting the complicated and labor intensive process in place, when it would all be a sham, anyway.

On her way to her waiting car, she literally bumped into Reilly, who was blocking her way.

"Oomph! Excuse me... Reilly Mitchell?" She looked at him closely. He looked like he hadn't slept in a week, and she barely recognized him in a trench coat and baseball cap. "I almost didn't recognize you. What the hell do you think you're doing here?"

"I need to talk to you," he said urgently.

"Are you out of your mind?" she said, continuing toward her car. "We can't talk here."

"Well, let's go somewhere, then," Reilly said.

"I can't be seen with you." She pulled open the door of the town car and slid in. Reilly threw himself in beside her.

"What are you *doing*?" She pushed him away.

"Please, I just need a few minutes."

"Fine. But close the door." Even as she said it, she reached over him and pulled it shut herself. They were safely hidden behind the car's tinted windows.

"You look like shit, you know that?" she said, incredibly irritated that he would risk talking to her in public—in front of her office, no less. He needed to learn the rules, if he was going to survive at *her Banner*.

"Candace..." he began as the car pulled out into traffic.

She pulled out her cell phone. "I'm calling Margolies."

"No! Wait. Hear me out."

She glared as he reached over and grabbed her cell phone out of her hand before she could make the call.

"You are way out of line, Reilly. It's not too late to pull the plug."

"I just need five minutes."

"Fine. But we can't talk here," she whispered, indicating the driver, who was easily within earshot. "Wait."

They sat quietly for the remainder of the drive downtown. Reilly's fidgeting annoyed Candace to no end. She really needed a drink.

"Follow me," she said, leading the way to her brownstone, looking both ways to see if they were being observed. She felt a little silly, but she couldn't be too careful. She wouldn't put it past Margolies to be spying on her.

Candace threw her briefcase against the wall and made her way to the open kitchen off the main living room. She poured herself a bourbon on ice, not bothering to offer one to Reilly. As she took a deep sip, she eyed him standing awkwardly on the edge of her living room.

He had seemed so confident when it all started. Now he looked nervous. Just another victim of the Margolies Effect. She finished off her bourbon and poured herself another, filling the glass to the brim. On an empty stomach she could already feel the bourbon working its magic.

She made her way over to the couch, taking her time so as not to spill her very full drink, and intentionally making him wait. It was a trick she'd learned from Margolies, a power play, and it seemed to be working.

She sank into the couch, put her feet on the coffee table, and slid over a stack of newspapers to make room for her feet. She considered asking him to sit down but decided not to. He wasn't a welcome guest after all. It feels nice to be powerful, she thought. It has been a while.

"What's so important that you had to see me and risk ruining everything?" she said, finally.

"That's just it." He took a seat on the edge of the chair across from her. "This plan. It's ruining everything for me. It's ruining my life."

"I find that hard to believe," she said, taking another long sip. "I'm offering you a life. A life as the chief theater critic at one of the largest papers in the world." She spread her arms wide, the ice clinking in her glass.

He rubbed the stubble on his chin and looked at her with desperate eyes. "I know, but the truth is, I can't go through with it."

"What...did...you...just...say?" she said coldly.

"Well...um." Reilly looked down at his hands.

She took her feet off the table and leaned toward him. "We will bury you, Reilly Mitchell. You have no idea how deep we will bury you."

"Can we just talk about this? I thought you might understand," he pleaded.

"Talk," she said, sinking back into the couch.

He looked her in the eye. "Do you know that *Swan Song* is my girlfriend's show? Do you know how long she's worked on it? There has to be another way." He looked at her pleadingly.

"You think I give a shit about your girlfriend and her little show? This is way bigger than all of that. Didn't you hear anything Margolies told you last week? We are giving you a chance to play with the big boys, to join the ranks of the Broadway elite."

"I know, and I'm ready. I just thought..." His voiced tapered off.

"*What* did you think?"

"I just thought that maybe you didn't want a corrupt critic, either. You're a journalist at one of the top newspapers in the world. I see what Margolies has to gain from paying off the critic, but, if you don't mind me asking, what do you gain?"

She stared at him. After a moment, she finished her second drink and started to stand up. She felt surprisingly wobbly. She must have poured more than she thought. She stayed seated, leaning forward, looking Reilly in the eye.

"That's none of your business," she said, but her tone belied her ebbing conviction. She'd be a fool to throw in her lot with Reilly and risk Margolies' vengeance. But Reilly appealed to her better self. She set her drink down. She needed to focus. "It's this or nothing," she said. Margolies would be proud of her.

His face hardened. "I could still expose you."

Candace suddenly didn't like the direction the conversation was going. "No, you can't. I know for a fact that you don't have proof."

"Maybe I do. Maybe you and Margolies and your thugs didn't get everything."

"You're bluffing." In her anger and drunkenness, she was slurring but didn't care.

"Maybe. Maybe not." He leaned forward and met her gaze. "What are you going to do about it?"

"I don't believe you," she said, looking away.

"Fine, don't."

She looked back at him carefully. He sounded like he was telling the truth, but she couldn't be sure. Margolies would have made sure there was no proof. For once, she wished he was there.

Candace pulled her phone out of her pantsuit pocket. "I'm calling Margolies!"

Reilly whipped out his phone. "And I'm calling the *Manhattan Journal*."

"You wouldn't dare!" She was enraged. Not her best self after all.

"Try me," he said with an edge to his voice she hadn't heard before. His eyes were steely.

They had reached an impasse. A tense moment stretched on, neither of them willing to concede the point. Finally, Candace broke the silence.

"I know it won't mean a lot coming from me," she began with dull resignation in her voice, "but I respect your integrity."

"Then help me," Reilly said, the lessening tension in the room leaving them both fatigued.

"I wish I could," Candace said honestly. "But I don't need to tell you how powerful Margolies is. He has us both backed into a corner."

She saw the light of an idea flash in Reilly's eyes.

"He *thinks* he does." Reilly got up and started pacing. Candace remembered having energy and hope like that, back in the day. "Margolies' whole plan revolves around what gets printed in the paper —the *Swan Song* review, the contest winner, all of it. But only you can dictate what actually gets published."

"So what are you saying?" she asked. "Tell him you're going along with his deal but then print a positive *Swan Song* review…and *still* have you win the critic contest? I don't see how that helps. He'd come after me. He'd come after you."

"But what could he do to us? If he revealed your involvement in the Kanter corruption, he'd be implicated as well."

She could see Reilly getting excited about his idea. "I need to think about it." It made sense. Of course, it did. It was what she had wanted in the first place. An honest critic. But Margolies was a formidable force to be reckoned with, and she had yet to prove herself up to the challenge of crossing him.

Reilly came over to the couch and sat next to her, looking her in the eyes. "You know this is the right thing to do. For the public. For the *Banner*. Together we can beat Margolies."

"I'll need to think about." She swirled the mostly melted ice cubes around her glass.

"You know this is the right thing to do," said Reilly quietly. "It's not too late—"

"Okay," she said, almost inaudibly, putting up her hand, still not looking his way. "Okay, okay, okay," she chanted, warming to the idea. She just wanted the whole mess to be behind her. "Now show yourself out. I'm tired."

"Thank you!" Reilly said, giving her an awkward hug before standing up. "You won't regret this." He practically danced to the door.

Candace heard the door click behind him. She felt drained. She closed her eyes. That was the last thing she remembered, until the late-morning sun hit her face through her open curtains the next day.

Scene 40

Margolies tried Candace again as he walked into the *Olympus* theater. He'd started thinking of it as *his Olympus* theater, since he intended for the show to run for a very long time. Not only did he want the show to run forever, but he actually needed it to in order to earn back the massive up-front capital he'd raised to get it off the ground. He couldn't take any chances with the whole critic debacle.

He hadn't heard from Candace in a few days. He was antsy to get an update. He knew that she'd been spending the week working with her staff on the online voting, and he wanted to make sure there wouldn't be a glitch in their plan once Reilly's review came out.

Olympus had taught him that technology could be his Achilles heel. He didn't want to take any chances. At least he was feeling good today. *Olympus* had made it through the first two weeks of previews with surprisingly few stops.

Of course, most of his shows didn't have to stop at all during preview performances, but considering the enormity of what they were trying to do and the new technology, he felt like it was a success. The audiences seemed to be enjoying it in the theater. Although he would have liked the online chatter to have been a little nicer the past couple of weeks.

The early previews of a Broadway show were always populated with chat room folks and bloggers. They hadn't been very generous to *Olympus*. Then again, he thought, it's not like those losers will be buying full-priced tickets, anyway.

He slid into a seat at the back of the house in order to oversee the crew and technicians run the trouble spots until they went smoothly. He expected the show to run all the way through that evening. He never knew when someone from OSHA safety board or the union reps would come through, and he needed them to see for themselves that everything on the show was working and safe.

He crossed his hands behind his head and leaned back. He was starting to feel like his old self again. Ticket sales were strong, thanks in large part to massive amount of press they were getting. Most of the coverage revolved around the "can he or can't he?" pull of the largest show ever attempted on Broadway. Audiences loved that kind of thing and couldn't resist seeing for themselves. A good thing, too, because with astronomical weekly running costs, he'd need to move a lot of full-priced tickets in order to pay back his investors.

A momentary dark cloud passed across his otherwise sunny mood. He didn't like having to answer to his new investing contingent. They were staying too close, breathing down his neck. He'd known they would be, but he had hoped they'd trust that he knew what he was doing.

He relaxed again. It would all work out. Reilly's guaranteed rave review on opening night in three weeks would seal the deal–and he'd be back on top!

Scene 41

Scarlett sat staring glassy eyed out the window of her apartment. It crossed her mind that if she didn't get up soon, she might fuse with the chair. On the other hand, that would be okay. She couldn't think of one good reason to ever get up again.

She heard her phone ring in her purse by the door for what seemed like the millionth time in the past twenty-four hours. She marveled that it hadn't run out of batteries. She didn't need to look at it. She could guess who was calling—Reilly. He might as well give up. He was the last person she wanted to talk to.

She should probably at least tell the Jeremys or Lawrence that she was sick. Or at least give them some excuse for why she had been a no-show at *Swan Song* the previous night. Maybe she wasn't technically sick, but she was heart-sick. That was the worst kind. They would wonder why she had stopped showing up to the theater with only a few days left before opening night. She slumped further in the chair. At least she'd run out of tears.

How could someone have it all one day—a good job, a great boyfriend, a Broadway-bound show—and nothing the next? She wondered again and again. And a bigger question plagued her: How could everyone outside her window be going about life as if everything was normal, when her whole life had shattered to pieces?

A knock on her door interrupted her pity-party reverie. She registered the interruption briefly but chose to ignore it. There was no one she wanted to see. Another knock, louder that time, soon turned to pounding.

"Scarlett, are you in there?" Lawrence's voice. "Scarlett?"

She half-heartedly turned her head to the door, debating whether to call out a response. She idly wondered how he had gotten in the front door. One of her neighbors must have let him in.

"Scarlett? We're all worried about you."

"Go away!" she yelled toward the door. Her voice sounding raspy after a full day and night of crying and not speaking to anyone. She knew she needed to get her butt in gear and salvage what she could of the situation. She had always prided herself at responding well in a crisis. But this one-two punch of bad news had really thrown her for a loop.

"Thank god you're alive. I thought I might have to tear hungry cats off your body." His attempt at a bad joke fell flat.

She turned back to the window, prepared to wait him out. He knew she was alive, and she saw no reason why he couldn't leave her alone. Forever.

"Scarlett? Bad joke, sorry. Will you please let me in?" He waited. "Scarlett?"

"No!" she yelled toward the door.

"I'm not leaving until you let me in."

She sighed and got up. "I'm fine. Go away."

"You don't sound fine."

"I'm not dressed," she said, looking down at the ratty robe she wore over nothing but cutoff sweat shorts.

"Nothing I haven't seen before, Gorgeous," he said, obviously encouraged that she was at least responding to him through the door.

"I said go away."

"Well, that's not going to happen. I'm prepared to wait for you to change your mind."

She could hear what sounded like his back sliding down the door as he sat on the floor outside her apartment, presumably to wait her out. He wasn't going to give up, she realized. Fine, she thought, if he wants to subject himself to my misery, that is his problem. What do I care? He'd hear about it soon enough, anyway, once the bad review hit. At least he could take his money and dump it into something else.

She didn't care. She had been so sure she could find her place on Broadway, become a player in the business she had loved her whole life. She had thought she could play the game, gave it her best shot, and still had come out a loser.

She wrenched the door open, and Lawrence, who had been leaning on it, flopped into her apartment. He looked up at her, upside down from the floor.

"Good to see you, Gorgeous." He flashed her his best smile.

She turned around and shuffled back to her chair.

Lawrence got up off the floor and dusted himself off as he came further into her tiny studio apartment, closing the door behind him.

"So this is where you live?" he said, looking around at her three-hundred square feet of Broadway show posters, unmade Murphy bed, and cluttered excuse for a kitchen. Not surprisingly, they had never spent any time there; Lawrence's penthouse was the more appealing and infinitely more spacious option.

"I didn't know you had my address," she said, her curiosity trumping her silence.

"I had to track it down," he said, clearly proud of himself. "Turns out it's not so hard to track down the one and only Queen Colleen in San Francisco. Your brother gave me your address."

"You remembered my brother's drag name?" At the moment, it didn't seem at all strange to be sitting in her bathrobe, talking to Lawrence about drag queens. Now that was an idea. Maybe she would move back to the Bay Area and produce drag shows at Castro dive bars. It cheered her up momentarily.

"It's not something one easily forgets. Besides, I was happy to hear that you had told your brother, or should I say, 'sister,' about me."

"Brother. Get over yourself," she said, but she had to admit that he was starting to improve her spirits, and she could see that he knew it.

"Now that I'm here, will you tell me what's going on? We've been worried about you. It's not like you to not show up at the theater." As he talked, he slid her chair around, with her in it, to face the bed.

He took a seat on the edge, amid the tangled knot of sheets and pillows.

"I don't even know where to start." She crumpled over, ending up with her head between her legs, feeling pathetic.

"Okay, here's what we're going to do." He pulled her to her feet. "Get up. We're putting you in the shower." He half-walked, half-dragged her limp body toward the bathroom.

"What's the point?" she whined.

"The point is that you're a mess, and we need to get you sorted out so you can tell me what's going on."

"Put me down," she said half-heartedly.

"Fine. But I'll be waiting right here." He set her down on the nearest surface he could find, which happened to be the closed toilet seat. He turned on the shower and got the temperature just right for her.

"Now get in."

She sat there, slumped on the toilet. Not as comfortable as her chair, she thought, but it will do.

"If you don't get in, I'm going to put you in."

That got her attention a little. "*Fine!*" she said with frustration. "I'll do it. Go away."

"I'll be right outside," he said, closing the door behind him.

She had to admit the steamy air felt good on her dry, scratchy eyes. She gingerly peeled off her robe and shorts and climbed in. She washed her hair and brushed her teeth. She was starting to feel somewhat closer to human again. She wrapped a towel around her hair and was about to put her ratty robe back on when she realized just how much it had started to smell. Before she could put it back on, an arm shot through the bathroom door with the purple satin fur-cuffed robe that Colin had given her.

She slipped it on. The satin and fur felt good on her skin, but one glance, even through the fogged-up mirror, confirmed that she looked ridiculous. She came out of the bathroom and struck a diva pose.

"Ah, that's more like it. You look like the Broadway producer you are...or soon will be!"

That sent her in a downward spiral again. She threw herself on the bed and put a pillow over her head.

"Was it something I said?" he asked, peeking under the pillow.

She squeezed her eyes shut. "Oh, Lawrence..." she said, though it just came out as muffled syllables. He came around to the other side of the bed and sat down. He lightly stroked her back with one hand and pried the pillow off her face with the other.

"Are you going to tell me what's wrong? Is it Reilly?"

"Ding, ding, ding. Ten points for you."

"Did you guys break up?" he asked.

Scarlett didn't sense even a hint of triumph in his voice. He really was a good guy. Maybe he was getting more mature at fifty, she thought. "If only that was the worst of it."

"Do you want to tell me what happened?" he asked again, gently.

She rolled onto her back and looked up at him. "I can't."

"What do you mean you can't?"

"It's too terrible. And anyway, I promised I wouldn't."

Just then a buzzer rang, indicating that there was someone at the building's front door for her.

"Hang on a sec," Lawrence said, jumping to his feet.

Before Scarlett knew what was happening, Lawrence had grabbed her keys off the counter and flown out the door. He returned minutes later with two bags of incredibly good-smelling Thai food. Apparently he had called for take-out while she was in the shower.

"Lunch is served," he said, unloading the bags. He'd gotten enough for an army.

"I'm not hungry," she grumbled as he continued to set out more cartons of yummy-smelling food. "My gosh, do you think I eat that much?" she said, slightly joking, slightly offended at the volume of food.

"Let's just say we may have reinforcements on the way," he said.

"I don't want to see anyone!" She put the pillow back over her head.

"I know, Gorgeous, but the Jeremys were worried about you, too. When I called to confirm that you were, in fact, alive, I couldn't say no when they begged to come over. You know they always cheer you up."

"Fine," she said, giving in. "You don't seem to listen to me, anyway."

"Now you're talking," he said with a grin. "Eat! That's an order."

Though she could still feel a dull ache in her stomach, the Thai food was calling to her and she gave in.

"You're getting some color back, at least," Lawrence said encouragingly, filling his own plate with pad Thai and green curry. "This is good. I wonder if they'd deliver to my place."

They continued eating. Lawrence did most of the talking while she picked at her food. They left the rest of it out for the Jeremys' imminent arrival. Lawrence put up the Murphy bed, with instructions from Scarlett, since he'd never operated one before in his life, while she dried her hair. She didn't bother to get dressed. The satin robe was surprisingly comfortable. I only look a little like a drag queen in it, she thought.

Lawrence made her a cup of chamomile tea. After the Jeremys arrived and devoured the last of the Thai food, the four of them gathered around her tiny apartment. Scarlett was pleased to see that four people could fit in her minuscule apartment at the same time. From the bed, the chair, and the floor, they looked at Scarlett expectantly.

"This isn't like you, Scarlett. What happened?" Jersey Jeremy asked.

"What can we do?" Buff Jeremy said.

"It's really bad, guys," she said, looking at all three of them. "And I don't even know where to start. I'm worried that it's somehow my fault."

"We'll be fine, honey," Buff Jeremy said. "Just tell us what's on your mind."

She felt tears coming to her eyes already but took a deep breath and charged on. "Well, you know how Reilly's up this week as a finalist for the *Banner* critic's job." They all nodded. "In a nutshell, the last critic, Kanter, had apparently been paid off by Margolies for decades to write good reviews for his shows." Three pairs of eyes widened. "Now Margolies is blackmailing Reilly into doing the same thing. Only to prove that he is the 'right guy for the job,' they're making him write a scathing review of our show this week."

They all stared at her in shocked silence. Clearly, it was far from what they were expecting.

"Well, of course he's not going to...right?" Jersey Jeremy said, trailing off as he realized that it was a silly question, given Scarlett's state.

"I can't believe I ever trusted him," she said sullenly.

"But he seemed like such a good guy. And he was clearly crazy about you. It just doesn't make sense," Buff Jeremy said.

"I guess his career came first. Let's just say we broke up." She stared at them in stony silence.

Lawrence was the first to recover. "I'm so sorry, Scarlett."

The Jeremys tried to echo his condolences, but Scarlett could tell that her announcement about *Swan Song* had knocked the wind out of them.

"I just don't understand why Reilly would do that you. To us," Buff Jeremy said, when he could speak again.

"He claimed he wasn't going to do it, but Margolies has threatened to kill his career if he doesn't go through with it. It's complicated," Scarlett said.

"I get that, but this would be really low. I mean, really, really low."

"And why would Margolies want to kill our show?" Jersey Jeremy asked.

"To punish me, I guess. I thought being fired was enough, but apparently not," Scarlett said.

"Actually," Lawrence said, "there may be more to it than that. If you've read the editorials, there's talk that if *Swan Song* came on to Broadway during this Tony Award season, we would actually have a shot at beating out *Olympus*. The Tony voters may shun Margolies' show for being too overblown, not to mention hard for the touring market."

"I hadn't thought about that," Scarlett said, relieved, in a way, that maybe it wasn't entirely about her. "But we don't even know if we're going to Broadway. Now, obviously, with the upcoming bad review, we have no chance."

"Scarlett, you're being modest," Jersey Jeremy said. "Thanks to you, we were perfectly set up for Broadway. The review would have been the lynch pin, but you positioned us perfectly. Lawrence's money didn't hurt, either." He nodded to Lawrence.

"Well, it's all over now," Scarlett said miserably.

Jersey Jeremy slid out of the chair to join Buff Jeremy on the floor. They wrapped their arms around each other. It was small comfort, after such devastating news.

"I don't know about you all, but I'm not willing to throw in the towel, just like that," Lawrence said.

"I love your enthusiasm," Scarlett said, "but I've wracked my brain and can't think of any way around it."

"Short of taking out Reilly…" Buff Jeremy said.

"Not going to happen," Scarlett said. "I'll admit I hate his guts right now, but he got himself in a bad situation. And, anyway, he'll get what's coming to him, if he has to spend the rest of his career wrapped around Margolies' little finger."

Jersey Jeremy shuddered. "Good point. I wouldn't wish that on anyone."

"Listen up," Lawrence cut in. "I don't think Reilly's our problem. The real problem—and I know this won't come as a huge shock to you all—is Margolies."

"But what can we do about him? He '*is* Broadway,'" Jersey Jeremy said, making air quotes in mock tribute to Margolies' constant self-aggrandizing claim.

"Actually, he's killing Broadway—or at least the Broadway that we love," Lawrence said. "When word got out that I had pulled my *Olympus* money, I started getting hit up by all the other major producers. I guess they thought I was available for fleecing." He smiled. "Anyway, those guys had some pretty interesting things to say about what's *really* going on."

"And you're only telling us now?" Jersey Jeremy asked.

"This all just happened," Lawrence said.

"Let him finish," Buff Jeremy said impatiently.

"Apparently, Margolies has done stuff like this before. When Scarlett mentioned that Margolies was paying off Kanter, it all started to make sense. I think he may also have been finding creative ways to keep certain other shows off of Broadway, too."

"You mean to keep his competition down?"

"Sort of, but there's more to it than that."

Scarlett sat up. That was interesting.

Lawrence explained, "Basically, Margolies' figured out that his big-budget, ultra-commercial shows—you know, some of those heavy handed movie musicals and spectacle shows that he's been doing—can command a faster increase in ticket pricing than your normal Broadway show. Tourists have heard of the titles, so they basically come pre-branded. And he has good enough street cred to lock movie stars into the lead roles." He paused to make sure they were following him.

"Now that ticket prices are no longer fixed but can, instead, vary widely based on demand, like airline tickets, Margolies has free rein to drive his ticket prices through the roof. When he has a hit, of course."

"Well, I hate to say it, but that just sounds like good business," Jersey Jeremy said.

"Except that it sucks up all the money that tourists used to spend on multiple shows. Now, more often than not, they can only afford to go to one. And if they only pick one, of course their first choice will be a Margolies hit since they want to see stars, stunts, and spectacle."

"Well, you could say they get what they pay for," Scarlett said.

"Yes, but it pressures all the other major producers to try to match his exorbitant production values at huge expense and in turn they have to raise their ticket prices too. In fact, each hit show that takes ticket prices to new heights sets the bar for the rest of the shows."

"I see where this is going," Scarlett said. "As Margolies systematically drives up costs and ticket prices, it gets harder and harder for the smaller and more obscure new shows and original musicals to survive. The shows that used to make it on merit alone… you know, great shows like *Next to Normal* or *The Drowsy Chaperone*… can't stay solvent."

"This is blowing my mind," Jersey Jeremy said, shaking his head. "I knew the guy had power but this is crazy!"

Scarlett looked at them all in disbelief. "So basically, the fact that Broadway is becoming a show-tune theme park is Margolies' fault and for the past four years I was helping him do it. I feel queasy."

"Don't be so hard on yourself, Scarlett," Lawrence said, gently. "A lot of people outside the theater world would think he was a genius.

He is a genius. Broadway is big business and money will always trump art in the end. We just happen to want to keep the art part."

Buff Jeremy cut in. "So, you're saying that all those original musicals that should have come to Broadway but disappeared were killed on purpose so the schlock from Margolies' office — no offense Scarlett — could take over Broadway?"

"It certainly explains a lot." Scarlett said. "I can finally understand why Margolies would tackle something as enormous as Olympus. He's simply raising the bar again."

"God, this is depressing," Jersey Jeremy said.

"So what can we do?" Buff Jeremy asked the obvious question. "Confront Margolies and tell him to cut it out?"

"Obviously talking to Margolies isn't going to do it. Between his goons and his influence, he'd squash us like flies," Lawrence replied.

"But what's the alternative?" Scarlett said. "Seriously, Lawrence, I've got nothing. I'm out of ideas."

"As it happens, I do have the beginnings of an idea," Lawrence said looking at each of them with a mischievous twinkle in his eye. "But it will only work if you're all in..."

Scene 42

Reilly felt like a wreck. The emotional rollercoaster he'd been on for days since Scarlett stormed off, and his subsequent talk with Candace, had left him feeling wrung out.

One moment he was elated that he was so close to accomplishing his goal, then in the next second, he panicked that Candace would renege on their plan, leaving him exposed to career annihilation. They hadn't had any more contact since he'd left her townhouse. He'd tried calling a few times, to no avail. He just had to trust her, which was no easy feat. Calls to Scarlett had been equally fruitless.

He got a new laptop up and running after his other one was stolen by Margolies' goons. That distracted him for a day or so, but now he was faced with a blank page and a flashing curser where his pivotal *Swan Song* review was supposed to materialize.

After a day of pacing around his apartment, he'd taken to the streets, walking what felt like the entire length of Manhattan. The following day, he'd searched the web for cheap islands he could retire to at a moment's notice with his meager savings. He felt foolish. But it didn't seem all that far-fetched, considering his situation if things didn't go as planned.

It didn't help that he had no one to talk to about his circumstances, his entire career on the line in epic make-or-break proportions. He thought about calling a shrink but didn't know where to start. And anyway, the information was too sensitive.

He called Scarlett for the hundredth time. "Scarlett, I *really* need to talk to you. Please call me back. I need you." He knew his messages were getting more and more pathetic and desperate. At that moment, she was probably getting ready to head to *Swan Song*'s opening night. His head hurt.

He glanced at the *Swan Song* ticket on the table. He had been expected at the final preview the previous night to evaluate it for his official review, but he hadn't even considered showing up. He couldn't face Scarlett in a public place and risk everything being exposed before things worked out. He had called Scarlett to tell her he wouldn't be there, but of course she hadn't answered. He'd already seen the show; not making an appearance wouldn't impact his ability to write the review.

He knew the *Banner* would be expecting his review to be submitted that day. They'd be scrambling to make their next day post-opening night print and online publishing deadline.

He sat down to write the review that would seal his fate one way or another, but he was interrupted by his cell phone ringing. He scrambled to pick it up, sure that it was Scarlett, finally throwing him a bone. But the number wasn't one he immediately recognized.

"Hello?" he said.

"Hello, Reilly." Reilly swallowed hard.

"Hello, sir." It was Margolies.

"It's come to my attention that you didn't show up at *Swan Song* last night. Are we going to have a problem?"

Reilly sat down hard on the couch. "Uh...no. No problem. I saw it last weekend with..." He stopped himself from almost mentioning Scarlett.

"I see," Margolies said, softly. "So you've had nearly a whole week to write your review and, yet, Candace told me that you haven't turned one in yet."

So Candace had been talking to Margolies. What did that mean about their plan? Had she changed her mind? Had Margolies somehow talked her out of it? He hoped she was still playing along. The uncertainty was maddening.

"I'm working on it right now." That wasn't exactly a lie. "My computer was stolen last week," he added with the slightest hint of an accusation. "I'll get the review to Candace soon."

"That's what I wanted to hear. I would hate to think that you had changed your mind," said Margolies, menacingly.

"Of course not, sir," Reilly said.

"Good boy. Oh, and Reilly..."

"Yes?"

"You look good with a beard." The line went dead.

Reilly's blood ran cold. How did Margolies know that he hadn't bothered to shave in almost a week? Reilly dashed over to the window and violently pulled down the blinds. What the hell have I gotten myself into? he thought for the thousandth time. Is this what Kanter had to deal with? The thought horrified him.

His adrenaline pumping, he sat down at the computer and began to write. The words came easily. He had been practicing writing reviews for weeks, after all, until things had gone south. He knew how to frame the review. He knew what the readers would want to hear, how to get the right pull quotes for the producers—Scarlett!—and how to keep them all reading to the end.

In less than an hour, the formerly blank screen was populated from top to bottom with words about *Swan Song*. He read it over only once for last-minute typos, opened his email, and sent it to Candace. The second he hit "send," he crumpled to the floor. It was out of his hands. He stayed there, face down, spread eagled, both relieved and petrified about what he'd just done.

The good news is, he thought, I've done everything I can to make things right. The bad news is, he had absolutely no idea what would happen to him next.

Scene 43

Scarlett adjusted her short, red strapless cocktail dress as she stepped out of the limo in front of the theater. She was flattered to see heads turn in appreciation as she stepped onto the sidewalk in front of the Manhattan Theatre Workshop. Despite the recent turn of events, Lawrence had insisted that they stick to their original plans for opening night, which included arriving in style at the theater.

Lawrence and the Jeremys were right behind her, piling out of the car, looking equally elegant in their suits. They made their way into the lobby, which was already crowded with many of their friends as well as several important patrons of the theater. A glittering opening-night crowd, everyone was in great spirits. Scarlett pushed through the lobby to check in with the artistic director. On her way, she overheard Broadway buzz about their show from numerous patrons.

She wondered for a second where Reilly's review was at that moment. Were his lethal words being run through the presses? It was common for reviews to appear online the same night as opening. She hadn't decided whether she'd look for it that night. Probably not. She wanted to enjoy one last night of glory before all their dreams came officially crashing down.

As patrons filed into the theater and took their seats, Scarlett remained standing at the back corner of the theater, where she could take in the audience and the stage. She could feel the positive energy and electric vibe pulsing in the room. The people knew they were in for a treat.

"You did good, Gorgeous," Lawrence whispered into her ear, standing beside her in the shadowy corner.

She squeezed his hand. "Thanks, Lawrence. I don't know what I would've done without you. I'd probably be at home right now with my head in the oven."

"You don't have an oven," he said.

"Good point. I've never thought of that as a plus before," she said, smiling at Lawrence before turning back to gaze out over the crowd.

"Look at them," Scarlett said. They both looked down at the Jeremys, who were whispering to each other from their seats, third row center. "I love those guys."

"They're the best," Lawrence said. "They deserve success with this show. As do you, Gorgeous."

"We'll see," she said, letting go of his hand. "Even if we can pull off your harebrained plan, it might be too late for *Swan Song*."

"I wouldn't be so sure," he said with a twinkle in his eye as the houselights went down, indicating the show was about to start. "We're changing history," he whispered. "There's no telling what may happen."

Scarlett and Lawrence stood side by side, watching the show for the entire evening. The opening-night party went by in a blur of champagne and compliments. Positive reviews in smaller publications had already started to come out, and the potential of a Broadway transfer was the talk of the evening, despite the conspicuous silence from the *Banner*. Scarlett had a great time; only in the limo on the way home did she allow herself to think about the review.

They dropped the Jeremys off at home first.

"No matter what happens," Scarlett said, hugging them goodbye, "you guys have shown the world that your talent is not to be ignored!"

"We love you, Scarlett!" Jersey Jeremy said, giddy from the evening's success and drunk from the festivities.

"To us!" Buff Jeremy said, raising the half-full champagne bottle he clutched in his hand.

"Do we need to get you guys into bed?" Lawrence asked, laughing as champagne splashed on the Jeremys as they staggered happily to the door of their building.

"We could ask you two the same thing!" Jersey Jeremy said with a devilish wink as they disappeared inside.

"They make a good point," Lawrence said, raising his eyebrows at Scarlett. "Shall we make a night of it? It's been ages since you've stayed over at my place."

Scarlett smiled, remembering how much fun she used to have with happy-go-lucky, no-strings-attached Lawrence—before Reilly appeared in her life. How did my life get so complicated so quickly? she wondered. "It's tempting. But I don't think it's a good idea, Lawrence. We're working together now."

"That never stopped us before," Lawrence said with a wicked grin.

"It's different now," she said with exasperation, then her tone became more serious. "And anyway, look what my last relationship did for my career. If that's not my cue to take a break from men for a while, I don't know what is."

"Just know I'm here, if the rebound mood strikes you," he said, stretching out his legs in the back of the limo.

"That's very generous of you," she said, smiling.

"I'm a generous guy." He smiled back.

At that moment, she just wanted to get out of her party dress, into her PJs, and sleep until the next day's inevitable disappointments for the theater and the cast had blown over. She hated to think how devastated everyone would be. At least the four of them had had time to brace themselves…not that that had really helped, but it was better than nothing.

Suddenly morbid curiosity got the better of her, and she couldn't resist knowing what the review said any longer—particularly when she realized that, without a computer, she wouldn't be able to check the online reviews when she got home.

"I don't suppose you've checked the reviews?" she asked Lawrence.

"I'll admit I've been keeping an eye on them all night. Really positive stuff from just about everyone." He pulled out his fancy phone. It was an even newer model than the one she'd seen him with just a few days before. He really was a tech nerd. "The *Wall Street Journal* could have been nicer, but that's no surprise. Their reviewer hates musicals."

"No one cares what he has to say, anyway," Scarlett said. "Is that a new phone?"

"Yep. Pretty cool, huh?" He held it toward her so she could see the screen.

"What did you do with your old one?"

"Nothing. Why, do you want it?"

"Maybe I could borrow it? I don't have a laptop anymore, and the internet is slow on my ancient phone."

"Sure, but if you need a computer, I can just hook you up with a laptop. I might have ten or twelve to spare," he said, ruefully.

"I'd love to borrow one, if you don't mind."

"Done," he said, and his attention became absorbed in something on his device. "Well, I've been checking the reviews all night, and there are some great ones, of course…but still nothing from the *Banner*."

"That's strange," she said. It was nearly 2:00 a.m. and the *Banner*'s online review should have been out.

"I guess the suspense continues," he said as the limo pulled up in front of her apartment building.

"Do you want to come back to my place and get the laptop now, so you have it for the weekend?" he said, in a last valiant effort to get her to come home with him.

"Nice try, but no," she said, sliding out of the car.

"A man's got to try. It's my job." He walked her to the door of the building.

"And you're great at it. All the girls say so," she said, laughing.

"What else do all the girls say about me?" he said, taking her teasing in stride.

"All I know is *this* girl is very grateful for everything you've done for her recently. I mean that. Thank you." She kissed his cheek and went inside, waving to him from behind the glass doors. He blew her a kiss before disappearing back into the sleek black limo.

She finally allowed herself to take her shoes off in the elevator on the way to her apartment. It had turned out to be a surprisingly great night. Who would have thought she'd enjoy the evening so much, given the circumstances?

As she turned the corner into the hallway, something caught her eye in front of her door. She leaned down and found a rose wrapped in a tube of paper. She let herself into her apartment and removed the paper from around the rose, curious as to what it could possibly say. More opening-night congratulations? Her parents had sent flowers earlier in the day and other opening-night gifts had been delivered to the theater. She'd have to collect them tomorrow.

She flipped on a light and sat down on the corner of her bed and unrolled the tube of paper. It was a printout of an email from Reilly to Candace earlier that evening.

Subject: Swan Song *review*

Headline: "Swan Song *Soars"*

Her eyes widened as she scanned the unmistakably rave review, with Reilly's perfect balance of acerbic wit and informed commentary thrown in for good measure. Everything a *Banner* critic's review should be, she thought—not to mention, it was everything that *Swan Song* deserved.

Scarlett took a deep breath. Does this mean what I think it means? Had Reilly just sacrificed his own career for her and her show?

Scene 44

Reilly woke up groggy and disoriented. He sat up and looked at the clock. It was dark, but he could see morning light peeking around his closed blinds. Suddenly the events of yesterday flooded back. He flopped back on the bed then changed his mind and scrambled to his computer.

Nothing in his emails from Candace, and more distressing, nothing from Scarlett. Maybe it is too late, he thought. He had waited in front of her apartment until nearly 1:00 a.m., but she'd never shown up. Either the opening night festivities had gone on into the wee hours of the morning, or she had already replaced him. Had she been seeing her money guy, Lawrence? He felt sick, thinking he might have destroyed the best thing that had happened to him in years. Funny how he hadn't realized it until it was too late.

A beep from his cell phone interrupted his thoughts. He pounced on it and, to his relief, saw that he had a voicemail from Candace. But it was the voicemail from Scarlett that captured his full attention. As the sound of Scarlett's voice on his answering machine filled his ears, all thoughts of Candace flew out of his head.

Scarlett had gotten the review he'd left on her doorstep and wanted to see him. Her message had come in at 2:00 a.m. She must have just been out late and hadn't gone home with anyone else. He felt like a silly school boy, so great was his relief.

He called Scarlett.

"Hello?"

He woke her up. It was 7:00 a.m. on a Saturday, after all.

"Can you ever forgive me?"

"Reilly! Hi! I tried to reach you last night," she said, coming fully awake. "I can't believe what you did for *Swan Song.*"

"How could I live with myself, if I built my career on a lie and hurt the person I care most about?"

"Thank you," she said quietly.

"Then you'll forgive me for being an ass? For getting myself into this situation in the first place?" he asked.

"I know Margolies. I know he put you in a tough position."

"I guess he'll be in for a surprise this morning when he opens his paper," he said with a feeling of satisfaction tempered with a lingering sense of dread.

"So you haven't heard from him? Or the *Banner*?" she asked.

The things that had seemed so important the previous night seemed insignificant in light of Scarlett's willingness to forgive him. But would she take him back?

"I don't care about any of that," he said, not yet wanting to face the inevitable fallout of what he'd done. "When can I see you?"

"Well...I'm still in bed, but I can get up and be at your place in a bit."

"I'm up now. Can I just come over?" he said, not wanting to wait another minute to see her again.

"Sure. Oh, and Reilly, grab a copy of today's *Banner* on your way here."

Twenty minutes later, she answered the door to her apartment wearing a purple satin robe he hadn't seen before. He wanted to take her in his arms right there, but he wasn't totally sure how things stood between them. He knew that just because she'd let him come over didn't necessarily mean they were back together.

"Your paper delivery, my lady," he said, presenting her a copy of the *Banner* with both hands.

She laughed. "Come in."

"Nice robe," he teased.

"Well, you didn't exactly give me time to get ready!" she said, though he could tell she'd brushed her hair and maybe even put on a little makeup. He took it as a good sign that she wanted to look nice for him. Maybe he could dare to hope that she still cared for him. "Coffee?" she asked. A pot was brewing.

She poured them each a cup as they both stared at the *Banner* laying between them on the kitchen counter.

"Ready to see your review in print?" she said, momentarily wondering if the Jeremys or Lawrence had been up early and seen it yet. She hadn't called them last night because it had been too late. But she was surprised that no one had called her yet.

He took a deep breath. "Ready as I'll ever be."

"Wait!" He put his hand over hers before she could open the Arts section. "I know it's probably too soon, but is there a chance we can give our relationship another try? I've been miserable without you."

"You betrayed me, Reilly," she said.

His heart sank.

"I trusted you." He could see the raw hurt that he had caused her.

"Just say that you'll give me a chance to make it up to you." He flashed her his signature charming smile that she had loved just the week before. He could see in her eyes that she was considering his request.

Without answering, however, she took her hand out of his and opened the Arts section.

"Oh my god!" she exclaimed, reading the headline. Her coffee cup hit the tiled floor and smashed to pieces.

Scene 45

Candace woke up in her own bed with a feeling of pure bliss. She had all but given up on waking up ever again with the wonderful feeling of a man's arms around her. Careful not to wake him, she slowly turned her head to take in Margolies' body next to hers. He was older than the last time they had been like that, twenty years before, but he was still the man she had loved more than anything, before he had irreparably broken her heart.

Having him here, in their bed again, she felt the pieces starting to click back into place. Candace's mind wandered back to the events of the night before:

Reilly's review had come in just before the print deadline. She was just beginning her final edits, but it was in good shape. Reilly was an excellent writer and would make a solid reviewer.

Margolies had appeared unexpectedly in her doorway.

"What are you doing here?" She felt her face flushing guiltily. She had minimized the document in front of her, hoping he couldn't see the deception that was written all over her face. She got up and pulled the door closed behind him.

"I found myself in the area and thought I'd get a sneak peek of Reilly's review," he'd said casually, though she knew it was not a casual visit. He had been checking up on her. It stung that he thought he needed to do it, and yet he was right to. After all, she had been attempting to double cross him.

"You shouldn't be here. This is risky."

"One visit in twenty years isn't going to raise any red flags," he'd said, helping himself to the chair across from her desk.

"So, what did our boy Reilly have to say about *Swan Song*? Was he suitably nasty?"

Candace had squirmed in her chair. That was not part of the plan, and she had never been good about lying to him face to face.

"Yep, all good. I mean, not good. A good bad review was what I meant." She was babbling.

"Candace…" He'd stood up and come around behind her desk. "What are you not telling me?"

"What are you talking about?"

"Can I see the review?" He was already bending over her desk to look at her computer.

"It's not ready yet..." she'd said lamely as he brought up Reilly's review. She spun out of her chair and stood facing the window. There had been no point in trying to stop him. She couldn't watch. Even with her back to Margolies, she felt the anger radiating through the room.

Minutes had passed. He had to have finished reading, but she couldn't bring herself to turn around. She couldn't guess what he'd do. She'd never betrayed him quite so directly before.

She'd flinched when she felt his hands on her shoulder.

"Oh, Candy," he'd said softly in her ear.

That certainly wasn't what she had expected. Her body craved his touch while her mind shouted, *Warning, warning!*

"I'm sorry," she whispered. As the sun went down she could see his reflection in the glass of the window. His faced looked grim, but his hands were gentle. He turned her around to face him.

"It must be hard to be in your position," he purred. "I should never have left this to you alone." It was a backhanded compliment at best, but his benevolent tone had been soothing.

She could feel her anxiety ebbing away. "Reilly came to see me."

"Of course he did. It's okay. It will be okay." He stroked her cheek. "I'm just glad I got here in time to fix this before you made a mess of everything."

"Fix this?"

"Candy, Candy." Still the soothing tone. "You know you can't print this review. You know better. We had a plan." He'd brushed his

lips on her neck. She wanted the moment to last forever... If only the nagging sirens hadn't been going off in the back of her mind.
She shivered in pleasure. She had trouble focusing on what he was saying. Reilly. The plan.

She turned away from him. "I hate you," she said, though her voice lacked any trace of conviction.

"I know," he said. His voice became suddenly hard. "But you need me." Then he'd sat in her office chair and spun back around to the document on her computer screen. Candace had stood rooted to her spot in front of the window, her body still quivering from his touch. She knew she had lost the battle. A mix of emotions washed over her.

She'd heard Margolies typing. He paused briefly. She could hear him going through her desk drawers, then the unmistakable sound of bourbon being poured into her coffee cup. She recognized that sound anywhere.

"Drink up, Candy," he said, holding the mug out to her. She'd taken it grudgingly but gratefully as he went back to clicking away on her computer. He was rewriting the review. She couldn't stop him. But that didn't mean she had to watch.

Margolies hadn't glanced her way again as she downed her first glass of bourbon in one long gulp and poured herself a refill. It hadn't taken him long to do his work. She knew that changing the *Swan Song* rave to a pan wouldn't be too hard, just a matter of changing a few key compliments into criticisms.

"Done!" Margolies had said with a flourish. "That was kind of fun."

She allowed herself to look at him again. She marveled that she could hate him so much in that moment and yet want him desperately. He had looked so smug. Pleased with himself. "Now, Candy"—He reached over and took her hand—"send this off and let's go home."

"We've nearly missed the print deadline... Wait. What did you say? Home?" She had no idea what he was talking about. Had she even heard him correctly?

"Of course, home. We'll get take-out. Catch up. Make a night of it," he said as he stood up and stretched.

She'd felt like she had missed something, like some seismic shift happened and she hadn't noticed. She looked at her half-empty mug. She hadn't had *that* much to drink. Last she checked, she had betrayed Margolies. Yet, magically, he was inviting himself over for take-out and a chat. As if they were a happy couple again. Was it a trick?

Candace took a deep breath. It might well be a trick, but she knew she was helpless to resist. She wanted it. She wanted him. She wouldn't pass it up…

Her reverie was interrupted by Margolies stirring and waking up by her side.

"Good morning," she said. She wished she had brushed her teeth and cleaned up a little. Mornings weren't her best look.

She saw a cold look cross his face when he opened his eyes. Was it just her imagination? It was quickly replaced by a tight smile.

He sat up and ran his fingers through his hair. "Has your paper arrived yet?" He got out of bed and pulled on his pants without a backward glance her way. It stung, but she felt grateful for a chance to brush her hair and fix her face. She hadn't had a chance to take off her makeup, as one thing had led to another the night before. At the moment she was sporting an unattractive raccoon look. Despite all that, she felt better than she had in years.

Fifteen minutes later, she joined Margolies in her living room. Or *their* living room, she thought wistfully. She was looking forward to coffee and reading the paper with Margolies. It would be like old times—if they had ever actually done that when they were married. Maybe it wasn't too late. People remarry their exes all the time, she thought. Funny how one night can change everything. She really thought she had hated him, but her current feelings were quite the opposite.

He held up the *Banner* proudly. It was open to the *Swan Song* review. "Maybe I should have been a critic!"

She took the paper out of his hands and kissed him gently on the lips. His kiss back was distracted.

"You better call Reilly and let him know."

"Can't we talk about this later?" She batted her eyes. "I think we have other things to talk about this morning." For once she was happy that it was a weekend. It would be much less lonely with Margolies back in the picture.

"What else would we talk about?" His question seemed genuine. He picked her cell phone off the table and held it out to her. "Call Reilly right now. Tell him he's got the job."

Her mouth dropped open. "But he... We..."

"He hasn't beat me," said Margolies, rising from the couch and putting the cell phone into her hand. "His life is about to get a whole lot less pleasant. But at this point, he's my best option. Where am I going to find another critic, with the contest next week? He's nothing I can't handle. Apparently, he'll just need a little more persuading."

The tone of his voice was starting to make Candace uncomfortable.

"Give him a call and then let's get to work. You and I have a contest to rig."

Her blood ran cold. Had the entire evening all been just a ruse to get his way? Had the last night's intimacy been his way of pulling the wool over her eyes? He'd gotten the *Swan Song* review he had wanted after all. But his words, his touch…it had all seemed so real, so sincere.

She watched him go to the kitchen to make coffee, as if nothing had changed in twenty years. She dialed Reilly's number on her cell phone and got his voicemail.

"Welcome to the *Banner*, Reilly Mitchell," she said. "We look forward to having you onboard as our new chief theater critic."

Scene 46

It had been a very strange few days for Scarlett since the review came out. She had been in and out of meetings with the various *Swan Song* artists and funders who, until that day, had been so hopeful about a Broadway transfer. It had been a challenge to sympathize with them, knowing that all hope was not lost. Their dreams might have a second chance. Of course, it was far from a sure thing.

That night, she and Reilly and the Jeremys were pow-wowing in Lawrence's living room for yet another strategy session, as events continued unfolding throughout the week.

As Lawrence poured wine all around to complement the pizza they'd ordered in, the Jeremys raised their glasses in a toast: "To Reilly. As of this week, the *Banner*'s chief, not to mention already-most-hated, theater critic."

"What's this crazy world coming to?" Reilly said, raising his glass.

"To this crazy world!" Scarlett said, as they clinked glasses.

"But seriously, Reilly, how are you holding up?" Buff Jeremy asked.

"Well, as long as I avoid the internet, the other newspapers, the late-night talk shows, and talking to anyone I know—present company excluded—I'm doing just fine."

The bad review of *Swan Song* had elicited a firestorm of criticism from people who had seen the show during previews and were outraged that the review could be so hateful, especially given all the positive buzz from other paper's reviewers and audiences.

"You're infamous, that's for sure," Scarlett said, knowing that despite the drama, a part of Reilly loved the publicity. His gossip column had prepared him to take flack, though this was extreme.

"No such thing as bad publicity. Isn't that what they say?"

"I don't know if the *Banner* would agree," Lawrence said.

The announcement had been made a few days after the *Swan Song* review that the votes were in and Reilly had won the contest for chief critic, and outrage erupted all over again.

"Do you think you really won the contest?" Jersey Jeremy asked.

Reilly couldn't help laughing. "Fat chance."

"Well, I voted for you," Buff Jeremy said.

"No, you didn't!" Jersey Jeremy said.

"He's right. I didn't," Buff Jeremy said with a rueful expression. "I just didn't want you to think you didn't get any votes."

"That's thoughtful, Jeremy, thanks," Reilly said, throwing a wadded up napkin at him. "Let's not forget that it's not *my* article they hated. You all saw what I really wrote about your amazing show—"

"Which brings us to the matter at hand," Lawrence interrupted. "Let us now call this meeting to order." He pounded the all purpose remote on the coffee table in place of a gavel.
"Scarlett and the Jeremys and I already have Project *Olympus* underway. We'll get to that in a minute."

"Aye, Aye, captain." The three of them saluted Lawrence. Scarlett winked at Reilly. She hadn't filled him in on all the details quite yet. He was only just beginning to regain their trust. Didn't he prove himself beyond a doubt by throwing himself under the bus for her? she reminded herself.

"So, Reilly, that leaves you to deal with Candace and the *Banner*," Lawrence continued.

"I should probably go to Candace's boss," Reilly said.

"Do you have any idea if he's in on it?" Lawrence asked.

"He was never at any of the meetings, so I'm guessing not. Though how she rigged the voting we'll probably never know," Reilly said.

"I think that's a good idea," Jersey Jeremy said. "If Reilly could get his good review in front of Candace's boss and prove that it was a set up, maybe they'd run a correction or something." The Jeremys' first priority was setting the record straight on *Swan Song*.

"But, honey," Buff Jeremy said to the Jersey Jeremy, "Reilly would lose the critic job if he did that."

Reilly jumped in. "You're all assuming I still want the job."

"Don't you?" That was news to Scarlett. While things had gotten unimaginably complicated for Reilly, she knew he still needed a job *somewhere*.

"Let's just say I'd like to sort this out; and whatever happens to me happens. Would you really want to start a job the way I have? I had already given up on it when I wrote my review." Scarlett reached over and squeezed Reilly's hand as he continued. "Who knew that Candace was a double agent! It's certainly given me a lot to think about. I know I did the right thing." He took a deep sip of his wine. "Anyway, I like this idea. I'll see if I can track down her editor tomorrow… unless we want to wait until after opening night of *Olympus* this week. Just think of what I could say about that with the pen of the chief critic!"

"Ooh, you're playing with fire. From what I've heard from friends who have seen it, it will warrant a bad review all by itself," Jersey Jeremy said.

"That does raise a good question," Scarlett interjected. "Who will review *Olympus* on Friday, if Reilly comes clean?"

They all looked at each other in silence.

"That's not our problem," Lawrence said, clicking away on one of his laptops.

"Finally! Something that's not our problem," Jersey Jeremy said.

Lawrence scribbled a phone number onto a napkin seconds later. "Reilly, here's the editor's direct line. Now let's go over to project *Olympus*. We're T-minus four days until opening night." Lawrence loved his action-game lingo. Their plans did feel a little like a video game, since their "*Olympus* Termination" plans were high tech —and yet so simple all at the same time. Their plans involved interrupting the wireless flying contraptions at a key moment in the show.

"I should have the technology ready to go by tomorrow."

"Are you sure this isn't illegal?" Reilly asked.

"It's a gray area. And anyway, it's worth it to give Broadway a wake-up call. Pretty soon everyone will have one these little gizmos," he said, waving an iPad.

"It looks like a regular iPad to me. You're saying it's some kind of supercomputer?"

"It is a regular iPad. Or, it was. I've simply souped it up to draw a lot more power and more bandwidth. Devices like these are going to be widely available any day now, and it's going to be bad news for any place that relies on unlicensed bandwidth." Lawrence's eyes lit up when anyone gave him a chance to talk geek-speak.

"Like Broadway theaters!" Scarlett said. She'd heard inklings about the whole "white space" issue and had done some research a while back for some initiative that Margolies was working on with the Broadway League. But the practical ramifications hadn't hit home for her before.

"Bingo," Lawrence said. "It's actually a wonder that something like what we're doing hasn't inadvertently happened already, just from someone walking by a theater."

"That could really happen? Someone could knock out a theater's wireless from the street?" Reilly asked in disbelief.

"It can and it will happen, unless the government does something about it. The problem is, the wireless companies are the ones who can afford to buy up all the unlicensed space for their devices. Theaters aren't their problem." Lawrence gestured again to the iPad. "I know you've heard about it on the news; it's called *white space.*"

"Sure," Reilly said. "I wrote a column for Journal when they pulled the *Phantom* stunt for the FCC, but I didn't realize an iPad could knock out the wireless. I thought it had to be some bigger device."

"Not if you know what frequencies they're using," Lawrence said proudly.

"How could you possibly know *that*?" Reilly asked.

Buff Jeremy leaned over and pretended to whisper in Reilly's ear. "He hacked the system."

"I have no idea what you're talking about," Lawrence said with a devilish grin.

"Can't Broadway just pull together some money and buy up some bandwidth?" Jersey Jeremy asked. It was a logical question.

"Even I'm not that rich," Lawrence said. That gave everyone pause. "But our little plan will certainly jump-start the conversation in the industry. That's for sure."

"See?" Scarlett said. While it had taken her a while to come to terms with the whole scheme, she was thoroughly convinced it needed to happen. "We're doing such a good deed."

"Something like that. Margolies can be the example that fixes things for the rest of the business. Won't he be thrilled." Lawrence grinned. "Now, back to the agenda."

"I was able to get a pair of opening-night tickets for our two secret agents on the inside," Scarlett said, leaning over to her purse and handing a ticket to each of the Jeremys.

"Wow, everyone wants tickets to the biggest opening night of the year. You don't mind if I sell these for cash, right?" Buff Jeremy joked. "How'd you score these?"

"You do not want to know," Scarlett said with a crafty smile. It hadn't been all that hard, actually. The intern was more than happy to help her, even though she hadn't told him why and had sworn him to secrecy. She'd only had to give him gift certificates for a year's worth of Dunkin Donuts in exchange.

"Do you have your tuxes ready?" Lawrence asked the Jeremys.

"Tuxes. Check!" they confirmed.

"Well, then, I say we reconvene on Thursday for a final rehearsal. Reilly, call us with any updates on Project *Banner* in the meantime."

Scarlett and Reilly helped Lawrence clean up, even though he had "people" who could do it. The whole week had been surreal, and Scarlett was ready for it to be over. On one hand, she felt guilty about what they were about to do to Margolies; but she knew she couldn't let him continue to keep Broadway in a strangle hold. She and the Jeremys, and all of the other up and comers in the city, had big dreams. If they wanted there to be any Broadway left in twenty years, something had to be done. And she knew that they might be the only people in a position to do it.

Scene 47

It was a double-header day of editor meetings for Reilly. While Scarlett and Lawrence were making final prep for Friday's big event, he'd been tying up his own loose ends. First, a meeting with his reluctant ex-editor and now a sit down with with Candace's boss, Tom.

After a brief phone call in which Reilly had indicated the general nature of his business, Tom had been more than happy to meet. *Happy* was probably not exactly the right word for it. He had been eager to hear what Reilly had to say. After all, Reilly was technically on staff at the *Banner* though, he hadn't—and wouldn't ever—officially start.

According to Tom, the fallout of the negative *Swan Song* review and Reilly's appointment as critic had caused a bigger firestorm from readers and execs at the *Banner* than Reilly had guessed. Tom was getting pressure from the very top to do something about it, before the theater section of the paper imploded all together.

They had met in an out-of-the-way hotel lobby, so as not to be seen. Reilly's third surreptitious hotel meeting in a month. Note to self, he thought: No more secret rendezvous in hotels…unless Scarlett is involved, he amended. Assuming she ever officially took him back. He'd settle for friendship, until she was ready.

His meeting with Tom had gone as well as could be expected. His disclosures about the Candace-Margolies-Kanter bribery scandal had been surprising and unwelcome news to the editor.

"I find this all very hard to believe," Tom said, unconsciously snapping his suspenders. "I've known Candace for a long time. She wouldn't do this."

"You don't know her ex-husband, then. If you knew him, you'd know what kind of power he has. She was simply no match for it."

"So you're saying she was forced into it?" Tom said. Reilly could see that he didn't want to believe that Candace was a bad person.

"I'm sorry to say that she was in on it, too. After all, she rigged the contest and got me the job."

That got a harrumph from Tom. "That's for sure," he said. "You have no idea how much everyone hates you."

"Gee, thanks."

"Just being honest," Tom said. "It's what I do. Or at least, what I thought I was doing."

"So am I," Reilly said. "And I'm really sorry to be telling you all this, but you needed to know."

"You said on the phone that you had proof."

"Just this." Reilly handed him another copy of his email to Candace with the real *Swan Song* review, including the send date and time. "But I think if you go back and look at the vote tallies, as well as Candace's phone records, you'll find more than enough proof."

Tom sighed and chewed his lip. "I appreciate you coming forward, Reilly. On behalf of the *Banner*, I'm sorry you got mixed up in this," he said gruffly.

"Well, as I told Candace in my interview, I'm interested in integrity in journalism. I just didn't expect the firmness of my beliefs to be tested like this."

"Harder than it sounds, apparently," Tom said, folding up the review and sliding into his pocket.

"Just out of curiosity, who's going to review *Olympus*?" Reilly asked.

"You just sprung this on me. I haven't had a chance to figure that out yet. I hate to think what Candace might have had in mind."

"We can only imagine," Reilly said. He had a feeling that Candace had given it a lot of thought. He had gotten the distinct impression after his last few conversations with her that her feelings for Margolies ran deeper than any of them had imagined.

"You know, that woman finalist did a really great job," Tom continued. "Might be interesting to have a female critic for a change."

As the editor got up to leave, Reilly stopped him. He'd had an idea on his way over.

"I know it's not my place, but can I offer a suggestion?"

"Offer away."

"What if you didn't assign anyone to review *Olympus*. What if, just once, you left this to the bloggers and chat rooms. Maybe just open a reader comments page online and let all those readers, who didn't feel heard after this critic contest debacle, offer their own reviews. Maybe leave it open through the weekend or even longer. Peer reviews at the *Banner*. Just an idea."

"I'll give it some thought," Tom said, mulling it over as the two of them headed out the lobby door. On the street, they turned to say their goodbyes.

"I'm sorry to have to tell you this the day after you were selected as the chief critic, but you're fired," he said with a kind smile.

"You can't fire me, I quit," Reilly said, returning his smile.

They shook hands before going their separate ways.

Scene 48

Scarlett finished up her makeup with one last glance in her bathroom mirror. All dressed up and no place to go, she thought. That wasn't entirely accurate, she knew. But her dress and makeup were probably unnecessary touches, considering she had no intention of leaving Lawrence's car that night. He'd be at her apartment any moment to pick her up for the opening night of *Olympus*—better known as *D-Day*—for their big plan.

She heard her cell phone ring in the other room and she rushed to grab it, assuming it was Lawrence letting her know he was waiting in the car. Despite everything, it still felt weird to think that *Olympus* was happening without her.

"Hello?" she said.

"*What's the story, morning glory?*" sang her brother Colin cheerfully.

She felt surprised but thrilled to hear her brother's welcome voice. "*What's the word, hummingbird?*" she sang back. It was a game they used to play for hours on family road trips. The goal was to have as long a conversation as possible using only lines from show tunes. Before he could return the parlay, she continued. "I'm actually on my way out the door. Can I call you tomorrow?"

"You can call me any time you want, *dahling*," he said grandly. "I just wanted to make sure you hadn't slit your wrists. Isn't that monstrosity of a show by He-Who-Must-Not-Be-Named opening tonight?"

"You can say his name," Scarlett said. "I'm not that fragile, and you know it."

"You're right," Colin said. "I'm the delicate flower of the family."

"I'm a little surprised you even remembered it was opening night for *Olympus*."

"I didn't, *dahling*, but it's on national news."

Colin had never cared about things like current events or politics. But if Scarlett ever needed the latest makeup trend, he was her man, so to speak.

"Since when do you watch the news?"

"Since this sad excuse of a drag bar won't turn off the TV while we're trying to rehearse for tonight's show," he said, raising his voice, making it clear he wasn't complaining for her benefit alone.

She could hear someone telling him off with a string of good natured profanity.

"My talent is woefully unrecognized out here," continued Colin with a wistful sigh. "I might just show up on your doorstep one of these days."

"I wish you would," Scarlett said, sincerely. It would be nice to have her brother nearby… and Colin would get a kick out of New York, she thought. "But right now, I really need to head out."

"*What good is sitting alone in your room*—" Colin began to sing.

"I'm hanging up now, Sally Bowles," cut in Scarlett.

"Just give me some dirt about *Olympus* that I can use in the dressing room later," Colin said, unfazed by her urgency to get him off the phone. "Your ex-boss couldn't possibly pull this off without you."

"You have no idea," Scarlett said cryptically. Her other line beeped. "Just... watch the news tomorrow, okay?"

"Two days in a row?" he whined. "Surely you jest."

"Trust me. Just do it," she said. "*Good night, my someone.*"

"*Goodnight, my love,*" he responded, per their show tune tradition.

Scarlett clicked over to Lawrence on the other line.

"Your chariot awaits!" Lawrence announced.

"I'll be right down," Scarlett said. She picked up her purse and her wrap.

As she reached her apartment door, she paused. Maybe her brother's overdramatic sensibilities had rubbed off, but she was suddenly keenly aware of the gravity of what she was about to do. Up to that point in her career, she'd kept her head down and toed the line. She'd always worked hard toward her dreams and waited for a break. That night, however, was a uniquely pivotal moment.

She supposed it was somehow appropriate that, in the spirit of *Olympus* itself, she was tempting the fates. Next time she walked through the door, she'd be a different person, for better or for worse. Scarlett took a deep breath and strode out of her apartment with renewed determination.

Scene 49

Margolies stepped into his current *Actress's* dressing room backstage at *Olympus,* to check his tux and comb his hair. He could barely see himself amid all the opening-night notes and cards from her friends and fellow cast members, which were crammed around the edge of the mirror.

"You look hot," she said, admiring him in the mirror. She was putting pin curls in her blonde hair and wearing only a lacy white bra and stockings.

And *you* look fifteen years old, he thought, not unfavorably. She was all the more appealing, after he had forced himself to make nice to Candace earlier in the week. It was just part of his job, but a particularly unpleasant part, as of late. That was over, since the contest was done. He was pleased that he hadn't lost his touch, even on such an easy target as Candace.

"Break a leg tonight," he said, kissing the top of her head as his hands brushed across her breasts.

"See you after?" she asked into the mirror as Margolies headed back into the hall.

"Yes. And bring a girl friend," he replied. It would be a night to celebrate.

Olympus had been running without a single technical glitch for a week. There had been more than a few personality glitches, thanks to his temperamental stars, but nothing he hadn't been able to iron out. Just to make sure, he decided to make a quick visit to their very separate dressing rooms.

He knocked and then popped his head in Cupid's dressing room.

"Come to wish me luck, love?" Cupid said, reclining on a ridiculous chaise lounge that he'd brought in. Two makeup artists applied special cover up to his arms, legs, and neck, to hide his extensive tattoos. That had been an expense that irked Margolies. But it had to be done. For all Margolies knew, Zeus may very well have had mermaids like Cupid's peeking out from under his toga—but not in this production.

"How are you feeling tonight?" he asked. Talking to Cupid always gave him an instant headache.

"I feel like a million bucks," he said, reaching around and squeezing the ass of the cuter of the two makeup artists. She glared at him.

A million bucks in sexual-harassment claims that I'll have to deal with, he thought. But Margolies was confident that the show would make them all millions, at which point they could all sue away. It wouldn't be the first time.

"Break a leg," he said, escaping out the door. One down, one to go.

He knocked on Psyche's door. No answer. When he tried to go in, he found it locked.

"Psyche?" he called through the door, feeling like an idiot having to do this in his own theater. "It's Margolies."

He heard the lock turn, and a mousy, wide-eyed costume assistant poked her head out.

"Sorry, sir. She's...uh...busy."

He could hear rustling and grunting through the open door. It didn't take a genius to know what was going on. He was partly repulsed and partly tempted to go back to his new blonde starlet's dressing room. Hadn't he upgraded her to a much-coveted private dressing room entirely for that same purpose?

"Never mind," he said to the red-faced costume girl. "Just tell her to break a leg."

As he turned away, he marveled at the range of people who found their way into the business. In one dressing room, a makeup artists was offended at a pinch from a lecher, and in another, a costumer sat idly by while her subject went at it with the understudy. Fortunately, he was too old to be surprised by any of it.

Here, tonight, in that theater, Margolies felt perfectly in control
—the real god of *Olympus*! He knew every second of the show, every
detail of every effect, the strengths and flaws of every member of the
cast.

He had already sent Candace his version of the *Olympus*
review, since he hadn't had time to deal with Reilly, yet. He couldn't
take any chances. His intern had gotten all the VIP tickets assigned
with only minor complaints from a few folks. The big bosses from
M_____ Corp would finally see the immense and thrilling spectacle
that their not-insignificant funds had paid for. On top of that, he was
opening in perfect time to be fresh on people's minds, heading into
awards season. The Tony Award would be his for the taking.

He loved opening nights when he had a hit. He wondered how
it must feel for other producers who didn't know in advance how their
shows would fare. How sad that must be, to have to wait and wonder
about their opening-night fate. He, on the other hand, would be off
with his little starlet, and hopefully one of her hot friends, while the
world learned of his triumph.

He checked his watch. Red carpet time. He never brought a
date to his shows, and not just because so often whoever she was was
in the cast. He didn't want anyone to infringe on his glory. He did it by
himself and deserved all the credit.

As he came out of the stage door, the paparazzi were already
lining the red carpet, which was surrounded by a network of velvet
ropes, flash bulbs popping as the first celebrities arrived. He enjoyed
hobnobbing with the celebrities, especially the women, but he never let
them forget that they were on his turf. He was the real star tonight.

Scene 50

Scarlett could only barely see the Jeremys' heads amid the star-studded crowd slowly entering the theater. The bright lights and flash bulbs were lighting up the block under the Olympic-sized *Olympus* marquee. Between the actual attendees and the hordes of onlookers, 44th Street was unofficially closed down.

"Testing, one two three," Jersey Jeremy said. "People are going to think I'm a secret service agent."

"Stop fiddling with your earpiece. People will see it if you keep putting your hand to your ear!" Scarlett chided. They had tested it a million times the night before. The pin-hole video cameras they were both wearing were also in working order.

She saw Buff Jeremy flinch as Lawrence adjusted the volume from the speakers that he'd rigged in the back seat of his Escalade. He'd been tricking out his car all week with listening devices, video feed, and computer systems. It looked like something out of Star Wars. His driver was only too thrilled to be given an unexpected night off.

"Too loud?" Lawrence asked.

"Better," Buff Jeremy said. From behind the tinted windows of the Escalade, amid the town cars and limousines lining the streets and depositing guests, Scarlett, Lawrence, and Reilly were perfectly hidden, right under Margolies' nose. The Jeremys had been elected to be the "men on the ground" inside the theater, since they were the only ones whom Margolies wouldn't recognize on sight.

Scarlett watched as the Jeremys disappeared into the theater right behind Sarah Jessica Parker and Matthew Broderick. From the way Jersey Jeremy was angling his body, she could tell he was trying to pick them up with his hidden camera.

"Thanks, guys, we can see them." Scarlett laughed. She didn't have the heart to tell them that she'd met SJP and Matthew on many occasions, since they had both done Margolies shows and were regulars at his opening nights. As were the line of other A-listers filing in past the gawkers and the press—Cameron Diaz, Robin Williams, Susan Sarandon, Whoopi Goldberg, Brad Pitt…the list went on.

For that particular opening, it appeared as though the celebrities outnumbered the normal audience members—if you could call the mega-wealthy investors "normal."

"Any sign of the M_____ Corp contingent?" Lawrence asked, still fiddling with one of the computers. "I'd hate for them to miss the action."

"Hey, Jeremys, any sign of shady-looking goons in designer tuxes?" Scarlett said.

"Hang on, I'll do a spin," Jersey Jeremy said.

"Wait a sec," Lawrence said, as he keyed in a few more codes on his laptop. The second laptop's screen flashed on, and the camera feed was live. "The video's up and running."

"Thank god it wasn't live five minutes ago. I forgot about the camera on my trip to the men's room," Buff Jeremy said, laughing.

With the video feed live, they could see what was happening in the theater, though at that point, the Jeremys were facing each other to appear as if they were talking to each other and not talking through surreptitious ear buds.

Jersey Jeremy started a slow, inconspicuous circle so that Lawrence, Scarlett, and Reilly could get a good look at the room. Scarlett recognized nearly everyone in the shot: investors, celebrities, and other VIPs. The room was awash in tuxes and twinkling gowns.

"Everything okay?" Reilly said, noticing the look on Scarlett's face.

"I'm fine. It's just a little weird to be watching all this from the outside," Scarlett said. She'd felt a momentary pang of sadness. She'd played a big part in making the show happen and wasn't even welcome at the opening.

"You'll have plenty of opening nights in your future," Lawrence said, reassuringly.

"I know, I know," Scarlett said, looking down at her red cocktail dress, the same one she'd worn at *Swan Song*. Lawrence had shrewdly suggested that they all dress up, in case anyone gave them trouble about parking the SUV so close to the theater. If they were in formal wear, it would be easier to claim they were guests and belonged there.

"Do you wish you were in there, Lawrence?" she asked.

"And give up all this?" Lawrence said, indicating his makeshift techie wonderland. "Not on your life."

Lawrence looked like he was born in a tux, Scarlett thought, and Reilly, since he'd gotten some sleep and was clean shaven, looked like something out of *GQ*. Too bad no one would see the attractive trio on that particular red carpet.

"The eagle has landed," Reilly said.

Scarlett and Lawrence peered out the window. Sure enough, Margolies was making his way up the red carpet, kissing cheeks and shaking hands as the paparazzi took it all in, one click at a time. He was the epitome of a Broadway mogul.

Pride cometh before a fall, thought Scarlett. She had been momentarily worried that she wouldn't be able to go through with their plans that night. But seeing him, there, a puffed-up peacock reveling in glory that was built on the broken backs of everyone involved, she had no qualms.

"Look behind him," Reilly said. Sure enough, the goon squad was hot on his heels.

"I bet he loves that," Scarlett said sarcastically, knowing how much Margolies must hate having a trail of middle aged, corporate suits, tailing him. She noticed Margolies ushering them in front of him and into the theater so that they wouldn't infringe on his red-carpet photo ops.

"What's going on in there, guys?" Lawrence said into the Jeremys' earpieces.

Scarlett looked at the video feed, currently focused on some guy's ass.

"Sorry, just getting some footage for later," Jersey Jeremy said as he adjusted position. The tight butt in question turned out to belong to Ashton Kutcher.

"Avert your eyes," Reilly said, jokingly putting his hands over the screen. "No girlfriend of mine should have to see that."

Scarlett knew he had meant to be funny, but the word *girlfriend* just hung in the air between them. She was still unwilling to discuss their relationship. The recent weeks had been exceedingly hard on their fledgling romance.

Lawrence came to the rescue, as usual. "I hate to be a killjoy," he said, talking to the Jeremys but eyeing the pair next to him in the car, "but it would be great if you could go to your seats, so we can make sure we have the camera angles right."

"If we must. I suppose our public can wait," Jersey Jeremy said grandly.

"Hey, look, there's Candace," Reilly said.

"Ooh, I need to see this Cruella D'editor! Tell me which one she is," Buff Jeremy said.

"She hasn't gone in yet, but you can't miss her," Reilly said. "Fifty going on eighty, blonde, tacky red dress, drunk as a skunk."

"Shouldn't she be in jail or something?" Scarlett asked.

"I'm sure they're still digging up proof before they nail her for fraud. I wouldn't be surprised if it takes a while," Lawrence said.

Candace had made it halfway up the block and then sagged against a wall. She looked really out of it.

"And to think, she was supposed to be my date for the evening," Reilly said.

"She clearly needs someone to prop her up. Where's her charming ex-husband?" Scarlett said, ungenerously.

"I wonder if she still has the extra ticket that I would have used," Reilly mused as if to himself.

"I don't like the sound of that," Scarlett said with a warning look in his direction.

"This is just too good to miss," Reilly said with an impish grin.

He leapt out of the car before Scarlett or Lawrence could stop him.

He wove his way through the cars inching up the street dropping off bejeweled guests, and he put his arm out to Candace. Her white knight to the rescue.

She looked confused initially, but after some sort of brief conversation she fished what appeared to be two tickets out of her tiny handbag, spilling various contents in the process, and allowed Reilly to escort her in. He tastefully steered her around the paparazzi and flashed a subtle thumbs up, along with a roll of his eyes, toward the Escalade, before disappearing into the theater.

"That kid's got balls," Lawrence said.

"Once a gossip columnist, always a gossip columnist," said Scarlett, more than a little annoyed that he'd ditched them just like that. True, he wasn't officially part of their plan, since he'd come into the process so late. But she'd wanted his moral support, at least. "But we aren't clear what Margolies does or doesn't know about Reilly's *Swan Song* review and his job at the *Banner*. We don't know what Candace has been telling him. What if Margolies confronts Reilly?"

"Well, luckily for Reilly, Margolies would never cause a scene tonight. You know as well as I do that there's too much at stake for him to risk overshadowing his masterpiece with a seedy showdown with Reilly in the lobby."

"You're right. Guess that just leaves you and me to hold down the fort out here."

"You won't hear me complaining. I haven't had you all to myself in a while," Lawrence said, taking a break from his electronics to give Scarlett a reassuring smile.

"Sorry I haven't been very fun recently. I really appreciate what you've done for me. All this..." She gestured to the high tech set up.

"Are you kidding? This is the most fun I've had in months!"

"Sorry to interrupt this charming tête-à-tête," Jersey Jeremy said, interrupting their moment, "but these are crappy seats."

"If you keep whining, I'm going to delete the Ashton footage right now," Scarlett retorted.

"Actually," Lawrence said, "you guys are perfect where you are." He winked at Scarlett. "Just do me a favor and sit up straight. Remember not to cross your arms or make any sudden moves." He pointed to the screen and said to Scarlett, "Look, they'll have a perfect vantage point."

From the Jeremys' seats in the balcony, the video feed gave Scarlett and Lawrence an unobstructed view of the stage over the gilt railing of the first balcony. The theater was majestic all by itself, and Margolies had pulled out all the stops. All they could see on stage at the moment was a large scrim with a projection of Mount Olympus and occasional flashes of lightning in the background. A hazer was already going at full steam, adding to the atmosphere and emphasizing each beam of light dramatically. Scarlett had to admit it was a cool effect, even from where they were.

They could hear the orchestra tuning up over the murmur of conversation picked up in the Jeremys' earpieces.

Scarlett glanced at the countdown computer. Lawrence hadn't been kidding about how many laptops he had. Eight of them had been called into action that night. One was counting down until 8:00 p.m. even though they both knew that opening nights never started on time. That was why they needed the Jeremys on the inside.

In order to precisely time their "attack," they needed to be able to see what was happening in live time. Scarlett thought it was ironic that despite all the technology, their plan was so incredibly simple.

"Let's get this show on the road!" Buff Jeremy said.

"It's 8:00 p.m. The show should be starting sometime in the next ten minutes," Lawrence laughed, sitting back to wait.

The sidewalk was starting to clear out. The paparazzi were packing up, preparing to wait in the lobby until they were allowed in to the theater for curtain-call photos—though Scarlett had a feeling that opening night, they'd get in before that.

The gawking tourists were shuffling away or heading into the Sardi's and Angus bars across the street to wait for people-watching opportunities during intermission. A few brave onlookers tried to sneak past the velvet ropes and take photos of themselves on the now-vacant red carpet. The theater security guards shooed them away.

Scarlett and Lawrence turned their attention back to the video monitor as the lights went down in the theater. The cameras took a second to re-focus then showed a crystal-clear picture of the scrim going up as the audience hushed and the opening number began.

"We're waiting for our cue," Lawrence said into the microphone. "Enjoy the show."

Scarlett felt nervous all of sudden. She shifted in her seat, suddenly uncomfortable in her stiff satin dress. "I can't watch," she said, turning to gaze out the window.

"Opening-night jitters?" Lawrence asked, patting her hand.

She gripped his hand back. "I don't know if I can do this."

"Of course you can."

"But why does it have to be me?"

"Because I need to monitor all this and make sure we're using the right frequencies. The Jeremys are in the theater, and Reilly is...wherever he is. And, anyway, it's only right that it's you. Artistic justice."

"But the cast and crew..." she trailed off.

"Will be just fine," he reminded her. She sighed. He placed an iPad in her hand. "Your weapon, m'lady!"

"Death by technology," she said, unable to muster a smile.

"Death by boredom," Jersey Jeremy whispered into his microphone. Scarlett had forgotten that they were being overheard.

"No one's dying of anything! *Shhh.* I'm trying to watch the show!" Buff Jeremy said.

Chastened, they all went silent and watched as Act One of *Olympus* proceeded. Margolies would be pleased, thought Scarlett. The show was beautiful. True, during the contrived scenes between the special effects, it dragged a bit. But a general audience wouldn't care; they came to see the spectacle that wouldn't disappoint. Well, maybe tonight it would.

Just as the first technical sequence went into effect, the video feed went blank. Lawrence jumped to attention, fiddling with buttons and dials.

Scarlett whispered into the mic, "Guys, are you there?"

Radio silence.

She looked at Lawrence in a panic. "What happened?"

"Best guess?" he said, not looking up from his frantic clicking and typing. "The wireless equipment on the stage bumped us out of available bandwidth. Pretty ironic, considering. I'm trying to find an open frequency for ours."

Scarlett kept her mouth shut and let Lawrence focus. The Jeremys probably wouldn't even realize they weren't broadcasting.

She checked the time, recalculating, prepared to guess at the right moment to put their plan in action in case the feed didn't come back up. Not ideal, but she was thinking on her feet.

"I've restarted the system, but it might be a good idea to talk about Plan B."

"Well, last I knew, Act One was a little over an hour. While they've probably made some changes, we could take a guess at when the finale will be in full swing."

"Too risky. If we miss our window, it all goes to hell. We *need* to know what's happening inside."

"What are we going to do about getting the video?" Scarlett asked, suddenly remembering the footage they were after.

"The cameras are still recording, so we should be fine on that front. It's just that they just lost their wireless transmission."

The computers started up again, and Lawrence frantically tried to get the feed going. "I think you may need to go into the theater."

"Uh uh," she said, shaking her head violently. "No way."

"We may not have any other choice."

"Why can't you do it?" she said.

"Because I need to get this up and running. And, anyway, theater security knows you and won't question it if you go in. Especially looking like that." He raked his eyes over her tight dress.

"Don't you think Margolies told them I was fired?"

"Not likely. Why would he think you'd try to crash his party?"

Lawrence has a point, thought Scarlett. Margolies was way too vain to think of Scarlett as a threat, once he'd cut her off from the office.

"Okay, but only as a last resort."

"Well, the clock is ticking, and I'm not getting a signal. He's eating up some crazy bandwidth in there. I have a whole new respect for the sound and tech guys on the show," Lawrence said, in awe. "Well, at least they won't have to worry about someone's cell phone ringing during the show."

"Really, they're using up that much signal?"

"Not quite, but pretty darn close. Which, let me remind you, is the good news for us—present crisis notwithstanding. Are you ready for your close up?"

"Please, please, please don't make me do this." Scarlett begged. "What if Margolies sees me? What if someone recognizes me?"

"Margolies won't see you. You know he always stays rooted in his box. He'll be easy to avoid. And if anyone else sees you, so what? You look great."

"So what's the plan? I just stick all this equipment down the front of my dress and wander inside?" Scarlett said, gesturing to the laptops.

"The equipment can stay here. Once I reset the frequency, all you'll need is this." Lawrence was in the process of wrapping the iPad in her shawl, trying to make it look like a bag of some sort.

"That's hideous."

"You have a better idea?"

She looked down at her tight little red number.

"Well..." She grabbed the iPad and slid it up the bottom of her short dress securing it against her stomach.

"That was so hot!" Lawrence said.

"Oh, please!" She turned awkwardly in her seat, giving him different angles to make sure the flat device wasn't detectable. "Can you tell?"

"I'm not sure. Can you wiggle a little more?"

"You're terrible," she said, blushing. "Please tell me I don't have to do this."

"This isn't just about us, Scarlett. You know that. And you are going to pull this off," he said, serious all of sudden. "I'll be right here when you get back."

She took a deep breath, feeling the cold iPad against her stomach as he handed her wrap to her.

"Here goes nothing," she said as she opened the door and swung her feet out onto the sidewalk, flashing the security guards with her sexiest smile.

Scene 51

Getting past security had been a breeze. But now, standing in the shadows at the back of the theater, she felt her heart pounding wildly.

Psyche was midway through her Act One ballad. It was one of the more emotional moments in the show that Scarlett had always thought would have been more effective with just Psyche, on stage alone, and some top-notch lighting. Instead, the pensive melody was lost within an overly intricate number involving a bevy of maidens singing backup around Psyche's feet, attempting choreography in what was basically an insanely expensive on-stage wading pool.

Despite her feelings about the show, Scarlett couldn't help but get a thrill standing at the back of the audience and gazing over their heads at the shimmering stage. Even given the unthinkable circumstances, she still felt her best inside a Broadway theater.

The iPad had started sliding down her stomach. Her nervous sweat dislodged it—a thought that grossed her out. She looked around. The only other people at the back were the ushers, whose attention was turned to the sexy Aphrodite scene now occurring on stage. She sidled behind the narrow lobby bar and ungracefully birthed the iPad from under her dress.

Scarlett scanned the audience. She couldn't see Margolies' box from her vantage point. She crossed her fingers that he was still in his usual seat and not lurking in the dark somewhere where he could spot her. No sign of Reilly. But from the back of the theater, it was hard to pick out any individual from the sea of men in more or less matching tuxes. Candace should be easier to spot, but for all Scarlett knew, she was slumped over in her seat somewhere.

By Scarlett's calculations, she had about ten minutes to go before the first-act finale. Her cue. If she timed it right, their revenge would be truly spectacular.

While the back wall provided the most concealed spot, she wasn't able to see the flying space, since the balcony overhang obstructed her view. Their best laid plans, wiring up the Jeremys, had all been for naught. She'd have to do it the old-fashioned way—with her own two eyes.

During the next applause break, she reluctantly snuck up the grand stairs to see if she could get a better viewpoint from the first balcony. As she cautiously turned the corner into the upper lobby, she caught sight of two of Margolies' goons chatting in the lobby. Not theater fans, apparently. She snuck back into the stairwell.

She made her way back down the grand stairway, the plush carpet softening her footsteps. She was running out of time. She inched around to the right side of the audience, doing her best to avoid the notice of the ushers, who would probably wonder where she belonged. She didn't see a single empty seat in the house. Every single coveted seat in the theater was taken. The night was, for a number of reasons, the theatrical event of the season.

Cupid's finale was just beginning. Scarlett's hands were sweaty as she held the iPad in a vice grip. She slid the "unlock" button, just as they'd practiced the night before, and held the dimmed screen against her body to shield the light. She wished with all her might that she was back in the Escalade as they had originally intended, playing her role at a safer distance.

She slid her back along the side wall of the theater, just far enough to see out above the balcony if she craned her neck but still mostly in the shadows. She had covered as much of her red dress with her dark shawl as possible.

Cupid was taking extra time with his song tonight. Milking the crowd. Scarlett knew how maddening it must be for the conductor, but it didn't surprise her in the least. The audience was eating out of Cupid's hands. He hadn't achieved rock-star status for nothing, after all.

He looked better than usual. His Zeus costume, a flowing white toga, hid the flying harness well. Without his usual visible tattoos, he looked like he could almost pull off a convincing "Greek god" look, thought Scarlett, grudgingly.

Just then, to spectacular effect, the pyrotechnic cues started. Scarlett had the sequence memorized, and it didn't appear to have changed in the time since she'd been fired. Cued to a series of Cupid's high notes and grand gestures, fiery lightning bolts streaked across the stage.

Next up would be rain, as the chorus of gods behind Cupid built the intensity of the number. There it was—sparkling sheets of water, cascading onto the stage, right on cue. Scarlett could see jaws dropping throughout the audience.

In a moment, the high-speed flying sequence that had necessitated so many hours of rehearsal and negotiations with the safety board would launch Cupid over the audience in a dramatic crescendo that was guaranteed to send everyone out into the intermission buzzing.

Scarlett glanced up to make sure she could see what she was doing.

Margolies spotted her from his box seat on house left.

Their eyes locked. Scarlett froze where she stood, her fight-or-flight instinct kicking in. And yet the hatred in his eyes gave her the last bit of resolve she needed to do what she had come to do.

Their death stare was broken as Cupid whizzed through the air in a flash of toga and vocal key changes. He was in great voice that night. The chorus of gods was chanting at full volume from the stage, and the audience was already whooping and cheering.

Scarlett slid a few inches to the left, so as to be just out of Margolies' hawk-like view. She gently tilted the iPad screen enough to see the button that Lawrence had programmed. She allowed herself one more peek at Margolies, who was momentarily distracted by the perfectly executed flight sequence that was reaching its climax. On stage the other gods were also rising in the air on nearly invisible wires of their own.

She closed her eyes and pressed the button on the iPad.

Nothing happened. Maybe Lawrence wasn't able to get the system back up in the Escalade, she thought, beginning to panic. A million more thoughts passed through her mind in a split second. Maybe this whole plan has been too far-fetched, after all.

The fact that one patron could stop an entire show was certainly hard to believe.

But sure enough, she did.

The first thing the audience noticed was a change in the sound. The orchestra was illogically quieter and louder all at the same time, as the actor's wireless body mics went abruptly silent. The unenhanced voices of even the strongest singers were completely drowned out as the orchestra played on, not yet realizing what was happening.

In the next second, the audience looked up to where Cupid swung from his harness, stranded helplessly above the heads of the patrons in the orchestra section. The wireless remote signal that operated his flying wires had been effectively blocked.

It was all happening exactly as Scarlett and Lawrence had intended.

It all happened in a matter of seconds.

The orchestra petered out as the conductor realized he was no longer getting a microphone feed. Cupid began flailing and cursing as he realized he was stuck. Hushed murmurs passed through the crowd as they wondered if it was all part of the show.

A series of clicks and flashes broke the silence, coming from the cameras and phones of the audience members directly below Cupid. Those were followed by a few giggles from the audience, which quickly escalated into a roar. Cupid's swinging had stopped, and everyone watched as his face went through shades of red to purple in extreme mortification.

Scarlett watched as Cupid desperately tried to adjust his toga. It immediately became all too clear that Cupid, dangling limply from the ceiling, was giving the celebrity audience a prime view of his decision not to wear underwear under his toga for opening night. From her vantage point on the side, Scarlett couldn't entirely see what those directly below him were seeing. Thank god! she thought to herself. The shocking news passed up and down the aisles like wild fire.

Scarlett couldn't quite stifle a small laugh herself, though her glee was quickly tempered by a quick glance up at Margolies. He was leaning over the rail of his box, shouting orders to Cupid, the conductor, the stage manager—but his imperious commands were hopelessly drowned out by the audience members, who were in complete hysterics.

Scarlett inched her way back to the door as the stage manager come out on to the stage, ripping his now-useless headphones off his ears. No longer able to communicate with the rest of the crew through their wireless headsets, he had to resort to waving and screaming to the various technicians to figure out how to bring Cupid down to the stage and lower the rest of the cast. Of course, Scarlett knew all too well that the revolutionary wireless flying remote wouldn't work, either. Until the wireless system was back up and running, Cupid and the rest of the cast would be stuck.

Less than a minute had passed.

She was nearly to the door, desperate to make a fast escape. She heard the microphones come back on suddenly–exactly according to plan. They had needed less than a minute of wireless interference to make their point. It was a horrifying thought for Broadway theaters everywhere, but a brilliant revenge strategy, thanks to Lawrence.

The first thing to be heard was Cupid swearing up a storm, followed by the unmistakable "*I quit*! I'm never setting foot on a Broadway stage again."

Ironic choice of words, thought Scarlett as she pushed through the doors into the lobby, where the waiting paparazzi were just starting to catch wind of the drama inside.

Through the now-open door, they could hear the stage manager speaking into a backstage mic, asking everyone to remain calm as they rebooted the system.

"You might want to see this," Scarlett told the waiting press reps and photographers. She held the door open as they flooded in, cameras flashing and video cameras going. Scarlett was careful to stay out of their camera angle as she fled across the street.

Lawrence opened the car door and she slid into the back seat of the Escalade.

Lawrence greeted her with raised eyebrows. "Well?"

"Mission accomplished," she said, sinking down into her seat with a satisfied but exhausted sigh.

Scene 52

It was 3:00 a.m., and Scarlett, Reilly, Lawrence, and the Jeremys were still celebrating their triumph. They'd decamped to Lawrence's penthouse, where his extensive collection of multi-media devices were broadcasting the repercussions of their earlier evening exploits. They couldn't get enough, endlessly replaying the events.

"I can't believe Margolies saw you! Do you think he'll hunt you down?"

"He has nothing to hunt her down *for*!" Lawrence said. "The white space interruption is untraceable. It was just a blip for a few seconds. Oops!" he said with a shrug and wide grin. "All Margolies knows is that she was there."

"Too bad we can't take credit for our videos," Jersey Jeremy said. "That's Oscar material, if ever I saw it."

The Jeremys had gotten prime video of the whole thing as it played out. Considering the slight change in plan, things had gone extraordinarily well. They'd collected Reilly and the Jeremys into the waiting Escalade, after more chaos than even they could have predicted. Margolies had finally called off the performance after an hour of mayhem—all caught on video—and sent the star-studded crowd home.

They'd anonymously uploaded key portions of the video to YouTube, and the whole world was getting to experience the monumental disaster that had been *Olympus*. In fact, it was headlining news cycles worldwide, just as they'd hoped.

"What do you think will happen to Margolies?" Buff Jeremy asked.

"Well, there's no way the show will go on," Scarlett said. "If OSHA doesn't shut him down for safety violations, the unions will."

"And Cupid's flown away on his little wings," Reilly said, smugly.

"*Little* being the operative term," Jersey Jeremy said, referring to the hundreds of pictures of the exposed anatomy of Cupid that had appeared on Facebook and Twitter almost instantly, once the wireless connection came back to the theater and the audience could use their phones.

An hour earlier, the news had covered Cupid, *sans* Psyche, boarding his jet to the UK. "No one can do this to me! Are you watching, Margolies?" Cupid spat into the camera. He was still in his toga. "My lawyers will have something to say to you. You are over. *Over!*"

"I think Cupid might be over, too. Not exactly the sexy rock-star image that he's been so carefully cultivating," Reilly said.

"Good riddance," Scarlett said, with a knowing glance in Lawrence's direction.

"I wouldn't be so sure. I can think of a few reality TV shows with his name all over them," Jersey Jeremy said. They all groaned, knowing he was right.

"So, it looks like a theater will be available in the near future. *Swan Song,* anyone?" Lawrence asked.

"You make a good point," Scarlett said. "But, if it's up to me, let's find another theater. The Jackman has too much bad karma right now."

"Here, here!" Jersey Jeremy said. "I want Broadway more than anyone, but that has a seriously bad vibe, now that Margolies has slimed all over it."

They fell silent as their headlines were picked up by the BBC morning news: "...a fluke signal interruption cut the wireless signal for just a few seconds at Broadway's Jackman theater last night, causing catastrophic damage to the production and shuttering what sources are saying is the largest Broadway show ever attempted. Cupid, from the international sensation rock band Cupid and Psyche, will be in the studios later today with an exclusive interview, detailing the abuses he suffered under famed Broadway mogul, Margolies. Margolies was not available for comment. Also in the next hour, telecommunication and wireless experts will discuss America's plans to address the pressing bandwidth and white space issues which threaten the uninterrupted wireless access not just of live theater but professional sports and religious organizations..."

Their Broadway debut, so to speak, was officially a success.

Scene 53

Candace poked her head into her editor's office. It was Monday morning and she'd spent the weekend in bed. Despite the fever pitch of activity going on at the *Banner*, her editor had asked her not to come in over the weekend. But he requested her presence in his office first thing Monday morning.

"You wanted to see me?"

"Yes, Candace, take a seat." He indicated the chair across from his desk. "Close the door behind you." She didn't have a good feeling about that. The critic contest had been a disaster, and her editor had clearly taken the reins of her Arts and Culture section, at least for the weekend.

"Paper sales are through the roof, right?" she said, trying to start the conversation on a positive note. "I thought the editorial on the FCC and wireless issues was brilliant. That should be good for Broadway, and good for us. Puts it in the spotlight, so to speak…" She was babbling, trying to put off the inevitable she feared was coming.

He sat very still in his chair, a grim set to his mouth. "Candace —"

"Wow, I read the *Olympus* review. Or I guess I should say *reviews*. Was that your idea to open it up to reader reviews, rather than a traditional critic review?" Truthfully, she hated the idea.

"We're trying something new for a while. So far, it looks like it's going to be a success. Our critic gave just one person's opinion, and readers weren't always responding. Plus, critics are fallible, it turns out, and subject to political biases." He gave her a pointed look. "This way, with peer reviews, people can get a more realistic picture."

"You mean…" It didn't compute. "You're eliminating critics all together?"

"I like to think of it as expanding, actually. Based on the response for *Olympus*, it's going to be a huge hit. It will just be something we're going to try occasionally, but I think peer reviews are the wave of the future."

"But what about my job?" Candace asked, in disbelief that the *Banner* of all places would be a trailblazer for reader-generated content.

"Ah, yes. Your job," he said. He rested his arms on his desk and leaned forward. "I don't think you've been entirely honest with me, Candace."

"I don't know what you mean," she said, though she could feel her face redden. Where was a drink when she needed one?

"I think you do. We searched your computer and recounted the public votes for the critic contest over the weekend. I must say I was very disappointed with what we found. You rigged the contest, rewrote a review, bribed a critic… and that's just what we've found over the weekend."

She stared at him stonily. She didn't plan to admit a thing.

"Do you have anything to say for yourself?" he prompted.

"I want a lawyer," she said.

"I'm not the police," he said. "And though it may surprise you, I'm not going to turn you in."

"You're not?" Her mind was spinning.

"Lucky for you, the *Banner* can't afford this kind of scandal right now. However, your desk has been cleared out and your passwords have been changed." He paused for her reaction, but hearing nothing, he continued. "Needless to say, you are fired as of this second, and if we hear so much as a peep out of you ever again, we will bring the full weight of the paper and the law down on your head. As far as the public knows, your position is simply being eliminated." He spoke quietly but firmly. "Am I making myself clear?"

"I understand," she said, feeling dizzy.

He buzzed his secretary on the intercom. "Please send in security."

A burly security guard materialized in the doorway seconds later. She'd seen him waiting out there on her way in.

"Good bye, Candace," her editor said, as the guard took her arm roughly and firmly led her toward the elevators.

She didn't bother fighting. She knew she'd lost. The one small blessing was that at least her humiliation was relatively private. She couldn't help but smile, even at that moment, at Margolies' ultimate mortification. His disgrace and downfall was as publicized as his success had been.

She thought of the bottle of bourbon waiting on her kitchen counter. I am lucky, she thought, pleased with herself. My secrets are safe. This will all blow over.

Scene 54

Scarlett leaned back in her new desk chair and surveyed the scene at her new office. A bright, airy, two-office suite just off Times Square with windows overlooking street and sky, it was a vast improvement from her last digs. She couldn't be more thrilled.

Setting up the office, she'd wondered more than a few times where Margolies was keeping himself. After the *Olympus* debacle, she had bravely gone to his office, only to find it crawling with IRS agents, tearing through files and trying to track down Margolies. In better circumstances and with lots of cash, a big show could try to weather a disastrous opening night. But with the theater shut down due to safety violations, the loss of the star actor, and an avalanche of law suits from everyone from the theater owner to the showbiz unions, Margolies had apparently cut his losses and skipped town.

Once the dust had settled, Lawrence and Scarlett had decided to start their own production company, Scarlett Productions, Inc. It was a big, terrifying step, but Scarlett knew it was now or never if she wanted to make a go at being a Broadway producer in her own right. Luckily, she had lots of support.

"Got any more calls for me, boss?" Lawrence shouted from the desk he had parked himself at in the front room. He'd been more than generous with his time, as well as substantial start-up funds, getting Scarlett Productions, Inc. up and running. He wasn't willing to give up his jet-setting life for a day job, and would be around when she needed him, she knew.

She and Lawrence had pieced together a list of as many of Margolies' regular investors as they could track down to let them know that, though Margolies was gone, they were invited to join *Swan Song* or other future musical-theater projects of Scarlett Productions, Inc.

Fortunately, most of Margolies' investors knew both of them well and were only too happy to take their calls that week. While a few funders had run for the hills, in light of the massive *Olympus* losses and the IRS sniffing around, most were eager to back a winner and start making some of their money back.

"I just finished with my last call. That's it for today," Scarlett said, as she crossed the last name off her call list.

"I'm meeting some friends for a restaurant opening in Grammercy tonight. Care to join us?" Lawrence asked, pulling on his expensive-looking leather jacket.

"Would these 'friends' happen to be females of the fashion model variety?" Scarlett teased.

"Now, whatever would give you that idea?"

"Because I know you."

"You might be right," he admitted, with a barely concealed smile. "Please come. I hate eating alone."

"Well, maybe next time you shouldn't invite anorexic supermodels to a restaurant opening."

"Point taken," he said with a laugh.

"Can't tonight, but thanks. I'm meeting Reilly at Sardi's for a drink."

"Ah…" he said with a knowing nod. "Are you finally going to give that man a break and take him back?"

"We'll see," Scarlett said, with a blithe smile.

"Well, if you don't, you know where to find me, Gorgeous." And with a wink, he was out the door.

As Scarlett headed down the street and around the corner to the Sardi's bar, she thought about what she would say to Reilly. She'd told Lawrence the truth. She was still undecided about what to do with their unresolved relationship. While her heart wanted to take him back, her head was still wary. It will just take more time, she thought. Reilly seemed willing to wait.

Speaking of waiting, he'd already snagged their favorite bistro table in the second floor bar.

"Sorry to keep you waiting," she said, kissing him on the cheek before hopping onto the tall chair across from him.

"Perfect timing, actually," he said. "Would you mind proofing my article one more time before I turn it in?"

He spread out two pages in front of her. She read through the article while he ordered them each a glass of wine at the bar.

"I think your editor will approve," she said.

Reilly had met with his former editor at the *Journal* to offer her an exclusive story about the *Banner* scandal.

"I hope so. She said I might even be up for a promotion, if I can follow this up with the 'Inside the *Banner*' series I proposed."

"That sounds like the work of a true investigative journalist," she said.

"Why, yes, it does," he said proudly.

"So they're not mad at you anymore?"

"They were, but when they heard I stuck it to the *Banner* and then brought them dirt like this"—he gestured to the pages, grinning—"they got over it pretty fast."

Scarlett leaned in so they wouldn't be overheard. "Rumor has it that Candace was fired. It's all been very hush-hush."

"Well, her secret will be out when everyone reads my exclusive in the *Journal*." He grinned and grabbed their wine off the bar. "She always did respect the power of the pen. But enough about me. How's Scarlett Productions, Inc?"

For the past two weeks, Scarlett had been putting Reilly off, still not sure what she wanted from him.

"I have to pinch myself every day to remind myself that this isn't a dream. It's pretty amazing how it all worked out."

"Any news on *Swan Song*? I better get the exclusive on any Broadway transfer updates!"

"You will, I promise." She sipped her wine and eyed him over the rim of her glass. "Off the record, though, we're getting some very positive responses from investors, now that the *Banner* retracted the awful review and printed your real one. We're still waiting on a theater, but I have more meetings with theater owners next week, and I'm optimistic."

Reilly glanced at the Jackman theater out the window, and Scarlett turned her head to see what he was looking at. A blank marquee. In an unprecedented move, the theater owner had actually taken down the *Olympus* marquee at his own expense, rather than waiting for the next show to replace it. Apparently, despite a waiting list of new musicals looking for theaters, no producer had been willing to touch the theater while the hulking shadow of Margolies still loomed.

"So that just leaves us..." he said with a hopeful smile. "We're in the business of musical theater. Doesn't that require that the love story have a happy ending?"

"It would, yes," she said. "But that assumes that this is the end of the show."

The End

ABOUT THE AUTHOR

Ruby Preston is a young theater producer currently working on several new musicals on Broadway. She couldn't be more thrilled to be living her dreams in the Times Square trenches. www.rubypreston.com

ACKNOWLEDGEMENTS

This book would not have been possible without the brilliant and talented cast and crew behind the scenes. Thank you to my extraordinary best supporting actors.

Dress Circle Publishing
New York, NY

Made in the USA
Middletown, DE
13 November 2018